# A Matter of Life and Death

# by Matt Carrell

## Author's note

This book is a work of fiction. All characters portrayed herein are fictitious and any resemblance to real persons, living or dead, is purely coincidental.

**Linden Tree and Matt Carrell Books**

**Copyright © Mattcarrellbooks 2014**

**In paperback**
**ISBN-13: 978-1499188479**
**ISBN-10: 1499188471**
**And as an e-book from Amazon**

# 1

The rain had started around four o'clock and, on the back of a biting south-easterly wind, it swept across the town in near-horizontal sheets. By five it was drizzle, by six it had almost stopped. Icy puddles and a bone chilling sea fret were enough to deter all but the most determined early morning joggers. Only one had braved the streets of Coldharbour that morning, he cursed as an untied lace forced him to pause at the bus stop on Ranmore Road. At first he thought the girl was sleeping, he'd seen that before. When they've had too many Bacardi Breezers and don't even realise they've missed the last bus home. She was sitting on the ground, her back to the flimsy plastic sheeting that's supposed to shelter waiting passengers from the wind and rain of a late February morning. Legs stretched out to the front, ankles modestly crossed; at first glance the only indication that anything might be amiss was the broken heel of a stiletto shoe. Second glance… she was soaked to the skin. The girl was hardly dressed for a night in the rain when the temperature had hit minus three. Her white bolero jacket was unbuttoned revealing a tight low cut top, her black skirt ended midway down her thighs… and bare legs.

"How do they do that when it's so cold?" The jogger muttered, as he reached down to nudge her shoulder. "Come on love, it's time to go home, you'll catch your death out here."

The girl's head tipped forward, a mop of thick, sodden, blonde curls slipped down over a face that would have been even prettier without the make-up. The rain had drenched her hair and mascara ran like ink black tears down her cheeks. The jogger nudged a little harder, the girl fell sideways and her head struck the pavement, just as the woman who'd arrived to catch the first bus started to scream.

\*\*\*

Jack Enright decided that he'd finally found the spot where he used to watch the game when he was a kid. It was hard to tell exactly, they used to stand in those days, but there was never much of a crowd so even when the fans in front were a good bit taller than him, it wasn't too hard to get a sight of the pitch. Now it was Row K, seat number 178, right behind the goal. Enright sat, put his elbows on his knees and cupped his face in his hands, knowing it would be the last time he'd have this view of the club he'd rescued from the brink of oblivion. It was twelve years since he'd seen the pitch from anywhere except the Director's Box and this was the final lap in his farewell tour of the stadium. It was a sombre moment but Enright had to chuckle quietly to himself as he thought of the question asked of one of his fellow Premier League Chairmen.

"When you were watching the club as a boy," the interviewer had said, "did you dream that one day you'd be Chairman?'

Allegedly, the man laughed and replied, "Not really, my family was so poor I had holes in my shoes and the toilet facilities at the ground weren't up to much. The fans used to relieve themselves at the back of the terraces and it all flowed down the steps. All I dreamed of was a win for the team and getting home without my socks being drenched in piss."

"Those were the days," Enright thought as he looked across at the stand he'd paid for out of his own pocket. He was a very lucky man, it was his partner Don who saw the opportunity in the mobile phone market. Jack was little more than the warehouseman but Don gave him ten per cent of the company. When it was floated on the London Stock Exchange, Jack retired; aged fifty-five, a very wealthy man. Don loved the sea and always liked to quote the old saying,

"Owning a boat is like standing in a shower, ripping up fifty pound notes."

Jack had learned that owning a football club was like throwing cash into a bottomless pit while twenty thousand people stood around calling you a clueless bastard.

4

"Jack, I've been looking for you everywhere. They'll be here in ten minutes." Dennis Hughes had been Enright's lawyer since the day he and Don formed PhoneZone back in the mid-90s. He was eager to get the contract signed and catch his plane back to Malaga. Hughes had promised his wife he was retiring for good this time and, once the sale was finalised, he could close his last client file.

"No rush Den, they're not likely to walk if we're a few minutes late."

"I guess so Jack, it's just the plane and Sue, you know…" the lawyer gave his old friend an imploring look.

"Five minutes Den, OK?"

The lawyer nodded and started to turn away, but Enright hadn't finished with him.

"What did I do wrong Den? It's only two years since we were doing the open top bus through the town. I was a hero. Now this…" He pointed to the back of the stand where two maintenance men were whitewashing over the graffiti. As Hughes looked round, they were starting on one that said, "Fuck off Enright, give us back our club."

"When did it become their club? We were about to go out of the League when I bought the last bunch out, now we're in the Premier and the Sixth Round of the Cup and they think I've let them down. We had three thousand coming through that gate if we were lucky back then. Now I've got twenty thousand telling me they want their club back. You know maths was never my strongpoint Den, but even I know that doesn't work?" Enright shook his head in despair.

"You gave them hope Jack. Nobody looks back any more, you won't get any credit for where you brought them from, they want to know where you're taking them next. They want European football, they want trophies, they want to wake up one morning and hear that Lionel Messi chucked it in at Barcelona and has signed for us. We beat Manchester City when they were down in the third tier and now they've got some bloody sheik with bottomless pockets, but if they don't win the League every year, everyone says it's a disaster. The people who write stuff like that," he nodded towards the graffiti at the back of the stand, "reckon if it's good enough for City, it's good enough for them too."

Enright ran his fingers through his thick mop of curly hair. Unlike most men of his age, it was all present and correct, but had gone from brown with grey streaks to pure white during his tenure as owner and Chairman of Coldharbour Town Football Club. His wife, Carol, had always loved what she called the laugh lines round his eyes and she'd got used to the ever deepening creases in his forehead, They were, he claimed, the product of his tendency to worry about the smallest detail. Since the acquisition of his local club, the wrinkles had grown and merged until now, Carol occasionally confided that he was a dead ringer for their pet bulldog. His hobby became an expensive indulgence and then a weight round his neck, he was a worrier and Coldharbour Town had given him a great deal to worry about.

"Den, we've run the club properly, always balanced the books, never gambled so the whole thing might blow up in our faces. It's been about building slowly for the future, in five years time we could easily be up there, challenging the top teams."

"They don't give a toss Jack. They want it now, they see one of our rivals buy someone for twenty million and they want to know why we can't do the same. It hasn't helped that this bloke Koloschenko has spent months telling people what he'd do if you sold him the shares. He's promised a fifty million transfer kitty. You can't compete with that."

"Dennis, it's my club, how can they drive me out like that? What next? Some Russian gangster tells my neighbours he'll trim the hedges better and mow the lawn more often and so they force me to sell my house. It makes no sense."

"Jack. I hear you, but this is football. It doesn't make any sense. Of course you can keep the club if that's what you want, but you'll still get the abuse, your grandchildren will carry on getting bullied at school and you won't be able to park your car in town without someone leaving you a message on the paintwork. It's time to sell up. Anyway, you're getting a good price, you'll have made a decent profit on your investment."

"Well forgive me if I don't get too excited about that Den. I didn't know what to do with it last time I came into a lot of cash. The only thing I could think of was to buy the team I supported since I was a kid."

"Jack, you're a rich man, but football's for billionaires now. You did an amazing job here, you gave the people of Coldharbour the best years this club will ever see in all probability." Hughes took a couple of anxious steps towards the stairwell, the clock was ticking and his plane wasn't going to wait.

"It's not supposed to be like this Den. What about all that 'Financial Fair Play" stuff they're supposed to have brought in? That's supposed to give teams like us a chance, it's supposed to bring an end to these lunatics throwing money at their club."

Hughes shook his head and stole a glance at his watch. "It's window dressing Jack. They claim they're clamping down but look at what they've done to the teams who broke the rules. A cash fine. It's hardly a punishment for an owner who doesn't care about what he spends. The people who run the game want as much money sloshing around as they can get. They're never going to stand in the way of another oligarch who wants a crack at Premier League glory."

Enright cast his eyes once more around the stadium. The mid-season transfer window had closed but Coldharbour had bought no one. They didn't have the cash. There was a bill from the local force for policing their last cup match; there was no money to cover that either. He looked up at the floodlights in the north-east corner of the ground, they were in need of major maintenance work and all around the ground, paint was peeling, wooden shuttering had come loose and the brickwork needed repointing.

It was as though Hughes knew what he was thinking.

"Jack, there'll be a few more bills to pay before the sale goes through. We got notification of a visit from the Health & Safety Executive; they're doing an inspection next week."

"Go on kick a man while he's down. So we'll have some little tosser with a clipboard, asking what we've done to stop the fans slipping on a discarded hotdog wrapper, or getting trapped in a stubborn turnstile or using a bloody toilet roll dispenser to slit their wrists when we get relegated at the end of the season."

"That's pretty much the size of it." Hughes offered a sympathetic shrug.

"Great, some ridiculous little bureaucrat has a quota, so we get a random list of stuff to do to stop our fans dying in their droves at the next home match."

Enright could cover it all with a personal cheque, but what was the point? All that mattered to the fans was what happened on the pitch and that could only be fixed, he'd been told, by a man with the means of Dimitri Koloschenko. He was waiting in the Board Room with a cheque for considerably more than Enright had put into the club and the Russian's PR people had suggested it was only the first instalment. Koloschenko was going to join the list of billionaires who knew that glory was a commodity that could be purchased.

Enright finally got the hint, as Hughes took another tentative step towards the exit. "I guess you're right. There's no point fighting the tide. Go on, I'll be there in two."

When the proceeds from the sale of Enright's PhoneZone shares came through, he and Carol had entered a state of benevolent paralysis. They had no idea what to do with all that cash. They travelled, toyed with the idea of buying a home in the Caribbean, but that was so far from their family, from their friends. Something kept drawing them back to Coldharbour, the town of their birth.

Years earlier Enright had picked up a history of the town. It had been a fishing village since before Roman times, a haven for smugglers in the eighteen hundreds and a thriving port when the British Empire was at its peak. The book claimed that Henry VIII used the eastern harbour to launch spying missions on France and that was where Anne of Cleves landed to make her ill-fated match with the King. Coldharbour, the author said, was the base for a series of top-secret missions by the SOE, precursor to the modern SAS in World War Two. Much of the book had to be taken with a pinch of salt but, like many southern coastal towns, Coldharbour had played its part in the extraordinary rescue of British troops from the beaches of Dunkirk as part of Operation Dynamo in June 1940. Everyone who owned a boat jumped at the chance to help to relieve the battle worn soldiers stranded in France. Cynics claimed that was the peak, after which the fortunes of Coldharbour took a decisive and probably irreversible turn for the worse. After the war, industry drifted away, merchant shipping found quicker and cheaper access points to the UK and unemployment started to rise at an ominous rate. The final nail in the ferry port's coffin was the opening of the Channel Tunnel in 1994. Who'd opt for a five-hour ferry crossing when they could make the trip in thirty minutes by train? Coldharbour had tried so many roads to prosperity and each was a dead end. The town was like an enthusiastic but untalented schoolboy, every time they raised their hand in class they got the answer wrong. In recent years they'd stopped bothering to put their hand up, accepting that success was meant for others, not them.

Enright was old enough to remember Coldharbour in the sixties. Mass air travel was still years away and his local town was a thriving holiday destination for those brave enough to put up with it's patchy weather and a beach that was devoid of sand. Kids built their castles out of pebbles. Enright even dabbled with being a 'Mod.' He had the tailored suit, the Crombie coat and briefly rode a Vespa, the soundtrack of the time was provided by the Who and the Small Faces. They partied all night and his more adventurous friends could often lay their hands on speed or LSD. Enright never tried anything stronger than beer or whisky, but plenty of those in his circle were living the rock star life. There may have been something going on outside of Coldharbour but for the young and carefree at least, how could it have been any better than what they had right there? Forty years on and the old and obese were weaving their way down the promenade on mobility scooters, to the sound of an empty bar pumping out Queen's "Another One Bites the Dust." Most of the bigger hotels had shut and the smaller ones had closed their doors to holidaymakers. It was easier to take block bookings from social services for broken families and immigrants awaiting the result of their asylum hearings. The town was all but dead during the week. On Friday nights, things picked up with an influx of stag and hen nights drawn to the heavily discounted drinks deals on offer in the pubs and clubs that were still holding on for an upturn in the economy. The locals usually saved their money for the weekends too. There was little fun to be had in a near empty bar.

Enright had bought a farm on the edge of the town back in 1998, there was something about Coldharbour that meant he could never abandon it completely, but his dream of turning the local football team into a trophy winning side had turned to ashes in his hands.

Hughes was right, it was time to move on.

# 2

Dimitri Koloschenko surveyed his new office and decided he'd not be back, until his interior designer had ripped everything out and put it back in a style befitting one of the richest men to own an English football club. He was no sheik and Abramovich had been there when the old Soviet Union was breaking up. It wasn't hard to make money in those days. Koloschenko had to be far more artful to gain any ground at all on his fellow countryman. Four years earlier, only about forty per cent of Koloschenko's wealth came from legitimate business. The rest was from what he described as shipping. The cargo was generally armaments; "mislaid" as the Soviet Union reorganised after the collapse of communism, drugs from South East Asia or women who believed that they were being offered a chance of a better life. They just had to hand over their passports while they were being transported to another country. Koloschenko had been a soldier for twenty years, his shipping business became the perfect test of the skills he'd learnt. The Army taught him the importance of meticulous planning, carefully executed logistics and the lesson that if someone stood between you and your objective they should be taken out of the equation. Koloschenko had almost completed his transition to legitimate businessman. He'd sold off most of his interests in the shadier activities, to men who were eager to emulate him and had paid top dollar for a foothold in drugs, guns or people trafficking and prostitution. He'd mastered the art of turning flows of illicitly obtained cash into money that he could flaunt with little fear of attracting the attention of the authorities. Bribes to local officials allowed him to purchase vast tracts of land on the Black Sea coast, on the Mediterranean and increasingly in underdeveloped areas of Africa and South America. Official documents showed the land transfers and subsequent construction costs to be at a substantial discount to the market price. These sums were settled by his legitimate Russian businesses. The balance was paid in cash from his "shipping" concerns. Dirty money had been turned into hard, legally owned assets. The process continued once Koloschenko had his chain of hotels and golf resorts. The books consistently showed a higher rate of occupancy than the staff would ever have noticed. Many businesses in the black economy take your cash and never declare it. He knew the secret to money laundering is to take the cash generated illegally and declare it as receipts of a legitimate company. There is usually some tax to pay, but that's a small price for getting money generated by the sale of machine pistols, methamphetamine and women into the global banking system. In any event, Koloschenko had hired a tax guru who understood how to use loans and inter company pricing to minimise what he euphemistically described as tax leakage. The Russian wasn't ashamed of the practice, he felt it was just another indication that he was closing on the likes of Google, Amazon and Microsoft who'd got it down to a fine art.

Koloschenko was delighted at the prospect of owning a football club. It was rapidly becoming the "must-have" accessory for the nouveau-mega-rich. He was a little disappointed that the only club within his budget was close to the bottom of the Premier League and in a town he'd never heard of, but he'd seen what an influx of cash could do to change the fortunes of an ailing football team. This was fun-money. He had no intention of committing the sort of resources that Abramovich had done at Chelsea, heaven forbid that he'd get anywhere near the astronomical sums spent by the Arabs. Buying the club would make his name in England, he'd have celebrity status and that would open the doors to a host of other opportunities. As for the club, he'd tart it up a bit, get it moving in the right direction and sell it for a decent profit in a few years. After all he didn't even like football that much. Ice hockey was his game, real men playing a proper sport not a bunch of feeble prima donnas who fall over if an opponent so much as looks at them. Football was an interesting stepping stone for a man trying to establish himself in the world but that was all.

Koloschenko checked his watch, Alina was waiting for him at their apartment in Knightsbridge and he didn't want to be late. They would only have a couple of hours together before he had to get home to his wife. She'd invited her appalling sister for dinner that night and he'd promised not to be late. His Rolex Oyster GMT Master II showed five past one, he had less than thirty minutes before he'd have to head back to London. Koloschenko stroked the face of the watch; he liked to tell people that it had a red and blue Cerachrom bezel insert, echoing the original GMT Master of 1955. Koloschenko wasn't entirely sure why that was a big deal but he'd read it on the Rolex web site so he was pretty sure it was important. The watch cost him a little under thirty five thousand US dollars. An aide informed him later that he could have got it for him for thirty if only he'd known Koloschenko wanted one. The man was fired that afternoon for suggesting that the Russian might be concerned by the amount he paid for a watch.

"So Dimitri, what do you think of your new toy?" Yuri Slatkin joined Koloschenko Industries straight from law school, initially in Moscow, then in New York and, in ten years, rose from legal assistant to principal advisor to the Russian businessman. At least that's how he thought of it. Slatkin was a huge fan of the Godfather series of books and movies. In his mind he was the *"consigliere,"* the trusted advisor and, most importantly, the wizard who could navigate his client through the labyrinthine complexities of the legal system both at home and abroad. It was true that he had a rudimentary grasp of the law, but his job comprised three main components. Finding the best external legal advisors to ensure Koloschenko could grow his business and stay out of jail, was his original task. Slatkin also organised the delivery of briefcases full of cash to people who could influence the Russian's business deals and he'd demonstrated an impressive flair for procuring young, willing women who might be interested in meeting a billionaire.

Slatkin was just five feet nine inches tall. Some said that was the source of his ambition, the relentless drive to compensate for an acute case of short man syndrome. His blond hair was cut short and his fashionably unshaven look took an age to maintain. A personal trainer helped him stay lean and fit, with five gym sessions a week. The man also offered a diet plan that Slatkin had no choice but to ignore. The main reason that he'd been admitted to Koloschenko's inner circle was his ability to keep pace with the Russian's insatiable appetite for red meat, vodka and the finest Bordeaux wines.

"Yuri, I think it will be an interesting diversion for a little while. There has already been some excellent coverage of the purchase in the English Press, they are talking about me as the new Abramovich."

"They will love you Dimitri, we need to work on your English a little but I think you will eclipse Roman in no time. He never speaks to the Press and how can I put it…? I don't think the camera really loves him."

The two men laughed. It was true that Koloschenko could be a PR man's dream. It was known that he'd been in the Army but little was known of his service record. That merely added to his mystique. In spite of his huge appetite, there was virtually no fat on his two hundred kilo frame and he could comfortably lift his own body weight in his regular work out routine. The Sun newspaper had done a lengthy feature on the Russian in the days following his takeover of Coldharbour Town. They'd dug up every paparazzi shot they could find, all of which were remarkably flattering. Stepping out of his vintage Ferrari… a black tie dinner on the arm of his ex-actress wife… even a shot of him sprinting through the surf on a private beach in Barbados. All carefully selected by Koloschenko's own publicist. The paper ran the photos alongside pictures of Robert Shaw playing KGB killer Red Grant in the Bond movie, From Russia with Love. The

14

resemblance was clear, straight blond hair in a military style short back and sides, clear light blue eyes set close together, and a deep cleft between the eyebrows indicating a man who'd spent a lot of time being very disappointed with the people in front of him. Both had a small mole low on their left cheek and a smile used more often to mock than in humour. Dimitri Koloschenko had the makings of a gossip columnist's dream and he was quietly thrilled by the prospect.

"Yuri, I will need you to turn this shit hole into a place that I can use as an office. I'll only be here when the team is playing but I need somewhere I can bring my guests. We also need to give the stadium a facelift, nothing structural, just something that shows it is under new management."

Slatkin was making notes. "Anything else boss"

"The cats."

"What cats?"

"Everywhere I look there are pictures of cats, statues of cats, there even appears to be a couple of live ones. You know very well it is not a good symbol in our country. Get rid of them."

"Dimitri, it's the nickname of the club. Everyone calls them "The Cats." It's all tied up with the history of the town. A big merchant fleet used to dock in the harbour and sailors love cats apparently. They bring good luck… they catch the mice… I don't know exactly why, but they adore them. I think you will have problems if you try to change such a thing, it's… tradition."

"Fuck tradition Yuri, it is a symbol of bad luck in Russia. I am allergic to the vile, disgusting, flea ridden sacks of shit and I will not have this club associated with them. We can be Eagles, or Devils or whatever you dream up, but we will not be cats. Do you understand?"

"Yes boss, of course. Anything else?"

"The colours. Who had the idea that we should play in black and white? There is a prison in Kiev that uses the same shirts for their inmates. I want my team to play in red, the colour of Russia." Koloschenko had a particularly vivid recollection of the prison garb, he'd worn it for two weeks before Slatkin's predecessor made a deal with the authorities.

Yuri looked at his boss with unconcealed despair. He'd done his homework and seen how other foreign owners alienated the fan base before the ink was dry on the contract. Page one of the briefing paper he'd finished the night before, focused on how important it was to get the locals on side. If the fans turned against the owner, the press would follow and in no time their carefully laid plan to make Dimitri Koloschenko the darling of the London celebrity circuit would be in tatters.

"Dimitri, the fans will go crazy. It's a tribute to Juventus, the Italian champions. They play in these colours apparently and they sent a team here before the Second World War. It's a tribute to them and it started nearly eighty years ago."

"So it's time for a change." Koloschenko thought that was the end of the discussion.

"But Dimitri… it's…"

"Tradition? Fuck tradition."

Slatkin nodded feebly knowing that it was the wrong argument to use. Koloschenko raised one eyebrow in the direction of his advisor. There was nothing more to be said. Slatkin vaguely recalled that he'd seen a look like that once before, it was in a James Bond movie. The villain was a Russian agent called Red something… he'd used it seconds before he slit someone's throat.

Slatkin got up to leave and the huge frame of Victor shifted awkwardly in his chair in the corner of the room. Koloschenko's bodyguard was only five feet eight inches tall but what he lacked in height he made up for in bulk and a look of barely controlled malevolence. He'd been in the Parachute Regiment with Koloschenko and many of those who served with him would say that Victor could have jumped without the chute, as long as he made sure he always landed on his head. The man appeared to be little more than a rabid pitbull who responded to nothing but his master's commands. Slatkin had

16

almost forgotten he was there. Victor was looking at a local newspaper... odd, as he didn't speak a word of English. On the front page was the smiling face of Annie Radford, the girl who'd recently been found dead at a bus stop close to the city centre. She looked a little like a young Ukrainian woman called Lyudmila Semolova. She too was on the front pages of a newspaper, this time back in Ukraine, about a week before Victor was sent to London as chief minder to Dimitri Koloschenko. She was found dead when a tram pulled into Demiivska Square just before midnight. When the ticket collector spotted her, she was sitting upright in her seat. Only when they moved her body did they spot the deep gash in her neck and the blood seeping through her coat.

***

"That must be ten grand's worth of watches, what made you buy four of them?" Tony Drake stared in awe at the slim leather presentation boxes and a familiar brand name etched in gold lettering on the covers. Watching his friend open them, he wondered why he was always the first to put his hand in his pocket when they met for a lunchtime drink. His pint of lager and Adam's orange juice and soda combined cost about the same as his hourly pay rate after tax. Adam probably earned that in the time it took him to open the boxes.

"I didn't buy them, I swear to God, they came in the post. This card was in the envelope."

It read, "To Adam Buckley, with our compliments."

Tony shook his head, this sort of gesture was beyond his comprehension. "They just give you this stuff and hope someone will see you wearing it. Is that it?"

"I guess so, Alexei told me a local dealership popped round with a Range Rover for him once. They put their logos on the spare wheel and across the back window, they just wanted people to see a famous footballer driving one of their cars.

"Awesome mate. Enjoy it while you can." Tony regretted his choice of words as soon as they left his mouth. It sounded mean spirited, as though he was trying to remind his old friend that a footballer's career is a short one.

"Yeah thanks. I will." Adam was never the sharpest tool in the box, but he'd picked up on the edge in Tony's words. "Here, have one. Fuck it, have 'em all."

Even as he pushed the watches in the direction of his best friend, he realised that it was his turn for regrets. The gesture was generous, but patronising. Each watch was worth more than Tony earned in a month in the local DIY store. Adam had recently signed a new contract at his club, one of the first actions of the new owner. Both men were now on slightly over twenty thousand pounds, Tony earned that in a year, Adam in just a week. It was just one of the many ways in which football defied the laws of economics. One man paid a meagre wage for a job few people would choose to do, the other paid a fortune for something most young men would do for nothing.

An awkward silence had descended over the two men. Tony decided it was time to break the ice.

"So the club's been sold then."

Adam nodded enthusiastically. "Yeah, it's some Ruski bloke. Another Abramovich I reckon, he says we'll be challenging for trophies in no time."

"Shame about Jack Enright though, he turned it all round when we were going out of the League."

Adam looked confused. "What that crusty old bugger? He's a bloody fossil, that bloke. We weren't going anywhere with him. Alexei said I'd never have got my new contract if..." he let the sentence hang in mid-air. He'd promised himself he wouldn't talk about the new deal in front of his oldest friend.

"Yeah, I saw the Merc outside your parent's place." Tony tried to inject a bit of enthusiasm into his voice but it came out flat with more than a hint of envy.

Adam looked embarrassed. "Bit of a pay rise, you know how it is."

"Not really mate," Tony replied. "In my job, you just hope you're still employed one month to next. Good luck with the new fella."

"Yeah, it'll be OK I reckon." Adam kicked himself for the slip, but it was hard to conceal his enthusiasm for the new owner. They'd made it clear that he was a big part of their plans and put money on the table to prove it. He knew he had to be careful in front of Tony. Four years earlier they played in the same team, there were plenty who said Tony was the better player and both were called for trials at their hometown club. Adam was offered a contract the same day, Tony never made it onto the pitch, he was still nursing a severely twisted knee. The club said he could come back when he was fit again but it never happened. Adam replayed it all in his head, it was a fifty-fifty ball and it was only in training, so maybe he shouldn't have gone in quite so hard. The turf was wet and, although he got the ball, the follow through took Tony with him. If they'd diagnosed the problem there and then, he might have got the right treatment, but Tony rested up and tried to make a comeback. That was when he snapped his anterior and posterior cruciate ligaments. Had he been with a top football club, keyhole surgery and the finest post-operative care might have got him playing again. As a shop assistant, standing in line for treatment on the National Health Service it wasn't going to happen. Adam could easily convince himself it wasn't his tackle that put an end to his friend's chances of making it as a pro. He didn't know what Tony believed, the two men never talked about it.

Tony had already noticed the two girls sitting at a table on the opposite side of the bar. He recognised the one that was facing him, she worked at the bakery where he often bought a lunchtime sandwich. Absolutely his type, big blue eyes, great smile and a terrific figure, not exactly voluptuous but everything was in perfect proportion and she knew it. He'd barely been able to take his eyes off her on the two occasions she'd strolled slowly to the Ladies room and back. Her clothes were all about half a size too small for her or had been tailored to each curve of her body, then shrunk a little. In the shop she wore a cardboard cap and a hair net. It took Tony a few minutes to recognise her as, now her long blonde tresses were loose across bare suntanned shoulders. It didn't take much to imagine that hair spread out on a pillow. When he bought his lunch she was generally polite but formal, today she was smiling. Tony caught her eye and nodded to indicate that he recognised her, she immediately jumped to her feet and walked towards his table. She was a couple of feet away when he stood up to greet her.

"Hello," she said. "I know you don't I?"

Tony smiled humbly and gestured towards the spare seat at their table. Then he realised she wasn't talking to him.

"I'm Becky, you're Adam Buckley aren't you. I saw your pic in the paper. My brother's gonna freak when I tell him I met you. This is awesome."

Adam grinned and shrugged modestly. He'd never been that good at talking to women, now he had the kind of job where it really didn't matter.

"Can we?" Becky pleaded, pulling out her phone.

Adam gave his friend a nonchalant smile. It said, "Look at this mate, happens all the time." In days gone by, Tony might have played some part in the exchange. The girl would have handed over her phone and asked him to take the picture. Maybe she'd have realised that he was almost certainly better looking than Adam, and he was capable of stringing a few sentences together when in the company of women. Advancing technology had conspired against him. In seconds, Becky attached herself to Adam, her face next to his for the first "selfie." The second was a tasteful snap of Becky licking the side of Adam's face and the third had the local celebrity giving her a chaste kiss on the cheek while she looked to the heavens in an ultimately unconvincing impression of a swooning virgin.

Becky was thrilled with her photo shoot but was not done with collecting souvenirs.

"Can I have your autograph please?" To Tony's amazement, Adam produced a felt tip pen from the inside pocket of his fleece. It was clearly kept there for exactly this sort of occasion, they'd known each other since they were eleven years old and Tony had never seen his friend with a pen outside a school classroom. The two men were looking around for something to sign but Becky was way ahead of them. She unbuttoned her top and pushed the top of her bra to one side.

"Here please," she said, then bit gently on her bottom lip while looking beseechingly at the local celebrity.

Adam still hadn't said a single word, but he managed a very broad and lascivious grin as he carefully signed his name on the girl's partly bared breast.

"And a little kiss please," she said as he finished. Adam obliged with a couple of crosses beneath his name.

"I mean a real one," Becky said pulling Adam's face into her cleavage. The footballer was happy to comply and Becky pretended to swoon with excitement.

"I'll never wash it… unless you're there to towel me dry."

With that she squealed and grabbed the beer mat from underneath Tony's lager. She scribbled a number and mouthed the words "phone me," as seductively as she could in Adam's direction. He gave what Tony would have described as a vacant smile but Becky whooped with joy and fled across the bar to where her friend was still sitting. Adam hadn't uttered a single word.

For Tony there could have been no more vivid example of how the tables had turned. In school, he was the one that got the girl. Some thought the men looked like brothers. Both had short dark brown hair, fashionably styled so that the sides and back were almost shaved and the top was what anyone over thirty might call a floppy mess. The facial similarity was marked although Adam's lips were a little thinner and his eyes a shade closer together. Tony opted for clean-shaven as soon as Adam got himself a beard trimmer and started carving elaborate patterns in his stubble. He was anxious to get on the cover of one of those lad's magazines he had delivered every month. Both men were fit and strong, but the professional disciplines were starting to pay dividends. Adam had nothing to think about, except how to keep fit and play better football, he suddenly looked as though he was standing a little taller than his friend, even though they were both exactly six feet tall. In photos from their teenage days, there was probably not much to choose between the two boys, Tony was more approachable and had a bit more to say for himself, so finding girls was never an issue. When relationships came to an end it was usually his choice. Adam never had the same luck and when he did find a girl it rarely lasted more than a couple of dates. Then he became a footballer.

At first it looked as though he was going to be just another hopeful who went through the sausage machine that processed aspiring superstars, only to come out the other end looking for any job that would pay the rent. He'd done alright in the reserves but there were at least three players ahead of him in the race for a first team slot. He was loaned out to teams in the lower leagues, again he did reasonably well, but not so well that the club wanted to keep him, not so badly that Coldharbour would cancel his contract. Adam was coming up to a crossroads, if a player hasn't made his mark at twenty-two it's unlikely he will. His contract was due to expire in the summer and most people thought he'd be released.

They say bad luck comes in threes, in the space of one week Coldharbour Town was struck with a series of blows that changed their season. Regular central striker Will Sutton was diagnosed with a stress fracture of the femur, he'd be out for the rest of the season. His strike partner Soren Berg cracked the fifth metatarsal of his right foot and first reserve Carlos Amato returned to Colombia, where his daughter was fighting for her life after a car accident. Amato's wife had left him and returned home just a month before. Adam Buckley had been propelled to first choice striker. Little was expected of him when they headed north for his first game, an FA Cup tie against opposition expected to brush the struggling visitors aside. The post-match analysis was stilted and confused as a team of highly paid pundits failed to provide any coherent rationale for the result they'd witnessed. Even the experts could not work out how Coldharbour had pulled it off. They had twenty-two per-cent of the possession, two shots on goal, only six per cent of play was in the other team's final third of the pitch. The pundits were truly lost for an explanation, they just played Buckley's goals over and over again. Then one of them made the connection that would launch the young man's reputation.

"Martin, it reminds me of Gareth Bale. Remember when he went to Spurs, I think he played a couple of dozen games before they won with him in the team. They say he was on the verge of being sold and then he got a chance because their regular left back was out. The rest, as they say, is history."

His colleague was unconvinced.

"You're not saying that Buckley is the new Bale?"

"Not yet, but there are similarities, the pace, the fearsome shot. Give the lad time, who knows?"

One game and Buckley was hot property. His name was being spoken in the same breath as that of the most expensive footballer in the history of the game. And it wasn't as though they could drop him from the team, there was no one else to take his place.

The episode with Becky was a landmark moment for Tony, the baton had well and truly been passed. He drained the last of his pint and stood to head back to work, when he noticed Becky waving from the door... at Adam of course. She was waiting for her friend to emerge from the ladies toilet. When she finally emerged, the girl turned as though she was trying to hide her face from the two men, but Tony was certain he recognised her. Natalie Simpson had been in their class at school and she was one of Tony's first "proper" girlfriends.

That was the term he used when he had sex with the girl in question. Tony had always thought it was going pretty well, they'd finished their GCSE exams and he was looking forward to the long summer school holiday with a seriously hot girlfriend in tow. She stopped answering his calls and didn't go back for the sixth form. He'd seen her occasionally around town, but she always blanked him. Just like today. Becky gave Adam another blown kiss and then tapped her left breast repeatedly with her fingertips to indicate that her heart was beating so fast it might burst. Natalie brushed past her to get to the door and the last they saw of the two girls was Becky shouting, "Hey, where's the bleedin' fire?" as she followed her friend into the street.

"So what's with the Bus Stop Killer then? … Lock up your daughters." Adam finally found his voice.

"Yeah, it's terrible. She was a local girl too. They've got no idea who might have done it according to the local paper."

Adam looked at his friend. "Thought it might be you mate."

Tony swallowed hard as his friend stared into his eyes. "What the fuck are you talking about?"

"Stands to reason, who runs the hand tools section down the DIY? You're the local expert on knives and stuff aren't you? Putting two and two together…"

"Why do you have to be such an arsehole Adam?" Tony pushed back his chair and grabbed his jacket from the hook on the wall behind him. He inadvertently kicked the table as he stood, spilling the four boxed watches into Adam's lap.

"I've got a job to go to, I'll see you around."

24

# 3

Toby Thomas had ten minutes before the start of the editorial meeting, there was time to put his feet up and enjoy a cup of Harrods Founder's Choice Coffee. Victoria, his secretary, had learned the hard way that he'd be unbearable if he suspected that she served him anything else. She also discovered that as long as the evidence was destroyed, she could always top up the stylish brown and gold container with the "own brand" variety from the local TESCO supermarket and he'd never know the difference. Thomas liked to imagine himself sipping the same coffee as Mohammed Al Fayed, the famous Harrods owner whose son dated Princess Diana in the days before her tragic death. Those were the kind of circles Thomas wanted to move in and imagining his favourite coffee had been hand-selected by Al Fayed himself brought it all a little closer. The founder of Harrods was actually a man called Charles Henry Harrod who died more than a century before the terrible crash in a Paris road tunnel, but Toby Thomas had chosen to make his way in the field of journalism and he wasn't going to let the facts get in the way of a good story.

It was a little more than three months since Thomas had taken over as Editor of the Coldharbour Echo. It was a huge step up for a man who'd only been hired as a reporter three years earlier. Like much of the rest of the town, the paper was in what appeared to be irreversible decline. It had completely failed to keep pace with the emergence of digital media and circulation had been in an ever-accelerating spiral for years. His predecessor had been at the helm for two decades when he was found slumped at the wheel of his car as the first employees arrived for work one cold November morning. They all said that Toby Thomas must have worked all day to produce the obituary, it was ready to go when they went to print that evening. In truth he'd been polishing it for months and knowing his boss had a heart condition, he was yearning for the day the old deadbeat would do the decent thing. When the publisher offered him the job, Thomas was delighted that he'd finally come across a man with the wisdom and vision to recognise his talent. William Fairhurst later told his wife that he couldn't afford anyone else and would be deeply suspicious of any outsider who accepted the role in a paper that would almost certainly be closed within the year.

Fairhurst soon admitted that he'd misjudged his new appointee. The previous editor had approved the creation of a modest web site but had no idea what to do with it. Thomas hired a team of young internet savvy students willing to work without pay, in return for a good reference and being able to claim any sort of job experience with a real newspaper. They were given free rein to make the site attractive to their own generation and advertisers began to take the paper seriously for the first time in years. The print version started its own revival. As the writing team lowered their standards, circulation rose in almost direct proportion. Thomas was of the view that any story could be accompanied by a picture of a girl in a bikini, or better still in her underwear. Coverage of rumours that the local branch of Marks & Spencer might close, merited a full page in one of Thomas's first editions. Only a quarter was text, the rest was a series of pictures of Tracy Miller, a local girl, wearing a selection of the M&S underwear that locals would have to drive twenty miles to purchase. The retailer denied they had plans to shut the store around the same time Thomas checked out of a London hotel with Ms Miller on his arm. The front page of each edition was generally devoted to unattributed claims that the local college was a hotbed of drugs and sexual deviance or anything that could be lifted from the gossip pages of the nationals. Coverage of the storylines of popular soap operas was intermingled with "real" news, giving further credence to the claims by Thomas's critics that he had no concept of the distinction between fact and fiction. William Fairhurst was thrilled, he'd planned to close down as soon as his tax advisor gave the nod, suddenly he was being approached by people who might even buy the paper as a going concern. It was a small price to pay to allow his new editor to refurbish his office. Two thousand pounds bought Thomas all the glass and chrome he could possibly desire from the local branch of Ikea and, with the help of his team of interns, it took only a single afternoon to stamp his personal brand on the editor's office.

Victoria, appeared at his office door, then left as suddenly as she'd arrived, having given a swift backward jerk of her head. The paper's section heads were due for a meeting and it would not do for the Editor to be there when they did. He'd have to engage in pointless small talk while they waited for the last person to arrive and that was not his style. Thomas headed for the bathroom where he'd sit and rehearse his carefully planned routine, arriving back no less than ten minutes after the rest of the team had gathered. Thomas took one last look around the office to make sure everything was as it should be. His desk was free of clutter; he was far too important and creative a man to be immersed in paperwork, and the TV was switched to CNN news with the sub-titles turned on. In pride of place, on a glass shelf he'd selected for the awards that were surely coming his way, was a picture of him shaking hands with Piers Morgan. It appeared to show the one time newspaper editor and perpetual showman, presenting Thomas with something. There was a scroll of some sort in the younger man's left hand and they were evidently shaking hands in front of a banner that clearly showed they were at the previous year's newspaper awards. Thomas had engineered the photo with the help of a friend and Morgan merely thought he was greeting one of his legions of fans. As Thomas never tired of telling his staff, "if you have a story you want to tell, it's not hard to get the evidence to fit."

It was twenty minutes before Thomas returned and, as planned, his team was there for his arrival. He'd been on a positive thinking course shortly before he joined the paper and one lesson really stood out. When making an entrance, behave as though you've arrived from an incredibly important meeting that is way above the pay grade of the people waiting for you. Thomas imagined that he'd come from a meeting where Rupert Murdoch had made him a multi million pound offer to head his media empire. Those who knew his pre-meeting routine would wonder whey such an important encounter took place in a cubicle of the Gent's toilets on the third floor of the offices of the Coldharbour Echo.

"So what have we got?" he demanded, fixing each of his team in turn with a look that he hoped was intimidating.

"Thought of this for the front page. Cameron and the floods." Eddie Taylor, head of news held up a picture of the British Prime Minister walking along the beach of an unidentifiable seaside resort.

"Great, I like it," Thomas enthused. "Out of touch Cameron on holiday again whilst the vulnerable suffer another month of floods that shatter their lives."

The team exchanged awkward glances. Eddie was first to speak, "Toby, he's on a trip to the worst hit places in Devon. This is his second day down there, he's leading the rescue effort personally, we've got a few shots of him shifting sand bags."

Thomas looked confused and not a little disappointed. "OK, put it on page three, with a piece about him being a media whore who'd do anything for a photo opportunity. Let's ask the British public if that's what we really pay the leader of our country to be doing, when he should be sorting the deficit. Next…"

Again the team traded glances. Toby Thomas was a Tory from the top of his head to the tip of his toes, without a socialist bone in his body. He believed that anyone could make it if they put in the effort and the poor and vulnerable could die in a ditch for all he cared. That was not, however, a philosophy that sat well with the people of Coldharbour. Their town had been in decline for decades but most of the local industry finally collapsed under the government of Margaret Thatcher. Anything that painted one of her successors as a cold-hearted toff with a callous hatred of the honest working man went down a storm.

"I said, what's next?" Thomas drummed his fingers on his desk.

Emma Davies had the latest story from Coldharbour University. It had been a mere polytechnic, until ex-Prime Minister Tony Blair decided the easiest way of achieving his objective of getting more people to university was to rename the 'polys.'

"Boss, they're trying to sell off a football pitch for development. Lots of locals are up in arms."

Thomas was incredulous, he gave his best "do I give a fuck?" stare and slumped back in his chair pretending to have fallen asleep.

"Dull, dull, and double dull. Raid the petty cash, get down the students union and buy some rounds. We need stuff on predatory lecturers trading A grades for blowjobs, sex games on the beach under a full moon or a secret drugs ring supplying the local high school with ecstasy pills. No names, no lawsuits, you know the stuff. Sports, come on, tell me you've got something we can work with." Exasperation oozed from every pore.

Rasheed Shah was Thomas's golden boy, promoted to head of the Sports team when the previous incumbent, resigned with the words,

"I'm a journalist not a fucking fantasy fiction writer, stick the job sonny."

Thomas congratulated him on his use of alliteration and mentally totted up how much he'd saved in severance pay. He'd already decided the man was a dinosaur who had no place at his newspaper. Rasheed was a wizard at rehashing the stories doing the rounds on the internet and Thomas had invested a lot of time in broadening his journalistic skills. After teenagers in their underwear and celebrity gossip, Thomas knew that football was the next best seller.

"Coldharbour's got Aston Villa in the Sixth Round of the FA Cup on Saturday, thought we'd go with that boss."

"Sounds OK but what's the back story? Where's the stuff they won't get anywhere else. Come on, we're the local paper, this is our chance to get a bit of national attention."

Rasheed smiled and gave a confident nod. He was sure he was getting the hang of this by now and had something he knew his boss would love.

"Boss, I've got three exclusive interviews from members of the team and Dave's been out and got a stack of pictures of the player's wives and girlfriends. We're planning a piece on the "WAGs" who'll be biting their expensively manicured fingernails while their men go for glory in the cup."

"Rashy, that's fucking brilliant, how did you pull of the photo shoot thing? I'm impressed, really impressed."

Rasheed did his best to appear modest and unassuming, but he was clearly bursting with pride. "Just asked politely boss, just asked politely."

"So where did they take the photos? You need a studio or you got them at their homes or what?"

Rasheed had more good news, there was no expensive studio to pay for.

"No boss, they're all round town. Taking their kids to school, shopping at TESCO, chatting to the butcher in the High Street, but all wearing the team scarf and waving at the camera, giving it the thumbs up… you know the sort of thing."

Thomas's face fell and he closed his eyes in a moment of silent contemplation.

"No Rasheed, I don't know 'the sort of thing,' shit like that has never appeared in one of my papers. You'll tell me next you've got one of the manager's wife cutting the cake at the local fete. I thought you meant proper pictures."

"Boss?" Rasheed was starting to get the idea, but still didn't trust himself to attempt a full sentence. His bubble was

30

well and truly burst and the young man shrank back in his chair as though that might save him from a further verbal assault by his editor.

"I'm OK with pics of them wearing the team scarf, as long as that's all their wearing. If you can't manage that then do something on that Daniella bird who's going out with the goalie. She used to be a lingerie model, there must be something on the net where she's got her tits out. Is that it?"

The incredulity that Thomas injected into the last three words went through Rasheed like a knife. Another painful lesson learned.

Thomas shook his head in disgust. "So we have nothing else... that's it."

Rasheed, eyes closed, shook his head.

Thomas stood and placed his hands palms down in the table in front of him. He'd learnt that on a course too, along with having all the guest chairs in his office set a little lower than his own. It was supposed to help him physically dominate his visitors.

"So what about the scouts from Real Madrid and Barcelona who will be at the next game to check out on our new superstar, Adam Buckley. What about that story? And the fact that Liverpool are planning to offer a player exchange to snatch him from under the noses of the filthy foreigners?"

Rasheed was tapping furiously at his IPad. Thomas wasn't finished, "And this," he dropped on the table a picture of Per Sunstrom, Coldharbour's captain and centre-half. It had been taken through the window of a pizza restaurant in the town centre. His face was clear enough, as was the back of the head of another man.

"Sunstrom rumoured to be discussing a return to his homeland with representatives of Swedish Champions." Thomas raised his right hand and made a dramatic sweeping gesture, as though he was visualising the headline.

Rasheed was still typing but finally found his voice, "It's great stuff boss but the locals aren't going to be happy, they're not exactly good news stories."

"Best till last Rashy, best till last. I want a feature on the three Russian internationals who are coming to Coldharbour now that Koloschenko's here. A source close to the club says that money is no object, that sort of thing."

Rasheed was overwhelmed. "Boss, I'm sorry, I've missed all of this stuff. Who are the three Russians?"

Thomas looked at him as though he was a favourite cat who'd soiled the carpet. "I don't know Rasheed, pick any three. It doesn't fucking matter does it. It's a rumour, like the Swedish thing and the scouts for the Spanish clubs. We're just reporting a rumour, but in a few days it will be round the net like it came down from Jesus Christ himself, carved on a big chunk of stone."

Thomas looked around at his team, they all avoided his gaze. The message he was trying to convey was "must try harder." They'd received it loud and clear.

"What else?"

Eddie Taylor raised his hand like a schoolboy needing the toilet in the middle of class.

"Well the Bus Stop Killer boss, obviously. The whole town's in a panic that there's a murderer on the loose. And we've got a bit of an exclusive on that one. Victoria remembered that the girl who was stabbed came in to see you about a month ago looking for an intern job, so we've got her CV on file. We've got loads of personal stuff that the other papers won't have."

The team braced themselves for a tirade, certain that Thomas would be well ahead of them with the line the paper should take. It didn't happen.

Toby Thomas waved his hand idly in Eddie's direction and nodded. "Sounds like you've got it covered, a few interviews with local women saying they're too scared to go out and we're there. Needless to say we don't need to mention that she ever set foot in this place. We report the news, we don't need to be part of it. OK everyone, let's get to work."

Each of the team gathered their belongings and made for the door before Thomas could change his mind. They had twenty-four hours to get the midweek edition ready and there was still plenty to be done.

Alone in his office Thomas caught sight of his reflection in the glass front of one of his bookcases. He liked to think he was better looking, but that he had the bearing of William Randolph Hearst, the Harvard graduate who built America's largest newspaper chain. Citizen Kane, the Orson Wells classic, was inspired by Hearst's life and Thomas had watched the movie thirty four times. When he looked in the mirror, Thomas saw a handsome, if slightly bookish, young man who wore the harsh responsibilities of being a newspaper editor with style and alacrity and had no problem staying in shape. In truth he was average looking at best. His hairline a little too high, his eyes too wide apart and his nose a shade too big. Thomas had won his battle with an expanding waistline by swapping key nutritional groups. He'd all but abandoned food in favour of alcohol and cigarettes. Behind his back they called him "Joe," ever since one of the interns did some background research for an article on neo-Nazis. She spotted that Thomas bore a striking resemblance to Joseph Goebbels, Hitler's Minister of Propaganda. There were only two subjects of conversation in the pub that night, 'Joe' and whether the assembled crowd believed in reincarnation.

Thomas stared out of the window of his office. He had a pretty good view of the cliffs and Ranmore Hill where publisher William Fairhurst owned a thousand acre estate. Directly between the offices of the Echo and the Hill was Harbour View, the mid-priced residential block where Thomas was renting an apartment. He'd failed to convince his wife that they should make the move permanent, she didn't want to take their kids out of a school she'd fought tooth and nail to get them into. Thomas usually managed a couple of days each week at the family home on the outskirts of Harrow. He'd never noticed before, but he could also see the bus stop where Annie Radford had been stabbed. It was just two hundred yards from his front door.

"Silly little slut, what did she expect going out dressed like that. She was asking for trouble." Thomas muttered as he turned up the volume on the TV set. He couldn't shake the image of the girl on the night she died, the bolero jacket, the tight top that barely kept her breasts in check and the bare legs. What was she thinking of, going out like that in winter?

The TV news concluded the business section and a bored looking male reporter began his account of the latest royal tour to Australia. Prince George was barely a year old but he was already waving to the crowd. This was indeed Breaking News. Toby Thomas was desperate to be on TV but he'd made a vow to himself. If they ever made him Royal Correspondent, he'd get the message that he'd done something to offend the bosses and he'd quit.

# 4

The centre of Coldharbour occupied around a kilometre and a half of seafront, and stretched inland for no more than half that distance. A relatively small space that offered an object lesson in the development of British architecture from the early nineteenth century to the present day. As the years went by, standards fell, function won out over form and nobody cared too much about the big picture. Like in so many British towns, sporadic bursts of development reflected the ebb and flow of the local economy. The result was an apparently random patchwork of quality and style. The seaside promenade was still dominated by Victorian terraces and huge Regency crescents with pale stucco exteriors, wrought iron balconies, bay windows and grandiose pillared entrances. Many of the private, half-moon gardens had their own access tunnels to the beach. Eighty years had passed since the majority were single dwellings, they'd been split into apartments in the 1930s and sub-divided still further in later years, to provide accommodation for the town's college students. As pictures on a postcard, they suggested class, sophistication, even opulence. The impression didn't stand up to closer scrutiny. Even those buildings were crumbling, as owners failed to keep at bay the harsh, salt-laden atmosphere and a forty-five degree swing in temperature from winter to summer. Two streets in, and Coldharbour had fallen to the curse of the British High Street. Identical chain stores dominated the landscape, as few sole proprietors could afford the rent, once even one or two of the big names set up shop. All individuality and character had been sucked out of the town, as mainly British visitors were offered the same cafés, the same clothing stores and the same opportunities to buy bargain electronics, as they'd get at home.

Market Square had been the commercial hub of the town back in the nineteenth century, where merchants and local farmers came to tout their wares. The central gardens were still maintained to some extent, but the local council had opted for savage pruning every few years rather than regular, careful maintenance of the trees and bushes. Flowerbeds were covered in mulch and gravel, as a further measure to cut costs. At the perimeter of the square and in the narrow lanes that ran off it, were the only businesses that appeared to hold their own. Bars, modestly priced restaurants and a few nightclubs catered for visiting soon-to-be-marrieds and their friends, and locals with a bit of spare cash in their pockets at the weekend.

The commercial district abruptly gave way to the residential area. In the 1800s, rows of small brick-built terraced houses had sprung up to accommodate the growing number of factory workers. Some had been renovated with double glazed windows and fitted kitchens. Others had slid into disrepair, their only toilet still at the bottom of the yard. On the outskirts was a series of council estates constructed in the aftermath of the Second World War. Most of the houses had since been snapped up by their tenants, as the Thatcher government gave owners the right to fulfil the ultimate dream of every Briton, to own their own house. For those who succeeded, they quickly realised it was merely the first stepping-stone. Having acquired a property on one of those estates, the next objective would be to get out. Successful people lived in the detached and semi-detached houses on the western edge of town, and anyone who made it that far, cast covetous eyes in the direction of Ranmore Hill. To the east was Coldharbour Stadium, home of the local football team.

To the west of Market Square was a wide tree lined boulevard. It ran for just one mile before reaching the A road and the route to London. The signpost had been covered over with a cardboard sheet that pointed the way out of town with an arrow and the word, "Civilisation." On one side of the road there were a few of the more desirable residential properties, on the other was a maternity hospital, a school, the local police station and the town cemetery. For many, the sequence was a metaphor for the lives of too many of the locals.

Inspector Maggie Davenport pushed the plastic cup of lukewarm coffee across the table.

"Here love, drink this."

The girl had barely strung two intelligible sentences together since the interview started. It didn't help that they only had a couple of rooms. Whether it was a serial killer signing his confession, the victim of some unspeakable crime or a little old lady reporting that her cat was missing, they all got the same hospitality. Room 1 was a dank, rectangular box with grey walls and a linoleum floor. The low ceiling and a cracked window with a view of the station's dustbins and perimeter wall made it even more oppressive. A single bulb lit the room and there was no lampshade. It might have been an economy measure, Davenport thought it more likely to be one of her male colleagues trying to evoke the atmosphere of a 1970s cop show that was doing reruns on satellite TV. They were not ideal conditions for interviewing a young woman whose best friend had just been washed up on the beach.

"Becky, you have to tell me what you know. We think you were the last person to see Natalie alive."

Her young witness sobbed and began to cry all over again with the reminder she'd never see her best friend again. Then came a stab of guilt as she realised that she was also worried about being late for work, her shift at the baker's shop had started half an hour earlier and she was already on a final warning. The policewoman had said they'd call and explain but that was only going to make things worse. Since the day she told him to get his filthy hands off her backside, the lecherous old bastard who owned the bakery had been desperate to get rid of her. It was another couple of minutes before the girl managed to compose herself.

"We went to the movies that's all. We didn't have much cash and Nat said she wasn't feeling that well, so she wanted to go home."

"Where was she when you saw her last?"

"The cinema's right opposite the pier. She went towards the bus stop, and I went back into town." Becky started to wail again. She lived two doors away from Natalie, had they gone home together, there might have been something she could have done. It was barely midnight when they said goodbye. It was after two when she got into a taxi with a guy called Gavin she'd met at Digital, the new club just off the town square. The police were waiting for her when she got home at seven thirty that morning.

"So she had to pass the entrance to the pier to get to the bus stop."

"I guess," Becky nodded, sniffed loudly and reached for another paper tissue.

"No texts, no calls, no contact with her at all after that."

"Well yes…" Becky looked pensive, Davenport was suddenly hopeful of even the smallest clue. The younger woman reached into her handbag for her phone, in a few seconds she'd found the conversation and passed the phone to the detective.

There were only two messages, the first was timed at eight p.m., Natalie saying, "ticket office at nine?" Then from Becky at 1.30 the following morning, "I pulled and he's soooooo hot," followed by a smiley face.

"Nothing *from* Natalie?"

Becky closed her eyes and gave the tiniest shake of her head. Then she sprang into life.

"I don't get it, why would she kill herself? She was a bit down the last couple of days, but we just booked up for Ayia Napa in July. She had everything going for her."

Davenport realised that they'd not given Becky the full story.

"Becky, she didn't kill herself. A young couple found her body on the beach, and she'd definitely been in the water, but she hadn't drowned. She was stabbed, probably up on the pier, then whoever did it, dropped her body into the water."

Becky would never have made it as a detective but it was the smallest of mental leaps.

"The Bus Stop Killer?"

"Maybe, we've got to check out a whole lot of things first, but it would be a terrible coincidence if it was two different people."

Becky felt as though her spine had turned to ice. She'd tortured herself about leaving her friend alone, a few short minutes before she died. What signs had she missed? Could she have talked her out of jumping from the pier had they been together? That picture was torn from her mind. Suddenly she imagined the two of them heading arm in arm towards the bus stop. Then a madman races up from the beach and starts slashing madly with a butcher's knife. They could both be dead. Or Gavin, she'd gone with him without hesitation. She'd never seen the guy before in her life, but he bought her a few drinks and he was incredibly cute... and that body! She'd seen Annie Radford at the bar in Digital a couple of days before she died, maybe that's how she met her end. Obviously it wasn't Gavin, but she could easily have walked out that door with a killer. Becky had been wandering the streets of Coldharbour late at night since she was fourteen, more often than not with a drink or two too many inside her. Never once had she felt even remotely vulnerable, suddenly she felt as though she was lucky to be alive. Nothing would ever be the same again.

The detective was talking but Becky had stopped listening.

"Becky did you hear me?"

"Huh?"

"You said she was feeling down. Did anything happen that might have caused that?"

Becky thought for a few seconds. "I can't think of anything. She told me work was going really well, something about a promotion and we were pretty excited about Ayia Napa, that's it."

"Boyfriend troubles?"

There was a dark brown stain in the centre of the table, a wet cup had been left there and nobody had bothered to wipe away the resultant ring. Becky suddenly focused on the spot as though it was the most fascinating thing she'd ever seen.

"Don't think so…"

"Becky, we're trying to find the person who killed your best friend. You've seen those cops shows when the police reckon they know when someone's lying?"

Becky nodded.

"Well that bit's real, it's the rest that's crap. I know you know something."

"She made me swear." There was real fear in Becky's eyes. As though Natalie's spirit was whispering in her ear, reminding her of the consequences if she broke her word.

"Becky, you walked in here as a witness, but this is a taped interview. If you don't tell me what you know you'll be withholding evidence and obstructing an officer investigating a major crime. I don't think I have to tell you what the penalties for that might be." Davenport hoped she wasn't going to have to elaborate, as she wasn't that sure herself and she doubted that they'd be that daunting anyway. Once again she was grateful for the imprint that televised police drama had made on the public. Becky nodded vigorously, she'd obviously recalled an episode of a favourite series where a character cracked under exactly that pressure.

"He was married, that's all I know… and he's well known round here. I think she liked the secrecy. It was all a bit of fun. Bit of glamour… you know."

Davenport nodded sympathetically, as though she knew exactly what Becky meant. The truth was that she'd never grasped why women went with married men. If they're not willing to be seen in public with you, then it said all you needed to know about the relationship and the man in question. Her own dad was a policeman and walked out on her mum and three kids when she was fourteen. It turned out he'd bedded a string of women, almost since the day he and her mum got married, mostly colleagues at work. Only one got him to leave his wife, but that relationship barely lasted a year before another young cadet caught his eye. Davenport recalled the comment by businessman James Goldsmith. "When you marry your mistress, you create a vacancy." Still it happened all the time, women who wanted to lure a man away from home or just have a bit of fun with a guy who had money to burn.

The latter option was more likely in Natalie Simpson's case. She was a nurse, good but not spectacular at school, everyone talked about a kind, gentle young woman who liked to party but was practically a nun compared with her extrovert best friend. Maybe at the age of twenty-two, she got tired of eking out her salary every month, saving her pennies to slum it in Ayia Napa once a year on her holidays and trying to make a battered old Ford Fiesta survive from one week to the next. A bit of luxury paid for by a wealthy local man might be a welcome break from bedpans and whinging patients.

"Do you have a name?" Davenport raised her pen, as though she expected Becky to have the details… address, mobile number and e-mail, the lot. "You said he was local. What? A businessman, a footballer maybe, a local politician?"

Becky shook her head vigorously as though the intensity of the movement would convey that she was telling the truth. "I swear… honest… I have no idea. She just said he was local and that he had lots of cash."

"You said she was subdued, did anything happen to upset her?"

"No, honest. Nothing." Then Becky started to think, as though a worm of an idea had found it's way into the back of her brain.

"Becky?"

"It's probably nothing, but she was fine right up until we met that footballer and his mate."

"Go on."

"We had a drink in that place in Market Square at lunchtime, you know… The Black Cat. I saw that Adam

Buckley who plays for Town and I got his autograph. He's so fit… I can't believe it." She shivered with the recollection. A sharp look from Davenport returned her abruptly to the present. "He was with another bloke, Natalie said his name was Tony Drake."

"Was there an argument?"

"No, I never noticed anything until we got outside. She was upset and when I asked her what was wrong, she just said the bloke was an arsehole. She said she hated him."

"This Tony… she meant Tony."

"Yeah, course. The other guy… Adam, he was lush."

"OK Becky we might need another chat, so don't go anywhere without checking in with us. You've been very helpful."

As the door closed and a young policewoman led Becky back to the reception area, Maggie Davenport checked her notes against the file she'd brought in. The name rang a bell and there it was exactly as she remembered. One of her colleagues had interviewed Natalie's parents. Neither said anything about a current boyfriend, certainly not a married man. As far as they knew, Natalie was seeing a young doctor at the hospital until about three months before her death. He was from Sri Lanka and had returned home at the end of his contract. Mr and Mrs Simpson both agreed that Natalie had taken it really well. Natalie was generally a pretty cool customer when it came to break ups, they had no recollection of her ever being too concerned when she split from a boyfriend. Except for the first one of course. They both liked Tony Drake a lot, he was polite, charming and really cared for Natalie. Then one day it was over and their daughter simply didn't want to talk about it. It was months before she was back to her usual self, but even then she said nothing about the reasons for the split. That was all so long ago, they said. Since then, boyfriends came and went and Natalie barely batted an eyelid.

Maggie Davenport drew a ring around the name of Tony Drake in her notebook.

# 5

It was hard to believe that she was the same girl. Back in school Annie Radford was a chubby little thing. Not fat exactly, but not the sort of girl you made a beeline for when the slow dances came on at the end of the evening. Her hair was a lot shorter back then, a little bob like a duck's rear end. Still she was pretty popular with the boys, it was the big blue eyes, the clear creamy skin and a raucous laugh that suggested she might have a wicked side if you could get the ratio of vodka to tonic right in her glass. The girl standing at the bus stop that night looked much taller, certainly more slender, the skin was still perfect and those eyes… so, so blue. She smiled, it was clear that she recognised him after all those years. He couldn't remember what he said, but she laughed and then cast her eyes towards the ground as though embarrassed that she'd laughed when she should have been offended. He stepped forward and gently grasped the collar of her jacket, bringing her closer. She didn't object at first, but then pulled back as though she'd had second thoughts. Her hand shot up to break his grip then she turned and started to walk away. That's when he plunged the knife into her back.

Tony Drake emptied the last of the contents of his stomach into the toilet bowl. There was no reason to cling on to the edge of the porcelain any more, so he allowed himself to slide to the floor and rest his aching head on the cold tiles. The dreams were alternating now, he couldn't decide which one he feared most.

"The apple didn't fall that far from the tree did it Tony? Just like your father, he was an evil bastard and you're going to turn out exactly the same."

He could barely remember what it was that he'd done wrong but it had sent his mother into another spiral of hatred that was directed at him, or the man who abandoned both of them. Alan Drake was most boys' idea of a pretty cool dad. He loved football, was always on hand with a ticket to the game and when his mother threatened her son with paternal discipline, his dad would give a conspiratorial smile and wag his finger in mock anger. Tony only heard about what went on between them when he read the coverage of the court case. His father was a drunk, a wife beater and spent most of his meagre weekly wage on what he described as "slow horses and fast women." Alan never denied killing the girl, the forensic evidence was overwhelming, he just said that he had no recollection of it. He'd woken up on the sofa of their two bedroom council house with a vague idea that he'd done something terrible, only when the police kicked down their door did it all fall into place. He was credible enough in the witness box but still got fifteen years in jail. Tony heard that he'd been released four years earlier, but there'd been no contact. He'd barely thought of his father until they found Annie Radford's body. Then they identified her as a girl who'd been in the year ahead of him at school. That was when the dreams started. Tony at the bus stop, seeing the smile, pulling her towards him, then as she turned away, he drove the knife into her. It was vivid, it was clear, there couldn't be any doubt at all that he was there when Annie Radford died. Then there was the other dream, his mother screaming at him that he was just like his father, the man who'd killed a girl but nearly convinced a jury that he'd done it while he was sleepwalking.

The newspaper was open where he left it the night before. The Coldharbour Echo used to be the midweek paper, recently they'd started putting out a weekend version. It was mainly sports coverage, with page after page devoted to the local team and synopses of all the unsubstantiated rumours that appeared in the press and on the internet that week. Local sport also got plenty of column inches, particularly ladies' hockey and netball or anything else where the paper's photographer could get pictures of buxom young women running around in short skirts. That Wednesday's edition had a single picture on the front page with the headline,

"Coldharbour Ripper Strikes Again?"

After one death, he was dubbed "The Bus Stop Killer," the second murder earned him a soubriquet more fitting an up and coming serial killer. That, at least, was what the Coldharbour Echo wanted their readers to believe was in their midst.

The front-page photo was from Natalie Simpson's personnel file at the hospital and the first six pages of the paper were devoted to the murder that had taken place on the morning before it went to print. It was as though the paper anticipated another killing. There were detailed accounts of serial killers who'd terrorised people across Britain, interviews with psychologists offering insights into the minds of the perpetrators and a host of interviews with locals expressing their horror at the death of another beautiful young woman. Anyone checking the electoral roll for those who claimed to be concerned local residents would have drawn a blank. One of the Echo's interns wrote the quotes, another picked names at random from the London Phone Book.

Natalie Simpson's best friend Becky looked sombre in the picture of her on page three. She'd always wanted to see her face peering out when she flipped the paper open, but she had something more glamorous in mind. This time, there was no make up, her hair hung like rat's tails round her shoulders and her eyes were red and puffy. The headline was designed to invite a gasp of shock from readers.

"'He nearly got me too,' Local girl tells how she was moments away from being slaughtered by the Coldharbour Ripper."

Tony turned back to front page. The picture didn't come close to doing Natalie justice. She was a beautiful girl. Long dark hair and steel grey eyes. Tony loved the combination. She said something about having Italian grandparents on one side of her family, that's what gave her that fabulous olive skin and a wide sensual mouth. She was a modest girl but there was always a tiny hint of vanity lurking beneath the surface. Tony liked to tease her,

"So you say you've got olive skin?"

"Yes, light olive, that's why I tan so easily," she replied proudly.

"But olives are green."

Natalie rolled her eyes in frustration and returned to applying her make up.

The paper's exclusive picture of the victim was a standard photo booth shot taken for an ID card. No smile, no make up, hair tied back in a severe looking ponytail, so tight it stretched out her features. What his mates called a "Streatham Facelift." It could have been a mug shot from a Wanted poster. The team at the Echo concentrated on the narrative, they were yet to find any other photographs. Natalie's Facebook profile was set to Private and an exhaustive search by one of the Echo's interns failed to come up with any personal pictures. Fifty quid paid to a temp working at the hospital secured a copy of the picture on her HR file, they'd have paid a lot more. Another intern was despatched to find a friend of Natalie who might have pictures they were willing to sell. He was authorised to go to a hundred for a regular picture, two hundred and fifty for anything compromising.

Tony had stared at the picture for an hour the previous night until he finally drifted into a fitful sleep. The dream about Annie Radford was even more vivid than usual, her face was turned towards him and contorted with pain and rage as he plunged the knife into her. Then he was sitting on the corner of Natalie's bed watching her put on her make up. Her face was green, dark green and twisted with hatred. Suddenly he was standing at the entrance to the pier, two girls were locked in an animated discussion barely fifty yards from where he stood. The blonde was definitely that slut he'd seen in the pub, the image of her licking Adam's face floated in front of him. Then she hugged her friend and tottered back down the promenade. The other girl turned, it was Natalie. As he stepped out of the shadow, she saw him for the first time, then smiled. She was genuinely happy to see him. Tony beckoned her for to follow him to the railings. When he turned she was standing no more than two feet from him. She opened her mouth, then hesitated. It was like there was something she wanted to tell him, but couldn't find the words. Then she spoke and the words came tumbling out, but he couldn't hear them. The waves were crashing on the beach, the wind was howling round the clock tower that stood over the entrance to the pier. She leant forward so he could hear her better, then stopped. The look on her face turned to confusion, then pain and then she dropped to her knees. Tony was standing above her with a knife in his right hand. The blade was covered in Natalie's blood. The first splash was the knife hitting the water, the second was the body of his ex-girlfriend as he slipped her over the railings into the ice-cold surf lapping gently on the beach. No waves… no wind… just a deathly silence.

Tony dragged himself into the shower and managed to set the taps to deliver a steady stream of tepid water. He had no idea how long he sat with his back to the wall of the cubicle, legs stretched out in front of him, ankles crossed, in a parody of the position in which the jogger had found the first victim. Only when the water turned to an icy stream did he stagger to his feet and grab a towel from the rail by the door. Days earlier Tony convinced himself that he was Annie Radford's killer, now he was replaying the murder of Natalie Simpson in his head. It all stacked up. His mother's tearful rant that he was a carbon copy of his father; a man who claimed to have killed while in a trance, the recurring dream that he'd attacked Annie as she walked away and now the images of Natalie falling to her knees as he stabbed her in the chest. A ringing phone dragged him back to the present. He'd missed a call while he was in the bathroom, it was British Telecom's 1571 service with a message.

"Tony, it's me… it's your Dad. I'm back son and I need your help."

47

# 6

Jack Enright looked at the wine list with utter bemusement. He'd chosen a fillet steak, his companion had ordered something he didn't even recognise, but it looked like he was pointing to the fish section of the menu as the waiter scribbled on his pad. Red with meat, white with fish, that's what he'd read, but what was he supposed to do now? One of each, he guessed, but it was only lunchtime and his car was parked outside. Sam Chalmers had worked for Enright for more than a decade and knew it was time to rescue his host.

"Jack, they do a terrific Malbec here, great with beef and it's fine with the fish too,"

Enright nodded as though he was about to come to the same conclusion. The waiter took the wine list and left the two men to their aperitifs.

"Thanks for coming Sam. I suppose I want to say sorry for selling up, but I need to find out what's going on at the club too. I can't bring myself to go back there since the sale went through."

Chalmers shrugged as though he wasn't sure he'd have the answers Enright was looking for. Eighteen years as a player, four on the coaching staff, then eight as team manager, he'd never been employed by anyone except Coldharbour Town. In his heyday locals liked to draw parallels with the only England captain to lift the World Cup. Bobby Moore was as stylish a defender as ever played in the English Leagues and Chalmers would have been thrilled had he been half as good. He was… just. He and Enright had dragged the club from the lower divisions into the Premier League, playing entertaining football. The motto was, "if they score three, we have to get four." There was little science, no flipcharts and no statistical analysis of player performance. They tried to play with discipline at the back and a bit of flair and movement going forward. The rewards were there in the trophy room. Coldharbour had won the championship of each of the three lower divisions and had taken half a dozen scalps of top clubs in the cup competitions. The Premier League, unfortunately, appeared to be a step too far. When they went a goal down in the lower leagues, it spurred the players on to hit back. In the Premier, all too often, heads went down and the defence took on the air of a battered child. So used to being hit, they flinched at every approach. A point above the relegation places, there was still hope but the bookies had quoted them odds on to be playing a level lower at the start of the following season. At least until Dimitri Koloschenko bought the club, now they all agreed there was hope, as he could bring to bear the one factor that everyone appeared to believe could guarantee success in football. Money.

"Jack, I'm not sure I know any more about it than you do. Nominally I'm still in charge of the team but I reckon they're just waiting until we get knocked out of the cup or we take a real battering in the League again and that'll be it." Chalmers looked remarkably at ease with what he anticipated to be his fate.

"Sam, I'm really sorry. It must be a nightmare."

"Jack, to be honest it's a relief. Even if you'd still been around I think I might have been knocking on your door at the end of the season. The joy went out of this a while ago. Football's no fun any more."

Enright was shocked, he'd expected Chalmers to be at Coldharbour Town until they carried him out in a pine box. The fans certainly thought the same.

"I had no idea you thought like that, you're planning to walk out?"

"If you were still there, we'd have had a chat about how to find a successor. With the new guy I reckon I'm on my way out anyway. They've got some Russian bloke… called Boris would you believe? He's taking training now and they've just handed out a stack of new player contracts, I wasn't consulted on any of them."

"You won't know what to do with yourself after all these years." Enright was certainly concerned for his friend, but

50

the comment simply echoed his own feelings at being ditched from a club, around which his life had revolved for so long.

"Jack, I've got grandkids in California, my brother lives in Brisbane and I've made more money in the last few years as a manager than I did for eighteen as a player." He raised both hands as though he was about to embrace his old boss across the table. "And I know I've got you to thank for that. It's time to move on. I'll be happy to turn my hand to something different."

"But what about the day to day stuff? Working with the players, matchday preparations, you loved all that."

"The fun's gone out of that too Jack. I remember handing out pro contracts to youngsters when I first started. Those kids would have done anything for you, they were that grateful. Now we're paying half a million quid a year to eighteen year olds and if you're not wiping their backsides for them they're in the press saying they want a transfer. Then there's all the bullshit the FA comes out with, all the PR to make out we're doing the right stuff."

"Like what?"

"Like Kick it Out, the racism campaign."

"It's a pretty worthy objective." Enright was surprised at his old friend's vehemence, Chalmers didn't have a racist bone in his body. He was shocked that he'd object to such a campaign.

"Yeah, I wouldn't argue with you, but there's something that sticks in the throat when I hear a footballer on a couple of million a year saying how dreadfully he's been impacted by racism. That lad Vinny Johnson had a terrific game last week, but came off the pitch almost in tears complaining he'd been abused by the other fans."

"Well he shouldn't have to tolerate it Sam, he's got a point."

"Of course he shouldn't. But the blokes who are doing it are Neanderthals, they haven't got a brain cell between them and they only resort to name calling because they're too stupid to string two sentences together. Why would a lad like Johnson give a rat's arse what people like that think? He's the one with the Porsche 911, the six-bedroom house and more women chasing him than he could shake a stick at. I told him to ignore it, give a couple of interviews where he says that he couldn't care less about the inane jeering of an ignorant minority and they'll get bored with it. They target him now because they know it upsets him.

"I see the argument Sam, but you won't get a lot of people agreeing that you should just turn the other cheek."

"I guess so, but did you see that Dani Alves the other week, the Barcelona player? Someone threw a banana at him so he picked it up and took a bite. The bloke's a genius. He was sending the message, 'go on, do your worst, I don't give a fuck.' Racism's a problem Jack, but if you want to run a campaign for the victims, footballers aren't that high on my list. Help the kids who can't get a job because of the colour of their skin, the ones who get picked on by the police just because they're black or the local shop owners who get targeted by thugs, because they're Pakistanis or Vietnamese or whatever. I'll buy the argument that they're victims of racism but Vinny Johnson? Do me a favour."

"Everyone deserves respect Sam."

"It shouldn't happen for sure, but it's not the top priority. We're so obsessed with these celebrities now, it's like they're the only people who matter. That's what gets to me. We've raised these people up onto pedestals and they're not worth it. And it makes my job a nightmare."

Enright laughed. "I've seen a few interviews that would make your skin crawl, for sure. I blame Sky, you create a twenty four hour sports channel and you've got to fill the hours somehow."

"That's my point exactly." Chalmers slapped the table so the cutlery jumped. In seconds a waiter was at his side asking if there was anything he required. He disappeared as quickly as he arrived with a wave of Chalmers' hand.

52

"All those ridiculous interviews, where they get asked about the game. Do you think Sky realise that we train them to give one of six answers whatever they're asked, 'taking it one game at a time,' 'happy to have scored but it's about the team, not about me.' We have to keep it simple because half of them are too stupid to remember more than half a dozen responses. Then they get the idea that their opinion matters. All of a sudden I've got some teenage upstart second guessing me during the team talk and if I put him in his place, it's on Twitter that afternoon as a dressing room punch up."

"Not like that in your day then Sam."

"No Jack, I shut my mouth and did what the manager told me. If I got dropped I worked even harder to get back in the team, I didn't get an agent to leak it to the press that I might be looking for a move." Chalmers was almost breathless after his rant, he looked at Enright and smiled.

"Jack, it's been great working together but this is definitely for the best. I've had enough. I'll hang around until the end of the season, I'm pretty sure that Dimitri Kolo'what'sit will have given me my marching orders by then. If he hasn't, I'll walk."

"So what are you doing for the rest of the day?" Enright asked. It had crossed his mind that an afternoon in the company of his old friend might be just what he needed.

"Oh Jesus, now you've gone and spoiled it all. I've got a Respect Workshop.

Enright looked bemused. "Do you need a hammer for that?"

"Jack if I took a hammer in there, there'd be no survivors."

"Go on, tell all, why does that piss you off?" Enright was trying to keep a straight face. Chalmers' trademark was his composure and calm authority, he'd rarely seen his old friend in such an agitated state.

"It's the FA and their bloody campaign. We all have to do these seminars to tell the players they have to respect opponents, respect the officials and don't karate kick the opposition's fans even if they're twenty four carat gold arseholes."

"Come on Sam, it's a problem, we see it every week, they have to do something about the way the players behave."

"Jack they could fix it in a week if they wanted to. This Respect campaign is just a PR stunt, no way is it a genuine effort to bring a bit of discipline to the field."

"Sam, I don't get it, why do they bother?"

"It's all about appearances. They want to look like they're doing something when really they're sitting on their hands. It's often the very top teams that are the worst offenders, they never accept the referee's decision if it goes against them. 'I got the ball,' they'll scream, then the action replay shows them take both the guy's legs first. Instant yellow card for dissent and you'd stamp it out in no time."

"Only because there'd be no one left on the pitch."

"Maybe, the first week they did it, but even footballers will cotton on if they see a genuine punishment. Today their clubs are sending them to Respect seminars and then coaching them to dispute every decision to get the referee on the back foot. A few sendings off and they'd soon change their tune."

"But Sam, why do they put up with it? If, as you say the FA could put a stop to it, why don't they?"

"Because it's not sport any more Jack. It's theatre. They want the confrontation, they want the publicity, they're desperate to be all over the back pages and preferably the front pages too. That's what sells match rights around the world, that's what gets people from every country where they've got TV tuning in to see the latest scrap. Did you hear Roy Keane the other day on TV?"

Enright shook his head and took his first sip of the wine. He'd have to write the name down. Handy if it was good with fish and meat.

"He said the Premier isn't the best League in the world, it's just the best brand. I'd call him an intellectual but he'd probably chin me. They've been killing the game for years, it's theatre now."

"Like Gladiators?" Enright meant the long abandoned Saturday night TV show, Chalmers read a deeper insight into the question.

"Absolutely, that's exactly what it's like. Can't remember who said it but it was some bloke in a long white dress, he reckoned Rome kept it's people in order with Bread and Circuses. Keep them fed and entertained and they'll put up with any old shit. Well we've got Fast food and Football. Nice one Jack, I'll have to get that into an interview sometime after I quit. They'll think I'm an intellectual too."

"Tread carefully Sam, You know what happens if you appear too smart in this game, they start saying you're gay."

"I'll cope… anyway thanks, and sorry for getting all this stuff off my chest." The food arrived and the two men raised their glasses in a toast before starting to eat.

"There have to be a few positives though surely." Enright said as he cut into his steak.

"Of course, football can be a fantastic influence on young lads. Hear some of England's top players talk and you know they'd be in prison if they weren't playing the game. Then there are the ones who are genuinely amazed at the privilege of getting paid to do the only thing they've ever wanted to do."

"Like Adam Buckley?"

Chalmers' brow creased and he rolled his head slowly from side to side as though he was weighing up what he'd heard.

"To be honest, that Buckley lad is right on the cusp. He was in tears when I gave him his contract, he couldn't believe we were signing him up, but I'm worried for him."

Enright looked puzzled. "He's the town golden boy now. What's the issue?"

"That's the problem Jack. He was a skinny, spotty little kid when we signed him. Scared of his own shadow, every time

I went to talk to him he'd get all tense. I reckon he thought I was going to tell him to pack his kit and get out."

"Not any more surely?"

"Definitely not. I'm just a bit nervous that he'll start to believe his own publicity. Remember when he first came, he had a nickname amongst the lads… they called him Mary."

"You're kidding, what was all that about?"

"He was a virgin, they all thought it was hilarious. He was awkward, shy… a nice looking lad but he couldn't get laid. Now half the women in Coldharbour would do him in the frozen food aisle of TESCO if they got the chance. They say George Best was the same as a kid and look what happened to him."

"He's got you to watch over him Sam, I reckon he'll be fine."

"He'll be OK as long as I'm there, but I don't know how long that'll be Jack. It'll be a hell of a waste if he does go wrong. The boy's got a lot of talent."

"Things have moved on since Best's days, nobody had ever seen anyone like him before, they didn't know what to do with him. Now all the clubs have got counsellors, advisors… even our little club wised up to that sort of thing."

"I guess so, even the Russian won't squander a talent like that. Jack I can't tell you how good it is to see you again and it's great to chat, like the old days."

"No problem... so this workshop, not that important then."

"God no."

"Well how about we get them to set up another bottle of this red in the bar and we can spend the afternoon really putting the world to rights."

Chalmers raised his glass, "I'll drink to that."

\*\*\*

56

Toby Thomas was horrified when he discovered that his secretary had been withholding a large portion of the mail he received every week. The phone had rung just as she was about to shred a huge pile of letters and, fortuitously, he'd walked past her desk before she could get rid of them.

"What're you hiding from me Vicks? You know I want to hear what our readers have to say."

Victoria blanched at the abbreviation of her name, she hated people calling her Vicky, Vicks was bordering on the intolerable. She'd been named after one of England's greatest monarchs, not some little slapper off the local council estate.

"Toby, I make sure you get the... constructive ones. I didn't think you'd want to see... these." She pointed towards the letters as though they should only be handled with suitable protective clothing.

"Come on... read to me." Thomas chuckled as he headed back to his desk. Victoria followed with a selection of the letters, her elegantly shod feet dragging on the carpet as though she was about to meet her maker.

Thomas sat and put his feet on his desk. "Hit me," he said. His secretary desperately wished she could.

"May I paraphrase?" Victoria was anxious not to have to read the letters word for word. Toby was well aware of her discomfort.

"Come on Vicks, I want to hear what our readers have to say, just pick the best bits."

Victoria took a deep breath. "Mr Wilson from Ranmore Hill says you are a... 'vile, odious little scumbag who is intent only on poisoning the minds of the ignorant masses. You should be flogged and thrown out of town.'"

"Ouch, that hurts." The smile on Thomas's face suggested the pain was transitory. "I'm guessing there are some that are a bit more cutting than that though."

Victoria had hoped to get away with one of the gentler letters. She shuffled through the pile and picked out another. "Mr Thomas from Pennywood says you are a... ummm an 'effing' disgrace to humanity and you should burn in hell for the filth you peddle in your lousy excuse for a newspaper."

Thomas laughed, "God, I hope he's not a relative. I guess he might be from my father's side, some of them were notoriously rough. Still that's more like it, is that the worst they can come up with?"

Victoria flushed with embarrassment and dropped the remaining letters on the desk. "Toby, if you want to read them go ahead. There's stuff in there about what people would do to you, your wife, your kids. I checked with legal to see if we should send them to the police but they just said it was par for the course. That's when I started shredding them."

Thomas shook his head. "No keep them, the police might want to take a look if you find me in the car park one day, my body riddled with bullets." He started to leaf through the letters and then yelped with glee. "See this one, if they find my body and there's a recently cooled poker protruding from my rear end, you'll know that A Friend from Stonehaven has to be a prime suspect."

"This doesn't upset you?" Victoria was incredulous.

"Vicks, I'd be gutted if they weren't saying this sort of stuff. We're getting to people, making them respond, that's what this job is all about. What's that saying? 'The only thing worse than being talked about is not being talked about.' It's brilliant, I'll keep these for a bit, but make sure you put the worst ones in my in-tray every day."

Victoria closed the door and returned to her desk. Her husband was up for a promotion that would enable her go part time, preferably with another company. She was suddenly eager for a bit of reassurance that he still had a good chance. As she picked up the phone she heard Thomas whoop with joy, he'd obviously got to the letter from Mr Saheed who lived in Eastwood. This particular correspondent was very angry indeed and was calling on divine intervention for the bloody retribution he planned for the editor of the Coldharbour Echo.

# 7

Jack Enright poured his third cup of coffee of the day. He'd not been able to face any food. Sam Chalmers had wisely suggested that they reject the waiter's offer of a fourth bottle of Malbec, not so wise was the decision to switch to Armagnac. Taxis were called around seven p.m. and Carol tucked him up in bed, then threw his dinner in the bin. She'd normally have been furious that he hadn't called but, for the moment, her principal emotion was concern. She'd spent over forty years with a man who'd always been confident and composed, suddenly her husband looked a little lost.

Enright emerged from the bedroom just before midday, he'd been awake since eleven but the flowers he'd ordered from beneath the bed covers, shortly after he came to his senses, wouldn't be delivered for an hour. He decided it was safer to skulk under the duvet until the deliveryman had been and gone. He'd never been that good at apologies, so he hoped the flowers would do the trick. As he made it to the bottom of the stairs, Carol gave him a quick peck on the cheek and picked up her car keys.

"Lunch with Moira, try not to do yourself any more damage while I'm out." There was the merest hint of a smile. He was forgiven.

Enright spent the afternoon flipping between the sports channels. Anything with a ball would capture his attention, those were the sports that demanded real skill. Motor racing was all about the car technology and the quality of your legal team. A casual observer might believe that as many world championship points are decided in front of the appeals committee as on the track. Boxing was too violent and horse racing and athletics were just dull. Football, golf, rugby, tennis and cricket were all proper sports, requiring athleticism, skill, tenacity and strategy. That's what Enright loved. He'd have given all his wealth for one season in the first team at Coldharbour Town. Ideally they'd win the League and Cup double and he'd score the winner at Wembley, but he'd be handing over a lot of money, so he felt justified in expecting something special in return. At sixty-eight the idea was clearly preposterous. It hadn't been that much more credible fifty years earlier. Enright never rose above the lower reaches of the local Sunday Leagues. At his peak he was a tough, combative centre forward for the Harbour Arms pub team and after scoring a crucial hat trick, the Coldharbour Echo might have been mocking when they described him as the Geoff Hurst of Division Nine. It was 1966 and Hurst had recently become the first player to score three in a World Cup Final, Enright notched his on local marshland where twenty pitches were marked out within a few feet of each other. The paper commented on the fact that Enright didn't even have the pleasure of seeing his goals hit the back of the net. The local parks authority couldn't afford them.

He and Carol were married a year later and for twenty-five years they lived a modest but comfortable life on his salary as a warehouseman and hers as office manager for the same company. He'd almost said no, when Don asked him if he wanted to help start a new company. Enright had a pension, it was ten-minute drive to the office for him and Carol, and they still had a mortgage to pay. It was his wife who gave him the push he needed.

"The kids have nearly finished university, we've worked at the same place for what feels like decades and who's to say those jobs will be there forever. It's time for a change. Besides Don has offered me something too and I want to take it."

Jack was forty-six when he joined PhoneZone, inside ten years he was worth slightly more than sixty million pounds. They bought a new house, two new cars and started to indulge their son, daughter and grandchildren in a way they could never have imagined when they started out. Nothing too fancy, just some nice holidays, help with the latest generation's schooling and the safety net of knowing that there's someone in the family with very deep pockets, who will always be on hand when money runs low. Inside a year, Jack and Carol Enright ticked off everything on their list of "things to do when we're rich," except one. It took him an age to convince his wife that buying Coldharbour Town was a good idea, but in the end she couldn't think what else they might do with the money either. They never imagined the road could end in the Premier League and when it did; Jack and Carol Enright became the toast of Coldharbour. The following year they escaped relegation on the last day of the season with an improbable away draw against Tottenham Hotspur and once again the crowd rose to cheer their Chairman and his team. Then it all changed, it was as though the fans had said,

"The first season's always the tricky one, now the Chairman just needs to bung in thirty or forty million and we'll be in Europe in no time."

Enright knew he was paraphrasing one of football's more outspoken managers when he responded privately to a reporter who asked him about the fan's hopes.

"If they want to be in Europe, they should write something for the Eurovision Song Contest."

Ron Atkinson of Manchester United coined the phrase, talking about Brighton, his team's opposition in the 1983 FA Cup Final. It probably laid the foundations for his career as a TV pundit. Enright said it about his own team and when the story got out, it was the start of the campaign against him. Six months later he felt he had no choice but to sell the club to Dimitri Koloschenko, billionaire darling of the gossip columns.

Enright took a sip of the coffee and decided he'd recovered enough to risk some food. His first instinct was to find Carol, normally a baleful look and some aimless rooting around in the fridge would encourage her to sit him down while she rustled up a tasty snack. In his wife's absence, he wasn't willing to be much more adventurous than head for the biscuit tin. Armed with the coffee and a handful of chocolate digestives, he returned to his place by the TV set. Enright's generation was brought up on Match of the Day on Saturday night and the Big Match on Sunday afternoon. Highlights of one game plus a bit of goal action from a couple of others. Back then, Coldharbour Town rarely made it onto TV, but the pulses raced if he passed the ground on a Friday afternoon and saw the gantry being erected on the East Terrace. That's where the main camera would be positioned. Fifty years on and every match is televised and grounds have permanent camera positions. The viewing public is inundated with live football and the days between games have endless reruns of the previous match day's action. Enright was dubious about whether there'd be a massive audience for live football. The people who really want to watch are at the game, and what Liverpool fan wants to watch Cardiff play Crystal Palace? He never anticipated the monumental success of the initiative, not just in England, but around the world. His conversation with Sam Chalmers came back to him, although the detail had been slightly dulled by alcohol. Maybe that's when football really changed. When it all went crazy, it stopped being about the glory, suddenly it was all about the cash.

Even if Enright had anticipated the success of live TV, he'd never have foreseen the success of what he found on Sky Sports. He wasn't sure that watching live football would have mass appeal. Yet Sky had launched a show for Saturday afternoons, where the cameras are trained on four or five ex professional footballers who are each watching a live game and relaying what's happening to the viewing public. Britain was so football crazy, people were now paying to watch people watching the games. The madness was complete.

Enright was actually disappointed with himself, a few minutes in and he was hooked by the banter of the ex-players and the almost frightening energy of the presenter. The man appeared to be able to speak faster than Enright was able to hear, but he'd got the gist. The three teams below Coldharbour Town were all leading at half time, if that situation didn't change within forty-five minutes, his old club would be back in the relegation zone. Town would have a game in hand because later that afternoon they were playing in the Quarter Finals of the FA Cup against Aston Villa. The new owner had invited Enright to the game, but having seen that Koloschenko had told the Echo the club he'd acquired was a "shambles," Enright declined. The marathon session with Sam Chalmers was still weighing heavily on his system. Enright's eyes grew heavy and with no one to complain about the snoring, it was close to six p.m. when he woke. Flipping quickly through the channels, he found the Coldharbour – Villa game. It was half time.

"So are we on the verge of a massive upset here?" the host in the studio sounded as though he'd sprinted up a dozen or so flights of stairs before asking the question.

"It's not the goal that will do it Martin. It's the one-man advantage. I'd still be putting my money on Villa if they had eleven men out there. Down to ten, I think they have big problems." Gianni Zambretti had played for two of the top English sides and had won a few caps for Italy. He was the channel's top studio pundit.

"Let's see it again shall we?" The host still hadn't recovered his breath. "Talk us through it Gianni."

Enright watched as the camera showed a hopeful ball being pumped up field by Per Sunstrom.

"Martin, this looks very easy for the defender, he has time to clear, even to roll it back to the keeper, but see… here, he stumbles. Then Buckley just gets a foot to the ball. Then it's a race."

"Is it a foul? It looked as though the defender got plenty of the ball."

"Martin, I've watched the replay dozens of times. We've slowed it down, we've magnified it. There's contact with the player, but is it enough to bring him down? Did he get the ball first? Only Buckley really knows."

"But the referee was clear, it was a penalty and a red card."

"For sure, that's why Villa are struggling. Coldharbour have parked the bus. They have everyone behind the ball and Villa just can't find a way through."

Enright watched the replay again. A few weeks earlier and no doubt he'd have been on his feet screaming for a penalty and a lifetime ban for the psychopath who'd savagely dragged his player to the ground. He'd still not worked out how he felt about the club, since Koloschenko took over. To him it looked like a dive.

His watch showed six p.m. and Enright suddenly realised that Carol was yet to return from her lunch. He picked up his phone, the call was answered on the third ring. Carol had obviously seen the caller ID.

"Hello, you're through to Alcoholics Anonymous."

Enright chuckled. "Am I forgiven?"

"Moira told me every husband is allowed ten mistakes, then he should be tossed out."

"Sounds good to me."

"Not really Jack, that was number ten. You'll be fine as long as you don't screw up again."

"You are too kind dear lady. Talking of alcoholics, when are you planning on finishing lunch?"

Carol feigned horror at the suggestion she might still be drinking.

"One glass of Pinot that was all. I'm at the station. Don't tell me you've forgotten. Katie, your favourite granddaughter, we're going to be lavishing gifts and attention on her all weekend. She's got her place at Oxford, remember?"

"So you're picking her up."

"Well done Sherlock, the head's clearing then is it?"

"What time will you be back?" Enright asked, ignoring the jibe.

"Train get's in at six thirty, so let's say… about seven."

Enright picked up the remote control, it was tempting to watch the second half of Coldharbour's game with Aston Villa.

He shook his head and turned towards the bathroom. There was time for a shower before Carol arrived back with Katie.

Jack Enright was every inch the happily retired grandfather by the time he returned to his spot in front of the TV. A long hot shower and a shave banished the remaining fuzziness from the night before, a carton of milk settled his stomach. Chinos and a neatly ironed long sleeve shirt replaced the jogging pants and rugby shirt he'd worn earlier. Enright picked up the remote control and switched to BBC Sport, there was no need to wait for an update on the score at Coldharbour. The crowd scene was unmistakable, it was a replica of the one he'd seen nearly twenty-four month's earlier when the team won promotion to the Premier League. A sea of black and white scarves as the fans left their position in the stands and swarmed towards the tunnel. The scoreline was there on the screen.

Coldharbour Town 1 - Aston Villa 0.

Had Jack Enright not known the meaning of the phrase bitter sweet, it would have come to him there and then. The team he was forced to sell less than a month earlier was in the Semi-final of the FA Cup. The reporter had better news still for Coldharbour fans, their rivals had all squandered their half time advantage. Coldharbour was still one point above the relegation zone but now with a game in hand on those in the final three places. It was one of the great days in the history of the club, and the first home game for nearly sixty years that Enright had missed.

As the fans milled around the player's entrance, the camera focused for a second on the face of Sam Chalmers, he looked bemused but pretty content with the world. Enright was pleased for his old friend. His phone was vibrating on the table right in front of him. It was Carol.

"Hi darling."

"Jack, it's Katie, she wasn't on the train."

"Huh." It wasn't what he expected to hear and the calm in Carol's voice threw him slightly. Her voice conveyed no greater urgency than when he forgot the milk on his irregular trips to the supermarket. Then the floodgates opened.

"Jack, what am I going to do? She's not here, she's missing, we've lost our grand daughter. Oh my God, how am I going to tell Robert? It's that madman, he's got Katie... oh sweet Jesus, what are we going to do?" The words tumbled out.

"Carol, try to stay calm. Maybe she missed the train, phone Rob and see if she's been in touch, have you got her mobile?"

"Jack, I spoke to her twenty minutes before it was due. She told me herself she was on the train, she told me exactly what time she was going to get in. I waited until all the passengers were off and she wasn't one of them."

"Did you call her mobile?"

"For fuck's sake Jack, of course I called her mobile. What do you think I am, a fucking imbecile?" In over forty years it was the first time he'd ever heard her swear. "It went straight to voicemail, as though it had been cut off. I should have gone to London to collect her, Oh my God Jack, that lunatic is out there and we've practically handed our grand daughter to him."

"Wait there, I'm coming straight down."

# 8

Toby Thomas spotted Carol Enright as he stepped from the train. She was the last person he wanted to bump into, but it did confirm the instinct he'd had earlier. It was the girl in his carriage. There was something about her mannerisms, her face was roughly the same shape; the chin a little pointy, the mouth a bit too small but she was still a cracking looking girl. Those legs went on forever. Thomas was tempted to ask her if she fancied doing a bit of modelling, but there was something familiar about that face that made him hold back. Then he decided she was an Enright, a dead ringer for the wife of the great man himself. Asking her to get her kit off for the Echo was out of the question, but it wouldn't stop him having a little chat, seeing if she was single. For the life of him, he couldn't see why it all went so horribly wrong.

Thomas raced across the station concourse to find his car, Carol Enright was hopping from one foot to the other and craning her neck, to see if she could spot her granddaughter over the heads of the other passengers. Inside ten minutes he was pouring himself a very large whisky and it barely touched the sides. The second nearly drained the bottle, so he poured the last half centimetre straight into his mouth. The harsh liquor caught on the back of his throat and he coughed until his eyes were watering and his face was an unhealthy shade of pink. The train's heating had been jammed on and he refused to remove his jacket knowing his armpits would be dark with sweat. Now the shirt was clinging to his back and perspiration turned the fabric from light to dark blue.

Uncharacteristically, Thomas had left a third of the Rioja he'd opened to accompany his Chinese takeaway the night before. By taking a couple of large sips from the glass he managed to empty the bottle, before searching the cupboards for his last box of duty free Marlborough Lights.

"Fuck, where's the lighter?" He lit one gas ring on the cooker to get his first cigarette going.

Thomas threw open the balcony window and slumped into the cheap leather sofa, placed directly in front of the wide screen TV that dominated his living room.

He had a routine for occasions such as this, learned on one of the dozens of self-improvement courses he'd attended over the years. An American professor had explained how it didn't matter how crazy life had become, somewhere deep inside there was always a "rational you," with whom you could reason things out. That persona was smart, calm, intelligent and would, by any measure, be a vastly improved version of the sweating mass of nervous energy now slumped in front of the TV. Toby liked to call him Tobias.

"So what's gone wrong then? It was all going so well." Toby spat the question at his more rational self.

Tobias took a moment to ponder. "It's your cock mate. While you were focused on your career, it was all going great, then your cock got in the way."

It was tough to argue the point. Tobias continued.

"That Annie was a little slut, hard to summon a lot of sympathy for her, but Natalie, she was a cracker. That's a real pity man."

"Look, Annie came on to me, it was her idea to come round to the apartment. She did all the chasing." Toby was anxious to paint himself as an innocent victim of circumstance.

"So she forced herself on you?" Tobias sounded incredulous. Toby really had to do better than that.

"No, I'm not saying that. I was planning to hire the girl and I don't poke the payroll. It bumped into her in town and she suggested we went for a drink. I said no."

Tobias was incredulous, "Only because you didn't want to be seen with a girl who was dressed for a night on the town and was already drunk. Not good for your image?"

"I was the perfect gentleman. We were right by the Queen Victoria Gardens so I said we could chat for a few minutes on one of the benches, then she ought to go home."

"But that's not what happened is it?" Tobias had adopted the demeanour of a prosecuting counsel quizzing a man who'd been found standing over the body with a knife in his hands. He was supposed to be on Toby's side.

"Look mate, I had a glass or two myself. I wasn't really thinking straight and she suggested coming back to the flat." Toby pointed to the floor with both index fingers, as though his other self would have any doubt about the property to which he was referring.

"And you agreed."

"I was drunk and her tits where practically falling out of her top, and she kept crossing and uncrossing her legs... really slowly. You know."

Toby convinced himself that his rational counterpart had given him a nod of understanding, maybe even sympathy. He was ready to go on with his defence.

"I realised that I was being a dick when we got to the bus stop, she was already getting a bit antsy, because I hadn't sprung for a taxi. For some reason I decided that walking with her looked less suspicious than getting a cab." Toby shook his head as though that was his biggest mistake.

"And that's when it kicked off..." Tobias obviously knew the answer but he was keen to keep his other self focused.

"Yeah, she went fucking mental when I said I'd changed my mind. Offered her cab fare and everything. What was I supposed to do?"

"So what about Natalie? Should I be talking to you or your cock again here?"

"I was nuts about her. I told her I was going to leave the wife and kids and she could move in with me. That wasn't lust mate, I loved her, I really did. That's why I couldn't go through with shagging Annie Radford. I couldn't betray Natalie."

"But she wasn't up for it was she?" Tobias was supposed to be the calming influence but he was taunting.

"Natalie? No, she laughed, she said it was a bit of fun to her, nothing more. She liked the country house hotels, the fancy restaurants, but that was it. She said I could leave the wife if I wanted but it would be over with her. She wanted a nice uncomplicated fling, with no commitment."

"Isn't that what you're supposed to say?"

"That's what I wanted at the start. I didn't think I'd fall in love with her." Toby looked genuinely crushed.

"OK," Tobias said. "It's almost a compelling argument, but what about the girl on the train? Don't tell me you can justify that."

Toby closed his eyes and tried to replay the events of the day in his head. Originally the plan was to be at the FA Cup game with Villa. At the last minute he decided to see his family. The whole thing with Natalie made him feel that his life was coming apart at the seams. He wouldn't be leaving his wife, so he decided to make a go of it. A day out with her and the kids might bring a bit of stability to his world. London traffic was always a bear, that's why he decided to go by train. If only he hadn't gone by train. Fuck it, if only he hadn't gone at all.

"I knew they were heading for London Zoo in Regent's Park, so I thought I'd surprise them. I waited near the main gate… hiding behind the coach stop. I was about to jump out and say 'Boo,' or some shit like that. And that's when I saw they had company. He was nothing special to look at, but every time the kids weren't looking, he grabbed my wife's arse like it was his personal property. I was going to rush in and fight for her honour… it was more than she was doing. Then it happened. The kids rushed off for ice cream and candy-floss, and the fat little slut stuck her tongue down his throat and pushed her pelvis against his as though she was trying to climb inside."

"So what did you do next?"

"Dunno really… spent most of the rest of the day walking through the park, and when I got on the train I could barely remember how I got there.

"So what happened?" Tobias was in a hurry.

"With the girl on the train?"

70

"Yes, the girl on the train."

"She smiled when she first sat down but I was so caught up with what I'd seen at the Zoo, I hardly paid her any attention. It took me half an hour to calm down."

"Then what?"

"Well it was so hot, and she was wearing this really sheer top and the skirt, it was almost indecent. Three more inches and I reckon I'd be staring at her knickers. It all started to cling to her, I guess I got a bit… overwrought."

"Overwrought, yeah that's the word. So you started chatting to her." Tobias could barely conceal his contempt.

"Well, the old 'would you like a little modelling job?' always goes down pretty well, but I was sure I knew her from somewhere. I thought she was an Enright and when I saw Carol at the station, I was certain. Granddaughter I reckon, but really gorgeous, not like that dried out old bag."

"And she blanked you."

"She was polite enough, but she didn't want to talk. Then she fell asleep."

"Or pretended to be asleep so you'd fuck off and leave her alone." Toby flinched. He couldn't even get his "other self" to see things from his point of view.

"Yeah I guess so." The shame was starting to course through him.

"So that's when you did it."

"It was an accident at first. I crossed my legs and brushed against her calf, and she squirmed a bit in her sleep. So I did it again and when she moved I noticed I could see right up her skirt. And the shirt it was just clinging to her, honest, you'd have to be a man of steel not to respond to that."

"So say it. What did you do?"

"I touched her leg."

"With your hand?"

"Yes my hand. It was only a little caress, I didn't think I'd wake her up."

"And that's when she screamed?"

"Not really a scream, more a shout really. Then she kicked me. She called me a slimeball, I was trying to apologise, but she wasn't having any of it. Everyone in the carriage was looking at us."

"And the doors opened."

"Yeah, she called me a fucking pervert and ran for the door, that's the last I saw of her."

Tobias was thinking, weighing up the evidence placed before him. Toby was still gripped with panic, unable to see anything but the terrible hole that he'd dug for himself. His rational side would shortly deliver a calm, measured assessment of the situation he faced. It was taking an age.

"I'd say you're fucked," Tobias said finally.

"But I've done nothing wrong, OK a bit of mild groping but there were no witnesses to that bit, they only paid attention when the little bitch started screaming at me. I could front that one up if the police ever came to call."

"It's not what you've done Toby, it's how it looks. You leave Annie Radford at a bus stop in the middle of the night. Then some bloke pops up and sticks a knife in her. You're shagging the lovely Natalie and days after she tells you to fuck off, she winds up falling off Coldharbour Pier with half a dozen stab wounds in her back. You can say it's all coincidence but if your face ever gets linked to this, there'll be the cute little lady from the train who will say you were the guy who tried to feel her up when she was asleep. No doubt about it, unless they find the guy who actually did all this, you are seriously fucked."

\*\*\*

Jack Enright was trying desperately to console his wife when Katie appeared at the exit to the platform for trains from London. She raced across to her grandparents.

"So, so sorry I'm late. You must have been worried."

Enright took over, his wife was holding on to Katie as though she'd disappear if physical contact was broken.

"Frantic Katie love. Why weren't you on the train?"

"It was nothing, just a nasty little pervert, who was trying to catch a glimpse of my knickers." Enright blushed, he still thought of his granddaughter as a little girl.

"But, to be on the safe side, I jumped off at the last stop before Coldharbour and waited for the next train." Her grandparents both stared at her open mouthed, relief washed through them. "I tried to call, but the battery went flat after I called you last. I'm really sorry if you've been worried."

Enright recovered a little of his composure.

"What about this bloke, would you recognise him again?"

"Sure. But don't worry about it. He's just a nasty little perve, I don't think he'd harm a fly. He nearly wet himself when I screamed at him. Anyway, can we eat? I'm starving."

*** 

Yuri Slatkin was grateful that he'd knocked. It took a few seconds for Koloschenko to call him in and even as Slatkin opened the door, his boss appeared to be zipping up his trousers. Perched on the near side of the brand new mahogany desk, was a tall, slender woman with classic Slavic looks. Huge green-grey eyes, small nose and chin but a wide and sensuous mouth. Her carefully applied lipstick was a little smudged and she reached for her handbag for a mirror to assist in running repairs. As she turned her head, Slatkin could see her magnificent mane of blonde hair, tied in a very loose ponytail. It still reached the small of her back.

"Yuri this is Alina. We were celebrating our success."

Koloschenko picked up a tall champagne flute and filled it from the bottle that nestled in a silver ice bucket on the corner of the desk. Slatkin thought he might be offered a glass and clearly failed to hide the expectant look. Koloschenko noticed.

"She doesn't drink. And neither do you when you're working."

"Of course Dimitri. I just came by to congratulate you. It's been an amazing start to your ownership of the club."

Koloschenko snorted. "But there were protests."

"The team played in red, the crowd has never seen that before. They arc upset that you have not respected their traditions."

"I want security at the next game, anyone bringing banners into the ground will be stopped, anyone who protests will be ejected."

Slatkin had rehearsed for this response but still found it difficult to find the words to contradict his boss.

"Dimitri, please trust me on this. Let them have their little protest, it will fizzle out in a few weeks, especially if we get a good result in our next cup match. We need to win them over, we don't want this to get into the Press. They love a story like this and they will not be on your side."

It was a subtle way of reminding Koloschenko of his reason for buying Coldharbour Town in the first place. This was not about building a club, it was about securing his place on the celebrity circuit. An unseemly falling out with the fans would not be a positive step."

"What about the cats?"

"Dimitri, we've got a wonderful idea. We're going to tell the fans that from now on the nickname is "Lions." They still have their cat, but now it's bigger, more powerful. What do you think? They are football fans and they are English, I think they will be stupid enough to fall for it."

Koloschenko nodded his approval.

"Anything else Dimitri?"

"What the fuck is this?" Koloschenko tossed a thin folder across the desk. Only Alina's very shapely thigh stopped it from sliding onto the floor.

Yuri recognised the file that had passed through his own hands a few days earlier.

"It's goal line technology Dimitri. All Premier League clubs have to have it for next year. You will see my note, I think we should wait until we are sure that the club will not be relegated but there is a small discount if we go ahead now."

"Over five years this will cost me half a million pounds?"

"It's compulsory Dimitri we don't have a choice."

"So we install some cameras and if the referee cannot see the ball cross the line this will tell him."

"Precisely, that's how it works."

"And how often is this a problem for the referee exactly?"

Slatkin shrugged. "Hardly ever boss, but it changes the course of a game when it does happen. They want to stamp that out."

Koloschenko shook his head wearily. "And the handball by the defender, the dive by the forward, the sneaky tug on the shirt, the offside that they did not see because it all happened so fast. Do these things not all change the course of the game when the referee does not see them?"

"Well, yes, I suppose... but," Slatkin wasn't prepared for this argument. Koloschenko was usually blasé with his money, but occasionally he'd challenge an expense to remind his underlings he wasn't a soft touch. It was always wise to be able to explain why a cost was to be incurred. Slatkin had thought, the "we've got no choice" argument was a good one.

Koloschenko continued. "Yuri, they already have the technology to answer all these questions. Every game is on television and every contentious incident is replayed a million times. Why do they not just look at a TV screen? They would solve more issues without costing me half a million pounds."

"Dimitri, they say that football is a fast game, they don't want to slow it down for replays. And they don't worry about the cost, they assume you will add a few pounds to the cost of a replica shirt, charge a bit extra for refreshments. It's the fans who pay, not you."

"We need to do that anyway Yuri, I bought this club as an investment and I expect to see a return on my money. But the argument that it slows the game? Bullshit. Instead it stops while one disgruntled team surrounds the referee and screams about the injustice of it all. It makes no sense."

"Dimitri, I agree it's bizarre, but this is the decision they have made. If we are in the Premier League next year we have to have this technology."

"I understand the imperative, I merely question the rationale. Yuri, I have learned that everything has a reason and if something makes no sense, there is something we have not considered. If there is already a perfectly good solution to a problem, but you choose another that is less effective and more expensive, then someone, somewhere has his hand out and someone else is filling it with cash. It is why there are so many very wealthy bureaucrats in this world."

"Dimitri, please don't ever say that in public." Slatkin could picture the headline, 'Coldharbour Town owner accuses football bosses of corruption.' There was a neat English expression he could not quite bring to mind, something about pots and kettles.

"Yuri, I have no proof, you merely present me with some facts and I have drawn a conclusion. As you say, we have no choice. Let's wait until our future is secure in the Premier League."

Slatkin nodded and backed away towards the door. As exits went it would not have been out of place in the court of a Tudor monarch.

# 9

Sam Chalmers took pride in the fact that he was almost always last to leave the training ground, even though his role with the team was now peripheral to say the least. Koloschenko had brought in his own man from the previous year's Russian Federation champions and Chalmers was reduced to dealing with administrative tasks. As he opened the door of his Volvo, he spotted Adam Buckley walking towards a brand new Mercedes SL Cabriolet, a snip at just over seventy thousand pounds.

"Adam, I wanted to say well done. You got us to the semi-finals, that was a hell of a run."

"Thanks boss," Chalmers hadn't been called that for a while.

"Not sure we approached the game in quite the way I'd have done, but I guess the result is all that counts."

"Boris had it all planned. Stay in the game as long as we could, hit them on the break, then shut up shop. It was brilliant, worked a treat."

Chalmers blanched at the mention of the new Russian coach. He was happy to give the credit for a great victory to a lad he'd brought through from the youth team, handing it to the new guy really stuck in his throat.

"I suppose so Adam, not exactly champagne football though, was it?"

Buckley's face hardened. "We got the result didn't we?"

Chalmers ignored the remark. "Course the Villa fans are saying you dived." He'd watched the replay dozens of times and still couldn't work out whether it really was a penalty. Chalmers wanted Adam to tell him his legs were scythed from under him, that he'd fought to stay on his feet, so he could score from open play. He feared that was not the case. Chalmers' teams were regularly criticised for not being sufficiently "professional." TV pundits would point out how a defender hadn't sought to block an opposing attacker's run into the box. How a forward failed to "draw" a foul in the opposition's penalty area. They'd lambaste his teams for surrendering a lead because they hadn't used the techniques that were second nature to their opponents.

"They should take it to the corner flag, run down the clock. This is no time to be going for another goal."

"That's lack of experience. The boy should have stayed down after the foul, get the trainer on, break up the opposition's rhythm, give his team time to regroup. He'll learn."

"Chalmers still has two unused subs, he should be bringing them on now. One at a time of course, the ref never adds on the time it takes to swap the players. They just need to hang on for the whistle."

Chalmers had heard it all before and he still didn't get it. He knew he was practically a museum piece who still believed that whilst there were rules, there was also a spirit in which the game should be played. TV regularly featured a famous clip from his last season as a player. Coldharbour needed a point to secure promotion and they were level with two minutes to go in their final game. He was chasing down the opposition's centre forward who was put through by a lobbed pass from one of their midfielders. The forward took it a little wide, then a clumsy touch meant he lost control of the ball. He still had the chance to cut the ball back across the Coldharbour box. Chalmers slid in to tackle and the ball flew safely into touch. It all happened so fast, the officials couldn't see who'd made the last contact, the opposing forward's arm went up instantly to appeal for a corner. Both sets of fans were screaming for the decision to be given in their favour. The ball struck an advertising hoarding and landed back at Chalmers' feet. He calmly picked it up and rolled it out towards the corner flag, then took up his position on the six-yard line, to defend the corner. The officials breathed a collective sigh of relief that the decision had been made for them. Chalmers' shirt was tugged just as the ball arrived in the area, he lost his man. Their centre forward got the slightest of contacts and the ball flew into the top corner of the net. Coldharbour were condemned to another season in Division Two.

Chalmers anticipated the furore his action would create, some sections of the crowd and all of the Press condemned him as a deluded old fool. The clip was replayed over and over again, when Jack Enright appointed him as manager of the club. It was considered to be conclusive proof that Chalmers was not fit to manage a modern football club. For Enright, it was the clincher that made him certain he had the man he wanted. Adam Buckley was barely nine years old when it happened and it was inconceivable that he'd not have seen it on TV. It was still played as a reminder of the way the game used to be played... in the nineteenth century.

Adam was spared the TV interview after the Villa game. After his two-goal performance in the previous round, he was ushered in front of the cameras for his first interview on live TV. He'd been coached in all the things a professional footballer had to say, 'delighted for the team,' 'it's not about me, it's the lads, they were all brilliant,' 'we're going to take each match as it comes.' All that training was supposed to kick in when the interviewer presented him with the Man of the Match Award and asked the big question.

"How does it feel to put your team into the Quarter Final of the FA Cup?"

Adam hadn't hesitated, he told the millions who were watching the interview around the world that it was "fucking brilliant." Mercifully, team captain Per Sunstrom was on hand to usher him away and pick up the interview. He told the interviewer that he was delighted for the team, that it wasn't one individual, all the lads did their job and that they were just going to take one game at a time. His banal clichés were replayed over and over again on the internet and reported in the written press as though they'd been handed down by the Pope himself. Adam's interview got far more attention on the internet of course, and the UK press feigned horror as they covered the story in great detail. There was no way that Adam would be risked in front of the cameras again, so the world was yet to hear his view of the crucial tackle, the penalty and the red card issued to Villa's centre half.

"I felt contact so I went down," he told Chalmers.

"You did what?"

"Boris says if you feel contact then you're entitled to go down."

"So you dived."

Adam looked genuinely confused. "I felt the touch, so I went down."

"But you could have stayed on your feet, if you'd tried."

"Boris said, if you feel contact..."

"You can cheat."

Chalmers turned away in disgust. Adam stared at the departing figure as though he'd had an encounter with an alien. He'd seen it a thousand times on TV, the best forwards in the world did exactly the same. When the occasion demanded it, they could ride the most aggressive of tackles, it was what they trained for, but if the chance was about to elude them and they felt a touch, that was a foul. They could go down. Plain diving was wrong of course, if you got caught at least, but if the other guy clips you, you're entitled to hit the floor. Gravity was no longer the deciding factor.

Everyone did it, Adam simply couldn't see where Chalmers was coming from. The dressing-room talk was no longer speculation, Boris would be taking over as soon as their future in the Premier League was settled. If they stayed up he'd get the credit anyway, as the guy who came in and sorted them out. If they went down, sacking Chalmers would send the signal that he was to blame.

"You're getting sacked you old has been," Adam said as soon as he sure that Chalmers was out of earshot.

He was wrong. Chalmers had gone to write his resignation. It said, "Dear Dimitri, Fuck you, I quit."

***

80

He'd only been doing it for two weeks but just as they tell you on TV, Special K can definitely aid weight loss as part of a calorie controlled diet. Tony screamed with laughter whenever he saw the adverts for the breakfast cereal on TV. His favourite jeans had been getting a little tight round the waist and he'd asked for some new shirts at work. Leaving the top button undone was against company rules and the old ones were starting to chafe. Then the dreams started, Annie Radford, Natalie Simpson and his frame-by-frame recall of how he killed them both. Every day was an ordeal, each time he stepped outside he was sure he'd bump into a friend of one of the girls who'd died, or the police would finally work it out. Someone must have seen him do it, he must have left some sort of evidence at the scene. They'd find him eventually, it was only a matter of time. Every night, over and over again, he'd replay the deaths of the two young women.

Then came the hope. The call that said his father was back in town. A convicted killer had turned up out of the blue and two girls are murdered. Maybe his dreams were some sort of guilt transfer, his father was the man they were looking for, but some astral connection had placed the images in his son's mind. In Tony's increasingly addled brain, that made a hell of a lot of sense. It was four agonising days before Alan Drake made contact again. He was looking at chisels in the DIY store where Tony worked when they literally bumped into each other. It was midday and the store was quiet, it wasn't too hard to get the manager to agree that he could have an early lunch. McDonalds had recently opened close to the entrance of the trading estate where he worked.

Tony didn't ask what his father wanted to eat and Alan didn't offer to pay. The younger man bought a couple of Big Mac meals and looked around to see if his father had found a table. In some ways Alan Drake had aged well, with a full head of hair, even if it was heavily streaked with grey. He didn't have an ounce of surplus weight and from a distance he still possessed the rakish good looks that had been the secret to his success with countless women. The clothes looked fairly smart too. Alan always had a taste for brand names and the jacket looked to be expensively tailored, the trousers were well pressed, but possibly a little too short, and the absence of a belt was a fair indication that corners were being cut to put his wardrobe together. At twenty paces Alan Drake looked like a well-to-do middle-aged man who'd done a pretty good job taking care of himself. Close up it all fell apart. The twinkling blue eyes had lost their sparkle, his cheeks and eyes appeared to have sunk into his face and his lips were white and cracked. When he smiled, his teeth suggested a man who smoked and had lost a fight. Two were missing, the rest were yellowed from a habit that was clearly affecting his lungs. The brief walk to the burger bar left him gasping for breath and twice he'd doubled over as his body was seized with a violent coughing fit.

Alan was seated close to the back of the restaurant, facing the entrance. He looked around nervously as though expecting an unwelcome visitor to arrive at any minute, then he'd check the door to his rear as though anxious to ensure he had an escape route should the need arise. Tony dropped the cardboard tray onto the table and took the seat facing his father. Alan's head bobbed from side to side as though he was frustrated that he no longer had an unimpeded view of the front door. Tony paused while his father fought to control another bout of coughing.

"What do you want?" Tony's voice was flat. He was desperately trying to control the rage that was welling inside of him. Whoever killed those girls, he was looking at the man who was to blame. Alan Drake had either done the deed himself or handed down the genes that had turned his own flesh and blood into a killer.

"Look son, I know I've been a really shit dad and I'm not claiming that I've come back to make it all right. But I will,

I promise. I just need time." Alan Drake was getting more agitated as he spoke. Unable to sit still for a moment he started to rub his nose and the area around his top lip as though he had a sudden and unbearable itch.

"So why are you here?"

"I need a bit of help son, a little loan to tide me over. You know how it is. A mate of mine's promised me a job, should start next Monday. Then I'll pay you back… I promise."

"Where did you get my phone number?"

Alan looked confused as though he had no recollection of ever calling his son. Then it all came back.

"Oh, I bumped into one of your old school mates. Can't remember his name now but he was in the Harbour Arms. I popped in there for a pint… you know. Lucky he recognised me, but he was still cagey about giving me your number. I had to use all my charm on him." Alan Drake pushed out his chest and raised his head proudly in the air as he uttered those words. For a moment it evoked the memory of the charming, irascible rogue that Tony remembered from his childhood. The image faded as fast as it came as Alan's body was racked with another coughing fit.

"So why didn't you call back?"

"I lost the number, no idea what happened to it. Then I saw your mate again and he told me you worked at the DIY."

"And you want money."

"Just a few quid son, till I get my wages at the end of the month."

"There are some things I need to know first."

This was going better than Alan Drake had hoped, it sounded like he'd have to answer a couple of questions but then his son would give him the advance he needed. There was no mate and no job, the following week he'd have to explain that it had all fallen through, but maybe Tony could spare another few quid.

"Anything son, you know you can ask your old dad anything you like." Alan reached across the untouched burgers to grip his son's arm. Tony pulled away.

"You killed Natalie and Annie didn't you?"

Alan Drake paused and cocked his head to one side as though he was going through the list of all the people he'd killed to see if there was anyone of either name.

"Son, what the fuck are you asking me?"

"You killed those two girls, I know you did." Tony was desperate for him to admit the crime. As far as he was concerned there were only two suspects and they were both sitting at that table.

"What girls? I have no idea what you're talking about."

Tony was struggling to keep his voice down, fighting to stop himself from reaching across and choking his father until he admitted to what he'd done. "Two girls were stabbed in Coldharbour in the last two weeks. I know it was you."

Alan sat back in his seat and went to pick up one of the burgers, Tony smashed his fist into the back of his father's hand sending meat, bread and relish flying across the floor.

"Tony, for fuck's sake, calm down. I read about it in the paper. It couldn't have been me."

"Why should I believe that?"

"Because I was inside," he was frantically searching his pockets for something.

"Inside what?" A cold mass formed in Tony's stomach, one of the prime suspects was about to claim his innocence and that left only one person who could possibly be the killer. Alan found what he was looking for and laid it out on the table between them, carefully ironing out the creases with a ketchup covered hand.

"It's my discharge notice. Lewes Prison. Dated last Monday, the day after that Natalie bird got cut up. I've got as good an alibi as you can get."

Tony's mouth gaped and a hoarse rattle came from the back of his throat. It was Alan who spoke next.

"What the fuck made you think I killed them?"

"You're a fucking murderer, and you got out four years ago."

"And I went back in, I had no money so I got caught up with some guys who said they'd help me out for a bit. The parcels I was delivering didn't have antique books in them after all." Alan tried a little chuckle to ease the tension, then gave a helpless shrug, trying to convey that, once again, someone had taken advantage of his good nature.

"That's why I need your help now son, I don't want to get stuck on that road again. You want your old man to go straight don't you?" Once again a tiny flicker of the man that Tony remembered from childhood.

"But you killed that other girl right? The one you went down for first time."

Alan nodded, as though the question he'd just been asked was no more significant than a query as to whether he took milk in his coffee. The anger appeared to have subsided in his son, so he made a grab for a handful of french fries.

"I guess I must have done son. She had a clump of my hair in her hand." He made it sound like he was the victim. "They got some fingerprints, they even found some of my blood and that scarf, I loved that scarf." It was the first point in the story where Alan Drake sounded regretful. So a girl had died, he killed her, but *he'd* lost a favourite item of clothing.

"And of course there was the bloke who saw me walk away from the scene. I woke up when they kicked my door down the next morning. I have no idea what I did that night but it sort of looks like I did it. Take your punishment and move on, that's what I say."

From his tone and body language, Alan Drake might have been talking about being caught driving away, after grazing the bumper of a parked car.

"Do you ever think about her?"

Alan Drake grabbed another handful of fries. He was trying to work out whether it would be safe to take the other burger, his son didn't look that interested in the food.

"Who?"

"The girl you killed for fuck's sake."

"Course not... can't even remember her name."

"Penny."

"Huh?"

"Her name was Penny, she was eighteen and she was about to go to college and you stabbed her."

"If you say so son. I paid the price, I don't give it a second thought any more. Except for the dreams."

Tony froze. He stared at his father with eyes and mouth wide open.

"Yeah, I used to get them all the time at the start, pretty scary to be honest back then. Really vivid they were, like I was replaying the whole thing in my head. Part of the reason I kind of accepted that I must have done it. But after a while I hardly got them at all. Found a little medication in prison that helped and that was it. Still get the odd flashback but it's no big deal."

Alan Drake gave his son a broad smile and finally found the courage to unwrap the other burger. Tony stood and grabbed the jacket he'd left on the bench seat next to him.

"Hey son, where are you going?"

"As far away from you as I can get."

"What about my money?"

"Stay away from me, I never want to set eyes on you again. You're a fucking monster."

Tony almost fell over the woman who was cleaning up the mess they'd left on the floor next to their table. As he reached the door, it felt as though a storm was raging in his head, but he could still hear her voice.

"Have a nice day."

Tony had tried to blot out the meeting with his father, when sheer willpower failed, he turned to extra strength lager, when that stopped working he tried vodka. Then a combination of the two. He awoke with a hangover, sleep was fitful, he murdered Annie and Natalie three more times that night. On each occasion the act was more vicious and cruel than before. Those dreams were interspersed with images of his father standing over the body of a girl called Penny. In his hand was a knife… he was laughing.

The meeting with Tim was an accident. Tony only made the trip to the Harbour Arms to stock up on Stella Artois and Smirnoff.

"Fuck me Tony, you look like shit. What have you been up to?"

"Drinking." Tony wasn't interested in having a chat, he was anxious for the server to get back with his supplies.

"No shit. I don't preach but haven't you had enough?"

"No mate, it's not quite had the effect I'm looking for, so I'm still working on it."

Tim waited all day every day for a chance like this. "Maybe you need some of this." He rooted around in his jacket pocket and having diagnosed his patient's symptoms he was sure he'd prescribed the appropriate medication.

"What is it?"

Tim gave a furtive look around the empty bar as he placed a cellophane bag on the table next to his pint.

"Ketamine."

Tony had read about it. Horse tranquiliser. Basically an anaesthetic, adherents talk about a floating sensation, about feeling that the mind was separated from the body, and that after one hit nothing was really that important.

Two weeks later and Tony had all but exhausted Tim's supply. It was awesome, but the effect was short lived. One hit might last two hours if he was lucky. Tony started taking it with food, he wasn't sure what else to do with the fine white powder, then he began taking it instead of food. The jeans were suddenly pretty loose and had he been going to work, his old shirts would have fitted a treat. He'd called in sick more than a week earlier.

The dreams were less frequent and when they came, they were certainly less vivid. It was actually quite hard to see the faces of the girls. Tony watched TV and when that breakfast cereal advertisement came on he laughed until his sides ached. He knew Ketamine like an old friend now and when he placed his order with Tim, he called it by its street name. Special K.

# 10

Zainab Mansour always had a smile on her face. It wasn't a question of whether the glass was half full or half empty, for Zainab it was as full as it needed to be and she wouldn't dream of asking for more. Her homeland had been torn apart by war, but whilst friends and relatives died, her immediate family made it to the Turkish border and, twelve months later. were accepted as refugees in the United Kingdom. Her father had saved a little, but everything he had went in securing their passage across Europe. He despised Saddam Hussein and often described life in pre-war Iraq as like living in an open prison. They had a good life, a reasonable income but lived in constant fear that something they said or did would be a real or imagined slight in the minds of those in authority. A neighbour and his family disappeared, there was talk of them being spies for the Americans. It was more likely that the Ba'ath party member who'd coveted their house for years had denounced them. The man took up residence within days of their disappearance.

Zainab's father initially welcomed the allied invasion, it would free them of the tyrant. Then he started to question their methods as more and more civilians died in the air attacks, later he questioned their motives. Western politicians spoke of Iraq's support of Al Qaeda and their readiness to use so called weapons of mass destruction. Hasim Mansour, like most Iraqis and a host of western academics, believed that Saddam considered Islamic fundamentalism to be as much of a threat to him as it was to the west. Nobody believed he'd spend money on nuclear capability, the Army wasn't that well equipped and the Hussein family was far too interested in new palaces, fast cars and expensive trinkets to waste cash on weapons they'd never use. Zainab's father decided that the west was not offering a war of liberation, but one of conquest. The reward was the vast oil fields of Iraq. He packed everything they could carry and headed for the border.

Hasim lost his wife to cancer weeks after they settled in the UK. He survived until Zainab, his youngest daughter, graduated from Imperial College and returned to Coldharbour to work as a laboratory technician at the local University. Zainab worshipped the man who'd risked everything to give his family a new start. There were dark days, loneliness, the fear she might not make the grade at university or at work and the normal day-to-day strains of making your way in a world that could not have been more different from the one she left behind. Then she'd think about the terror, when the bombs fell, the friends who'd not turn up for the school the day after an allied raid and the hushed tones her parents would use when they spoke, hoping their children could not hear. Then she'd decide that she was one of the luckiest people alive.

As she set out for home that night, her outlook on the world was being severely tested. An experiment had gone badly wrong, it wasn't just that it had to be repeated, the lab had to be cleaned and orders written out to replace equipment that was damaged beyond repair. When she got to her car, the battery was flat and the last of her colleagues had turned out of the car park on their way home. Zainab reached for her phone, then she could picture it… on her desk where she placed it as she put her coat on. The door to the lab was locked and she didn't have a key. It would take an hour to walk home, but there was a taxi rank about ten minutes in the other direction.

The rain had stopped but there was a cold easterly wind, Zainab pulled the sides of her hijab together for warmth. She wore the veil, not for religious reasons, but because she liked the colour and it was practical in the ever-changing weather of a coastal town in early spring. She spotted the shambling figure when he was still about a hundred yards away. His face was cast down, a hoodie covered his head. Zainab felt a chill run through her as she remembered the briefing they'd given at the university the week before. The Coldharbour Ripper was at large and everyone should take extra care. She pulled up the collar of her coat and used the cover of a couple of large oak trees to cross the road, she was sure the man hadn't seen her. When Zainab got to the other side she took one quick look around, the man had disappeared. She breathed a sigh of relief and turned to continue on her way. The taxi rank was no more than four hundred yards away, just around the next corner. The man wasn't shambling any more, he was standing right in front of her. She tried to scream but a hand closed across her mouth, with one twist of his powerful arms he spun her round so he was behind her. The only thing that she could focus on was that he was wearing gloves… she could taste cotton fibre. The man released his grip and Zainab thought she was free. That was when he plunged the knife into her neck.

***

The night shift arrived and handovers were being completed all around Coldharbour Police Station. Maggie Davenport had been at her desk since seven that morning. One of the constables had left a coffee at her elbow about an hour earlier. It separated in the cup as it cooled, leaving a thick film of scum on the top. She had nothing, no forensic evidence, no witnesses, no CCTV footage, not even a worthwhile tip from a suspicious neighbour or disillusioned girlfriend. They had plenty of calls. One claimed the murderer was Prime Minister Cameron, allegedly trying to strike fear into the poor to take their minds off the mess he was making of the country. Several suggested it was alien abductions that had gone wrong and then there were the most worrying ones of all. They were the people who claimed to be the perpetrator. Most were astonished to find the police at their doors, having traced the mobile phone or IP address from which the "confession" was made. Davenport suspected they were grateful, after all who'd do such a thing if it wasn't an attempt to get attention. They'd get plenty of that, in due course. In the meantime she was simply battling to keep her officers on the trail of the person who really did it and these interruptions were a pain in the arse.

Maggie Davenport had to admit that she joined the police having been captivated by their portrayal on TV. She took the fact that the reality was somewhat different in her stride. Fictional detectives are invariably deeply flawed individuals who solve crime in spite of their physical handicap and/or psychological issues, whilst battling against hostile superiors and jealous and uncooperative colleagues. They treat the rulebook with the disdain it deserves and generally win the day with intuitive brilliance or an improbable slice of luck. Davenport had no physical or mental issues, no dodgy home life or complex relationships and, on her bedside table was a copy of the Police (Conduct) Regulations 2008. She lived with an ex-soldier who understood the rigours of her job and didn't give her a hard time about long hours and dates cancelled at short notice. She channelled what maternal instincts she possessed for the benefit of an eleven-year-old Siamese cat called Cleo.

Davenport's parents had been horrified when she told them she wanted to join the police. The random shooting of PC Yvonne Fletcher outside the Lybian Embassy in 1984 was still all too fresh in their minds. She'd started patrolling her neighbourhood from the moment her parents allowed her to play outside, her favourite toys were a notebook and pencil for taking statements from friends, family and household pets. A determined child, there seemed to be little her parents could do but hope that she'd fail to attain the minimum height. A growth spurt in her late teens and the politically correct abandonment of the requirement in the 1990s left them disappointed. Their daughter's rise through the ranks was impressive but not stellar and one wise colleague noted that she was lucky to be pleasant enough to look at but no ravishing beauty. That would have made life in the force even tougher. Her ultra-pale skin was in stark contrast to jet-black shoulder length hair, cut straight just above full dark eyebrows. The look was a deliberate attempt to mimic her favourite English teacher. Miss Conway was both capable and intimidating.

Davenport won her spurs at police college with the type of calmness under pressure that was to become her hallmark. Her colleagues were drinking at the bar when she went out to call her then boyfriend. When she returned only two remained and they were giggling conspiratorially.

"So Steve, what would you call it?"

"Dunno mate, it's like a third leg."

"Here Maggie, come and inspect the evidence."

Davenport didn't need to be a detective to work out what was going on. She picked up her gin and tonic and walked back to where the two men were standing. As expected Colin Paston had unzipped and was cradling what he'd been assured on many occasions was his prodigious manhood.

"So what do you make of that then?"

Scratching the side of her head as though genuinely confused, Davenport finally spoke. "Well I guess it's like a penis... only smaller."

It was a second or so before the two men realised their bluff had been called and they both roared with laughter. Davenport drained the last of her drink and then turned towards the door. She gave them one last contemptuous look then said, "It looks to me like it would never stand up in court."

If it wasn't for the fact that her current case was getting nowhere, life was pretty straightforward but she'd resigned herself to the fact that they'd never make a TV drama called simply, Davenport. Her team had followed the book in all respects, they'd pursued every line of inquiry they could imagine, and drawn a complete blank. There was a tenuous connection between two of the victims but even that was challenged by the death of Zainab Mansour. The other girls were at school together, Zainab's family was from the other side of town.

Davenport had only two leads and she called her sergeant in to go over it all again.

"So what's the story with Drake?" Davenport still believed this was her best line of inquiry.

"We've interviewed him twice and there's nothing to go on. He has no alibi for any of the killings, but we have nothing to link him to the scene and he has no motive for Annie Radford or Zainab Mansour. He's a bag of nerves, but he just repeats the same thing over and over. Simpson was..."

"Natalie," Davenport corrected him.

"Yeah sorry, Natalie was his girlfriend. He's a mess, he might be guilty but it could just as easily be because he's upset. The Simpson family think he's a lovely lad. Until we get something concrete, it's a dead end."

"Where was he last night?"

"I went round to his place first thing this morning. He was there and we woke him up. To be honest ma'am he wasn't behaving like a man who'd killed someone a few hours earlier. I reckon he's using, downers not uppers and he was completely zonked. I asked him what he'd been up to and he just said 'I didn't kill Annie or Nat, I swear, it wasn't me.' So I asked him if he'd killed anyone else, and he looked confused. Either he's an awesome actor or he didn't even know that another girl had been murdered."

"So we leave him? Is that what you're saying?"

"We're waiting for forensics, that might turn something up, but all we've got on Drake is that he split up from one of the girls four years ago."

"And the train pervert?"

"Katie Enright's given us a description but she laughed when we said we thought he might be the killer. She said he was just a little creep who nearly pissed his pants when she screamed at him."

"Anything from the description."

"Nothing yet, but we're trying to get that Thomas bloke to agree to put it on the front page of the Echo midweek. It's been pretty hard to get hold of him."

"That's all we've got?"

94

The sergeant could only manage an embarrassed grimace. He knew that Davenport's frustration wasn't directed at him. It just felt that way.

*\*\*\**

Koloschenko's chauffeur driven Range Rover slowed only briefly. Security had been warned of his imminent arrival and a dozen thickset men wearing high visibility vests had formed a cordon to keep the protesters away from the gate. There were forty or so, all wearing the black and white shirts that were Coldharbour's home strip until the change of ownership. All were bravely resisting the temptation to put on a jacket against a cold wind that was blowing from the East. As a light drizzle began to fall, their leader began distributing scarves and woolly hats, again in club colours. It was like the old days, on the picket lines, when local union members stood up to greedy factory owners. Once again, wives and families were on hand with soup and sandwiches. Several of the protesters had been there over thirty years earlier and they reminisced of their glorious battle with their bosses. It was a pyrrhic victory, many of the factories they targeted were forced to close their doors when they withdrew their labour, most never reopened. It was just the incentive the owners needed to shift their manufacturing centres to Asia. The town had never fully recovered.

There were several banners, few risked spelling the Russian's name in full. "Kolo out," featured on several. "Ruskis not welcome here," was another popular choice, the maker of "Krauts go home," got high marks for effort but nothing for his grasp of colloquial abuse. Far busier than the protest site was the nearby school playground, empty for the Easter holidays and used as a car park at the weekends by those attending the match. At least two hundred people were queuing at stalls set up to sell what was being described as Coldharbour Town memorabilia. It wasn't intended to evoke a bygone age, it was supposed to remind people of the days when the club wore black and white and the club nickname traced its lineage to a ship's lucky cat. That was less than two months before. Striped shirts were selling at a rate that the top clubs would have envied. Cuddly black toy cats were the next most popular choice, followed by a range of t-shirts with snappy slogans like, "Cool Cats never lose their stripes," and "Dimitri's a lion bastard." And they were a bargain, about a third of the price of the equivalent product in the club's official shop. The promise that every penny raised would go the "Keep the Cat - Fighting Fund," gave a pretty heavy hint that a wealthy man had paid for their manufacture. Jack Enright wasn't picking a fight with Koloschenko, but when the chairman of the supporter's club asked him for help, he decided to do it in style.  On his trip to the ground, Koloschenko passed a high street shop that had been boarded up two weeks earlier. The "Keep the Cat," sign was above the door and the same stuff was on sale. The queue at the new place in town was a little longer than that at the makeshift market near the ground. As he passed the club's official store, the only activity was a desperately bored looking assistant taking a lengthy cigarette break. The Russian was close to boiling point by the time he met Slatkin in his office.

"Yuri, you advised me that we should be patient, cup success would banish any opposition to the changes I have made. Your lion was supposed to consign their flea-ridden cat to history. Today I need a team of security guards to ensure my safe passage into the club I have purchased, while that bastard Enright taunts me with his charity shops. Do you have a Plan B?"

Slatkin deeply regretted his plan to introduce the lion nickname, it made him an architect of the catastrophe rather than the trusted advisor making the best of his master's poor decision. He was desperate to remind Koloschenko that he'd advised against any changes until they had their feet under the table. He'd seen enough of his boss to know that was probably the equivalent of a resignation letter, maybe even a suicide note.

"Dimitri, it looks bad but we have to give this time. I've given a confidential briefing to the Echo to say that we are in negotiations for three or four world famous players. We have a home game coming up and the cup semi-final. If we could just get two victories, all this would be forgotten. Boris needs to know that it's in his hands."

Koloschenko nodded, the argument appeared to have worked. It was classic deflection on Slatkin's part. It was pointless trying to argue that he was not responsible for the mess, next best thing was to suggest that it was down to someone else to get them out of it.

Koloschenko leaned forward placing both hands, palms down on his desk.

"Yuri, I think I have been badly advised."

The words struck terror into Slatkin's heart. The man who offended Koloschenko by saying that he could have found him a cheaper watch had lost his job and been told he'd never work in Russia again. Slatkin heard that he was now a croupier on a cruise ship that ferried old age pensioners around the Mediterranean. Slatkin was instrumental in the multi million pound purchase of a Premier League football club. It was central to Koloschenko's plan to transition from gangster to legitimate businessman and part of the trendy London scene. Koloschenko was not happy with the advice he'd received.

"In what way, Dimitri?"

"Abramovich bought Chelsea, I am told they were already a successful club, he simply had to give them more impetus. And the location, could not be more perfect, it's two miles from my London apartment. Yuri, I could walk it in thirty minutes."

"But Dimitri…" Slatkin was grateful his boss ignored him, he'd started a sentence he didn't know how to finish.

"And Manchester City, they have history, they have a magnificent new stadium, it is the city of George Best. And what do I have? Coldharbour Town, a filthy run down little club in a filthy run down little town. Alina has refused to set foot in this place again, she says it smells of rotten fish. I have people telling me I am not welcome here when I have rescued the club from the brink. Yuri, I am very unhappy with the bargain I have made. Neither does it open the doors I expected in London. Did you see the Sun, they were calling me the "new Abramovich," this week it's the "poor man's Abramovich."

Slatkin was lost for words, Dimitri was talking about the collapse of his dream and he was holding his *consigliere* responsible.

"Dimitri, I don't know what to say. I ummm…"

"Yuri, I didn't ask for your opinion. I have made a decision and I am asking you to execute it. Nothing more or less."

"Of course Dimitri, anything you say."

"I've been approached by an American businessman who wishes to buy the club. He is willing to pay a modest premium as long as we secure the services of that Buckley boy. He is part of the deal, no Buckley no sale."

Yuri smiled for the first time since he'd pushed his way through the protesters to get to the stadium that morning.

"Dimitri, we already have him on a three year contract. It was the first thing we did when we took over."

Koloschenko sneered at his employee. "Yuri, the last couple of months have been a painful learning curve for me. Things a businessman takes for granted in the real world simply do not apply in football. I can be forced to buy equipment I don't need, I make changes to how my business operates and my customers demand that I quit. If you don't like the renovations in your local supermarket, you don't demand the sacking of the chairman of the board, you take your custom elsewhere. These people think they own the club that I paid for and I will not tolerate it."

Slatkin briefly considered explaining that allegiance to your local team can hardly be compared with the choice of where you buy your teabags, but then dismissed the idea. He didn't have the courage. What all this had to do with Buckley was truly beyond him.

"So Buckley has signed a contract."

"Yes Dimitri."

"And if he decided he wants to leave, we can hold him to it."

"Of course."

"But it never happens Yuri, does it? These little bastards go on strike, they whine to the press, they talk about their 'boyhood dreams,' and they make it impossible for the team to play, because one of their number has made it clear that he thinks he is too good for the rest of them. I've seen how it works and it will not happen to me."

"So what should I do, Dimitri?" Slatkin failed to keep the quiver out of his voice. Koloschenko wanted solutions not questions, but he was truly at a loss.

"Next week, we will announce that Buckley has signed a five year contract, that is the minimum the American will accept and you will ensure that the player understands that he cannot make a transfer request."

"But Dimitri, how can I…?"

"Tell him you'll have his sister killed, I don't care Yuri, just do it."

"Anything else boss?"

Koloschenko paused for a second. "Tell Boris I want to see him. I need to leave this club as a winner not a loser. The deal will only go through if we stay in the Premier League, but I think I'd also like to win this FA Cup. Get Boris."

Slatkin was almost crouching as he backed humbly through the door.

***

Adam Buckley waved the door keys in the air and then placed them on the kitchen worktop, so his friend could find them.

"It's meant to be a change of scene for you Tony. It's what mates are for. Rest up here for a couple of weeks, I've sorted it so someone will come in and keep the fridge topped up. If you need anything else you've got my mobile number, just call."

"Adam, I'm really grateful mate but you don't have to do this, I'll be fine."

Adam shook his head and laid a reassuring hand on Tony's arm. "You're not a well man. Just have a rest. It's a really cool apartment, great view, biggest wide screen I could find and a cute little Filipino to come in and cook your dinner if that's what you want."

"Cheers Adam, maybe for a week or so. I don't know what's happened to me the last few weeks. I get these dreams and I've been taking this stuff and... I dunno." Tony rubbed the corners of his eyes with the tips of his index fingers, then shook his head vigorously as though trying to dislodge an unwelcome presence in his skull.

Adam rested his hand on Tony's shoulder. "I ain't judging you man. I wouldn't take that stuff myself but you do what you have to do. Take a break that's all."

As the door closed behind his friend, Tony Drake caught sight of himself in the hallway mirror. His eyes had sunk into their sockets, his cheekbones stuck out and his face was drawn and pale. For a moment he thought he was looking at his own father, he had that same deathly pallor when they met in McDonalds. All life had gone out of his eyes. Lengthy experimentation had uncovered the perfect dosage of Special K. He was taking just enough to keep him in a place he dubbed "zombie." Even when the police had knocked on his door a few days earlier, he stayed calm, on the outside at least. There was something banging away at his brain telling him he should be panicking, there was another voice screaming at him to tell them everything. To throw himself on their mercy and explain that it wasn't his fault. The voices were fighting it out all the time the police were at the door. Then he watched himself say that he'd been there all night and then repeat that he'd not killed Annie or Nat.

He almost unravelled when he saw the news bulletin that announced yet another girl was dead, but a carefully measured dose of the fine white powder and zombie was back. That was how Adam found him and that's when his friend made the offer. Adam had bought the flat as a 'buy to rent' property, but he didn't have a tenant yet. Tony could move in and there was a young lady who'd come in and do whatever Tony wanted. Adam winked when he said that, but the point was lost on Tony. It was a change of scene. Maybe it would help him banish the dreams for good. Only time would tell.

Tony checked his supplies, he had only enough Special K for four more hits. Tim would be at the Harbour Arms, in the little cubicle close to the toilets. The bar staff couldn't see him, but everyone in the pub had a reason to wander past where he was sitting. They dropped the cash on his table when they went in and collected their purchase on the way out. Adam had left some cash next to the door keys.

"I know you're not working at the moment. If you need any of this, take it." Tony wanted to protest, but he knew he didn't have the money to get what he needed from Tim without it. He'd nodded and given his old friend a grateful smile.

Tony checked his watch again, Tim would be open for business in twenty minutes. He picked up the black fleece jacket that was part of his work uniform and headed for the door.

***

Maggie Davenport felt like she'd been asleep for less than an hour when her mobile rang. She was way off, it was a full seventy minutes since she climbed into bed, deferring the shower until morning, after another fourteen-hour shift. There was only one development in the case. The perpetrator managed to kill both Annie and Nat without leaving any forensic trace whatsoever. It was as though he'd touched neither girl. On Zainab, there were tiny threads on her back and shoulders and some cotton fibre between her teeth. It was consistent with someone holding her from behind and putting a hand over her mouth. The attacker must have been wearing a black jacket and a pair of gloves. Forensics said the jacket was almost certainly a fleece. Davenport desperately hoped that she didn't have a boyfriend who'd got frisky just before she left work. Nothing they found on her phone or laptop indicated that she had a man in her life but it still didn't mean the traces were from the killer. She rubbed her eyes as she picked up the phone.

"Davenport."

"We think we've got him, a girl's been assaulted but she survived. We're trying to pick the guy up right now."

Davenport checked her armpits and wrinkled her nose, then looked at her watch. The shower would have to wait.


Davenport arrived at the station as the custody sergeant was completing the formalities on the prisoner. Sergeant Gray was waiting to brief her on the arrest.

"So he just fell into our lap," she said. There was a trace of disappointment in her voice. It was a fantastic result if this really turned out to be their man, but they wouldn't be turning it into a case study for trainee detectives. She pictured the scene of the killer's arrest a thousand times, as the cuffs were placed on his wrists, he'd plead with her to explain how she'd tracked him down. Davenport would give a modest smile and wave her hand nonchalantly to indicate her sergeant should take care of the paperwork. She'd not share the secrets of her craft with a murderer.

"It happens sometimes… we got lucky." The sergeant wondered why he felt as though he was apologising for what seemed like the first break they'd had in the case.

"So have we got a statement from the girl?"

"She's doing it now, but she's pretty distressed, she was thirty seconds from being victim number four."

"So tell me what happened?"

Gray took out his notepad, but barely glanced at it, the story was still fresh in his mind.

"She was standing at that bus stop on Newlands Road. She didn't hear anything, she thought she was alone, then this guy seemed to appear from nowhere and grabbed her tits… sorry ma'am… he grabbed her breasts."

"Get on with it."

"So he was mauling her and she started to scream. That's when he tried to make her turn around and she managed to get a home run with her rolled up umbrella. Right in the nadgers."

"She hit him in the testicles with her umbrella."

"Yes sorry ma'am… in his testicles."

"And he ran away?"

"No that's the best bit. She'd phoned her boyfriend to say that she'd meet him in town and she was getting the bus. He went mental and he came to get her in his car. He and his mates turned up just as she whacked the guy in the balls."

"And then?"

"He pulled a knife on them ma'am, the one he was going to use on the girl. Then he had second thoughts and made a break for it. His car was next to the bus stop and he was off before they could stop him."

"And you're sure the man we have in the cell is the one who attacked the girl."

"No doubt ma'am. She works at Coldharbour Town and she's seen him wandering around there… the number plate checks out too. We found the address from the database and there was a squad car at his flat before he even got back there. We found a knife on him too, just as they said."

"So what's he got to say for himself?"

"No idea ma'am."

"You haven't interviewed him?" Davenport failed to hide the disgust in her voice.

"No ma'am, we're waiting for the interpreter, it could be hours yet."

"Interpreter?"

"Yes ma'am. He doesn't speak a word of English."

"Who exactly have we got back there?" Davenport couldn't hide her surprise and a little disappointment. She'd started to visualise the interview that was about to take place and, in her mind, the man on the opposite side of the table was Tony Drake.

"All we have is that his name is Victor. He works for Dimitri Kolsa… whatever his name is. That bloke who bought The Cats."

"Do we know anything about him?"

Gray smiled, he knew Davenport would love this. "There's no record over here boss, but we know from his papers that he comes from Kiev, so I gave them a call. Just to see if he had any previous."

"And?" Davenport could tell that the sergeant was trying to build the suspense ahead of a big payoff.

"They've questioned him about loads of stuff. He's often in the vicinity when people get hurt, but they've never been able to pin anything on him. Witnesses clam up or disappear, evidence goes missing, his boss has a team of fancy lawyers that are always ahead of the police."

"But you've got something right?" Davenport was losing patience.

"Yes ma'am, they had nothing concrete on him, but the woman I spoke to asked what we were investigating. I told her about the killings and she went to check something. She said they had an unsolved murder that wasn't that different. They found a girl on the tram system, knife wound in the base of her neck. A week or so later Victor moves to London."

"With his boss, he only moved because his boss came to the UK."

"That might be the case, but this girl was a model. She regularly worked for the same photographer in Kiev. Three times in the weeks before she died, she was picked up from work by a bloke who answers to the description of our little friend in the cells."

Davenport was impressed, "Let's go chase up that interpreter shall we?"

# 11

Koloschenko slammed his fist onto the desk. It was Brazilian Tiger Mahogany, amongst the hardest woods in the world, but the impact was still enough to rattle the cups and saucers his secretary had laid out for his next meeting. Slatkin stood in front of him, head bowed. It was the classic schoolboy reaction, he'd done nothing wrong but, standing in the headmaster's office, he could not suppress the involuntary body language that screamed "guilty." His tongue felt as though it was nailed to the roof of his mouth, his hands were clammy and he could not look Koloschenko in the face.

"How the fuck has this happened Yuri? There is a serial killer on the loose and my bodyguard is suddenly the number one suspect. What are you doing to get him out?"

Slatkin was gasping for breath, he only had part of the story and Koloschenko wasn't going to like what he'd discovered.

"Dimitri, this is not a straightforward situation, of course we know that Victor is not the killer…" There was a subconscious uptick in his tone at the end of the sentence, he'd turned it into a question. Slatkin managed to summon the courage for a quick glance at his boss. Koloschenko's face was set in stone… no clue there.

"The problem we have is that he sexually assaulted the woman, he was in possession of a knife and the police were at his flat when he arrived home. He had four times the legal limit of alcohol in his bloodstream. They have plenty of reason to hold onto him, regardless of who killed the other three."

Slatkin wiped his eyes, Koloschenko appeared to be physically swollen with rage. When the reply came, it was surprisingly calm and measured, as though Koloschenko knew that if he crossed the line and lost his temper, even a little, a bloodbath might ensue.

"Yuri, you will fix this. There must be someone we can pay, someone we can influence, who will make this go away. You will find that person."

"I will try, but there is more. They've contacted the police in Kiev."

Koloschenko had turned away, as though the meeting was over and the view of Coldharbour Town's training pitch was far more interesting than his conversation with Slatkin. On hearing the word "Kiev," he turned again towards his advisor. The move was slow and deliberate as though Koloschenko was applying every ounce of his self-control.

"Kiev." His tone was flat.

"They wanted to know if Victor had a criminal record over there. Of course there is nothing, but during the course of the conversation they mentioned the murder of a young girl." Slatkin paused as though he was trying to recall a name.

"Lyudmila Semolova." Koloschenko said the name almost under his breath,

"Yes that's it, Lyudmila… yes Lyudmila."

Slatkin paused, Koloschenko had turned to face the window again.

"Do they think he killed her?"

"I don't think they have anything, but the British police described the killings in Coldharbour and the officer in Kiev said they had one just like it. They're not going to let Victor go easily. These are provincial cops, if they issue a parking ticket it counts towards their crime clear up rate. If they find the Coldharbour Ripper and solve a case in Kiev at the same time, they'll erect a statue outside the Town Hall for the detective that does it."

There was a brief but heavy silence, broken by Koloschenko.

"Victor didn't kill Lyudmila Semolova."

The obvious question was to ask how his boss could be so sure, but there was no way that Slatkin was going there. Questioning Koloschenko was frightening enough, more

108

terrifying was the possibility that the man might answer. Slatkin had a strange feeling that he wouldn't want to know why his employer was so certain. He waited for Koloschenko to speak.

"So what will get Victor out of prison? What will stop them looking at the murder of this girl in Kiev?"

"Dimitri, they have nothing else. This is their only lead. They will be like a dog with a rabbit, they will dig their teeth in and shake until…"

"Until the real killer takes another victim." Koloschenko's delivery was flat and cold.

Slatkin gave a short nervous laugh, "I guess that would give Victor the best possible alibi. There is still the assault but we could get our lawyers to plant the seed with the girl that, should she drop the charges, we'll make it worth her while. There's no guarantee that the police are going to back off, and there's still the drunk driving charge, but then it becomes manageable.

Koloschenko gave an almost imperceptible nod in the direction of the door. Slatkin had learnt the hard way that he should take that as confirmation that the meeting was over.

***

Davenport was Gray's first female boss and it had taken time to adjust. Many of his colleagues remembered the halcyon days when women brewed the tea, comforted battered wives and rape victims and, hopefully, danced on the tables at the station Christmas party. The idea that they could climb the ladder and start giving orders was preposterous. In the event that one did make it to sergeant, the assumption was that she must be banging the Chief Constable. Davenport had got all the way to Inspector and she was clearly very good at her job but there was still that nagging doubt. How had she made the grade when so many men never made it past constable? Gray endured the taunts from his colleagues. Did they have to shut down their investigations once a month while she battled with stomach cramps? Did he have to stock up on Kleenex in case she burst into tears when a suspect gave her a hard time? Gray was a convert, he saw her as a police officer first and a woman second. She was as good as anyone at Coldharbour nick, better than most. There just wasn't a lot of street cred in sharing that opinion with his peers.

Barry Lewis had made sergeant in the same round of promotions that brought Gray his stripes. Lewis was still part of the uniform branch and never tired of telling his colleagues that the police force lost its edge the day it started giving women real jobs.

"What's up with Princess Maggie then Pete? She looks like it's her time of the month when she should be doing cartwheels because we caught the bastard." Lewis dipped another biscuit into his tea, bit it in two and then crammed the whole thing in his mouth. He made a half hearted attempted to brush the crumbs from his shirt before reaching for another. Gray had little time for his colleague, the man had an opinion on virtually every officer in the station and was always keen to share it. Not much of what he had to say was positive and he didn't have the wit to realise that his audience would invariably wonder what he was saying about them behind their backs.

"She's got doubts that's all. It's not open and shut."

"You've got to be fucking joking. Three girls killed by a lunatic, half the town is too scared to pop out for a pint of milk after dark. We catch a bloke with a knife red-handed who's just attacked another girl and she reckons it's a different perp." Lewis shook his head, hoping to convey a sense of incredulity combined with resignation. This was the kind of madness the police force had brought upon itself by promoting women.

"She's got her reasons."

Lewis laughed. "Yeah too right she has. If she'd found the bloke who did it, she'd have been a fucking heroine. Because it was us boys in blue that went and picked him up, it's spoiled her party. Pompous bitch."

"Barry, the MO was completely different. The guy who killed the first three girls was really careful. All we have is a few fibres from his clothing. This Russian guy was a mess. Out of his head on booze and he didn't care how many clues he left us with. He was all over the girl. Even if he'd got away, we'd have got some sort of DNA from her clothes. And there's the knife, the first three girls were almost certainly killed with a flick knife of some sort, the one this Victor bloke had on him was a different type completely. She's not saying it isn't him, she just thinks we shouldn't be too hasty in closing the case."

Lewis gave a low whistle. "Bloody hell, she's got you by the balls hasn't she? You're quite the fan. Fancy your chances do you? I hear she's got a bloke already, so you'll have to stand in line."

"Screw you Barry. She knows what's she's doing and she's got a point. The fourth attack is nothing like the other three, we shouldn't assume the Russian is guilty of all four."

Lewis sneered. "That's the problem with you lot, it's all checklists and profiling and patterns and bollocks like that. We're not talking master criminals here, this blokes a nutter who likes killing women. So he fancied a bit of fun with this one before he got the knife out. I've nicked plenty of villains in my time and I'm telling you, this is the guy. Copper's nose I call it. Instinct, you get that when you do proper policing." Lewis adjusted his tie and picked up the peaked cap that was lying on the table. The message was clear, real policemen wear uniforms, Gray and his like were a poor imitation.

***

Football teams don't play games any more. The press will describe any upcoming fixture as a 'clash' or a 'battle' and a player who nicks the winning goal is described as a hero. When the game is against a neighbouring team the press up the ante still further, trying to place a football match on a par with the political tensions between Pakistan and India or Iraq and Iran. Local derbies are war by other means... Liverpool v Everton, City against United in Manchester or Tottenham and Arsenal. These are rivalries that generate the greatest passions and the essentially tribal nature of the average football fan. Some Evertonians were happy to see their team lose a potentially crucial game as victory might have helped Liverpool to a long awaited championship. In Manchester, you are blue or red from birth, neutrality is not an option. Tottenham fans will give enthusiastic support for their own team and for anyone who is playing against their closest rivals. The only thing that comes close to the joy of three points for your club is defeat for your neighbour. The hatred is strong and it's mutual.

Coldharbour Town had a dilemma. Derbies are great for business but their nearest neighbours were miles away and over the years had rarely been in the same division of the League. A section of Coldharbour fans started to dub the match against Southampton, a local derby and the idea quickly caught on. The clock was ticking in Coldharbour's fight to stay in the Premier League and next up was a trip to their "local" rivals. The Echo ran a lengthy feature on the history of the fixture, a credit to the author, as the teams had met less than a dozen times. The first occasion was before the First World War, which gave some credence to the claim that it was a long and bitter rivalry. The missing ingredient was the lack of any recognition of the derby status of the game on the part of the Southampton fans. Their rivalry was with Portsmouth and possibly Brighton. Coldharbour had flown under their radar. It was just another game. One pundit picked up on the asymmetry of the rivalry and suggested it was like having a stalker but being completely unaware of their existence. Coldharbour Town was that stalker.

The Coldharbour fans were in ecstasy after only four minutes, a typical burst of pace from Buckley wrong footed the covering defender. The striker shaped up to shoot drawing his opponent into a desperate lunge to block. Buckley's left foot had never been as reliable as his right, so there was no shot. He dragged the ball back creating a yard of space on his other side. It was little more than a toe poke, but the keeper's outstretched hand fell a couple of inches short. The ball nestled in the bottom corner of the net and Coldharbour were ahead. It was the wake up call their opposition required. Southampton had been coasting, comfortably in the top half of the division, playing a team they were expected to beat, in a match that was of no great consequence. Most of the players were contemplating the imminent end to the season, all the important battles had already been fought. Some were asked, before the game, about the derby status of the game, most expressed bemusement. It was news to them. Suddenly they were one down, at home to one of the weakest teams in the division. It was time to pull their socks up and earn their money.

Southampton ran out four-one winners. They eased up once the fourth goal went in, the point was proven, the opposition fans had been silenced. Only Adam Buckley came out of the game with any credit on the Coldharbour side. He barely touched the ball again after his goal, but the pundits laid the blame firmly at the door of his team mates. Even Gareth Bale himself wouldn't have been able to do anything with that sort of support. Unable to keep possession, unable to service their lone striker with a decent pass, panicking with every forward thrust from the opposition. Buckley did all he could, they agreed. If he was playing for a decent side, they said, he'd be a hell of a player.

# 12

Angelina Miynarczik's body was found just after one a.m. She left the restaurant where she waited tables around eleven thirty. The owner said she got into a taxi. Since the killings, all his girls did that when their shift was over and he'd given them all a modest pay increase to help them with the cost. It didn't make sense that she was killed only six hundred yards from the restaurant door, she lived three miles away on the other side of town. Alberto, had not only seen the taxi stop to pick her up, he noticed a dent in the rear offside wing, so it wasn't hard to track down the driver.

When Sergeant Gray and a uniformed constable rang Gary Miller's doorbell the following morning, he was bleary eyed but totally unconcerned that a couple of strangers in suits were doing house calls at the ungodly hour of eight thirty. Miller appeared to have fallen out of bed seconds earlier. An ancient pair of faded pyjama bottoms was roughly tied at his waist. The vest might once have been white, now it was mottled grey with dark yellow stains where it hung loose below his armpits. Miller looked to be completely disinterested in the policemen's introductions, he was more concerned with finding the source of what must have been a very severe itch in his groin.

"Look officer, if it's the car, I know I need to get the dent knocked out. Licence rules and all that, but I'll book it in next week. Alright?" Miller made to close the door as though it was inconceivable that the forces of law and order would not be satisfied with the undertaking he'd given. Sergeant Gray placed his foot firmly between door and frame and gripped the edge, close to the Yale lock, with a gloved hand.

"Mr Miller, do you know a waitress by the name of Angelina Miynarczik?"

Miller's brow creased as though he was mentally running through his little black book of women's names and phone numbers. Then he gave a shrug that indicated he couldn't summon a face to match the name, a fact that was causing him no concern whatsoever.

"You picked up her from Alberto's last night."

Miller's eyes widened and for the first time he realised that he might have a bigger problem than a dented wing. Then the look turned to irritation and anger.

"The silly little bitch reported me did she? Is that the best you can do? Chasing down honest taxi drivers on the word of a little slut who shouldn't be in the fucking country anyway. I call your lot when I got burgled and you couldn't even be bothered to show up for two days. All I got was a fucking letter asking me if I want victim counselling. Then this little tart cries on your shoulder and you kick my door down in the middle of the night. It's a fucking police state that's what it is."

"Mr Miller, the girl in question was murdered last night. Six hundred yards from where you picked her up. Do you want to cooperate with this or do we have to do this the hard way?"

Miller's mouth was opening and closing in a passable impersonation of a pet goldfish, he even stopped scratching his crotch.

"Sorry officer, I thought she'd made a complaint that's all."

"And what did she have to complain about?"

Miller flushed with embarrassment and suddenly appeared to be totally absorbed by Gray's left lapel. Eye contact was out of the question.

The policeman eased the door wide open and, with his colleague, walked past the taxi driver into the living room of his flat. It was sparsely furnished, the sofa and a single armchair looked threadbare but the TV was a state of the art Samsung wide screen. A cardboard box on the coffee table contained the remnants of a half eaten pizza. Miller had covered it with a paper napkin as though saving the leftovers for breakfast.

116

"Mr Miller, I asked why she should complain about you?"

The taxi driver appeared to be racking his brains to determine how much of the story he could share with his visitors.

"She couldn't pay the fare that's it."

"That's it?"

"Yes." Miller made it sound like a question. As though he was hoping that that would be enough to make the policeman back off, but suspected otherwise.

"Well that clears it all up nicely. Thank you Mr Miller."

"Really?" Miller failed to suppress the astonishment and relief he felt.

"No not really," Gray stepped forward so his face was only a few inches from Miller's. "You think she might have complained. What did she have to complain about?"

Miller reached for a packet of cigarettes.

"Not until you've answered the question and we're out of here. No smoking in the workplace and the way your going Miller, our officers will be spending quite a bit of time here." Gray took the pack from Miller and tossed it into the corner of the room.

"She told me she didn't have the money after we pulled away, but there was a cash point a couple of hundred yards down the road. We stopped there and she went to the machine, then came back and said her card wasn't working. So I left her there, that's it. I've got a living to make, I can't go driving people around for free now can I?"

"When there's a killer on the loose?"

"Don't lay that at my door mate. It's your fucking job to catch him, not mine to keep the locals off the street."

The constable's radio bleeped and he stepped into the kitchen to answer it. Inside two minutes, he was back and beckoned the sergeant to join him in the other room.

"Sarge, he checks out. Inspector Davenport has been through it all at the taxi company. They have satellite tracking on all the cars. It shows that he stopped for a couple of minutes by the cash point and then drove in the other direction, away from the bus stop where they found the girl. They have an on-board gadget that lets him indicate to the office that he's available, he put that on and they gave him a job about thirty seconds later. And she checked with the bank, the girl tried to use her card just as he said. They even have some CCTV. It shows her walking back to the taxi, looks like they exchange a few words then she slams the door and he drives off."

The two policemen returned to Miller's living room.

"You're a lucky man Mr Miller. Your office has bailed you out. They tell us you got another customer just after you abandoned this girl to her fate."

"Yeah… yeah that's right I did." Miller looked relieved and walked towards the door to let the policemen out. Gray lingered, there was something not quite right about the driver, there was guilt for sure and a marked lack of sympathy for the girl who'd died. Nonetheless, they had nothing on him and his story was backed up by technology rather than the word of an equally suspect friend.

"I'm guessing our paths will cross again sometime Mr Miller. I'll be looking out for you." Gray scanned the taxi driver's face, he was hiding something but continued to avoid eye contact. His earlier aggression had dissipated, in spite of Gray's provocation. It was obvious to both policemen, he just wanted them out of the flat. The sergeant was sure he'd be seeing Miller again.

Miller closed the door and rested his head against the peeling paintwork. "Fuck," he thought, "that was close."

He wasn't concerned about the fate of Angelina Miynarczik, even though the girl had been in his car only the previous evening. He'd seen her around town too, but she never even noticed him. Stuck up little bitch thought she was too good for a humble taxi driver, but he had a skilled job, she carried plates around a restaurant.

The previous night was his big chance. She noticed there was no money in her purse as soon as she got in his car.

"We'll work something out," he'd said, but she'd not heard him. Spotting the cash point she barked at him to stop. She was back at the car door in no time.

"My card's not working. Could you pop by the restaurant tomorrow for the money. You know where I work and where I live, so you're not going to lose out." She gave him her best smile, there was even a tiny flutter of the eyelashes. He almost agreed. She'd owe him, she couldn't possibly blank him again after such a chivalrous act. Maybe he'd give her a free ride.

"Don't worry love, this one's on me. Hop in and I'll take you home for free, it's only a few quid." He rehearsed the line in his head. Then when they got to her place, he'd suggest a drink or a meal later in the week, maybe she'd invite him in. He'd heard what these foreign girls were like. Up for anything if a bit of cash was involved. It was one option, but the downside was that she might turn him down. Miller wanted a bit more certainty. He went for option two.

"Give me a blowjob darling and I'll take you back for free."

The girl called him a filthy creep and slammed the car door. It wasn't his fault she got herself killed. He'd been irritated when the police arrived, it was just like them to follow up a complaint from some bloody foreigner, especially one with blonde hair and nice tits. When he was burgled the response was, "what do you expect given where you live?" Irritation turned to fear when they said she was dead. The last place she was seen alive was in his car and in the boot was a small cardboard cylinder with ten cellophane bags and each contained five ecstasy pills. He had five more bags when he picked up the Polish girl, but the call that came seconds after he'd left her by the roadside, was from a customer. Miller used to bring the cylinder inside each night, until the burglary, then he decided he had to take his chances. If the car was nicked;

they'd never trace the cylinder to him anyway and if the vehicle turned up, he'd look confused and say that drug dealers had obviously stolen the car. What he could not afford was to have his car searched outside his flat. Had Coldharbour Taxis not given him a cast iron alibi, that's exactly what would have happened.

Miller laughed, if he hadn't got the call to deliver twenty-five ecstasy tablets to his number one client, he might be in the frame for a murder.

"Who says crime doesn't pay?"

\*\*\*

Adam Buckley was still practicing, the rest of the squad had long since gone home. A young Academy player was there to act as ball boy and to offer the attention and adulation that the footballer craved. Adam could hardly believe that at the age of twenty-two, he'd suddenly been thrust into the role of local celebrity. Every young lad wanted to be like him and half the female population had caught Buckley fever too. He had a hundred thousand followers on Facebook and the football club had taken over updating his page. Every morning he'd read what they wanted his fans to believe about him. Facebook Adam ate yoghurt, muesli and two bananas with green tea for breakfast. Real life Adam wolfed down a bacon sandwich and a large black coffee. Facebook Adam expressed his horror at the news that another girl had been murdered and offered a ten thousand pound reward for information that would lead the police to her killer. Real Adam hoped the club were going to put their hands in their pockets for that if it ever got claimed. His on-line persona also informed fans that his prayers were with the families of a group of coal miners, trapped two hundred metres underground in southern Mexico. Real Adam snorted his derision. "Praying," he thought, "is for poofters." The club had forbidden him from posting to the page or answering any of the private messages, but he was allowed to read them. That was his favourite part of the day. Susanna from Canterbury sent him a photo of her vagina and said that he could stop by to check it out any time he liked. Shereen from Rye sent her mobile number and a topless photo of herself, one arm modestly positioned to cover her breasts. Pauline from Yorkshire offered to show him things that would make his head spin. Adam was struck by how much the woman looked like his own grandmother. That was the secret of Adam Buckley's success, his appeal cut across the generations. He was tempted to jot down Shereen's number, the club would never know, but what was the point? If he wanted a woman, all he had to do was crook his finger the next time he walked into a bar… or a supermarket, or the local newsagent for that matter.

Three years earlier he was trailing in the wake of his best friend. Tony Drake was the one they tipped to make it as a pro, he always had the pick of the girls and, on a lad's Saturday night out, Tony was the one telling the stories, he was the centre of attention. Adam sat quietly and sipped his beer. Well things had changed and Adam Buckley was in no doubt as to why. Tony had been unlucky, the injury was a big factor, but he'd never put in the hours, he'd never done the practice, he thought he had some God given gift and that would carry him through. Adam knew you had to do the drills. Training finished over an hour earlier. Adam took a mesh sack of twenty balls and stood at the edge of the centre circle. For twenty minutes he practiced trying to hit the cross bar from fifty yards. The Academy kid was there to knock the balls back to him. From the edge of the penalty area, he worked at hitting a cleaner's bucket that he'd attached to the inside of the right hand stanchion that supported the goal netting. He finished the session, playing two-man "keepie-uppie," with the star struck youngster. That was the difference between him and Tony Drake, he was willing to work at his craft. It was the reason he could put his arm round the young lad and tell him,

"If you're willing to train as hard as me, one day you could have all of this too."

Tony Drake, on the other hand, hadn't bathed for three days and was slumped on the sofa of an apartment for which Adam had paid cash. The only contact he had with the outside world was satellite TV and a regular call to Tim the dealer to top up his supplies of ketamine.

Adam thought about stopping by to visit his old friend after training, but decided he had other priorities. He didn't have a lot of time before he was due to meet his new agent. When he first signed a professional contract, he knew nothing about such things, he'd just heard that all players had someone to negotiate their deals. His Uncle Mike used to work at an estate agent, so Adam asked him to take up the role. There were no big sponsorship deals but Coldharbour had given him a new contract and he was getting a handsome cheque from the manufacturers of his boots. Uncle Mike pocketed ten per cent and couldn't believe his luck.

He had Yuri Slatkin to thank for the change. Adam had seen Slatkin around the ground and assumed he was part of Koloschenko's Security detail. Then came the suggestion they have a chat. Adam had not seen the inside of the owner's office since he'd signed his first contract with Jack Enright and Sam Chalmers. It wasn't just that the furniture was a big step up in quality, somehow the room looked bigger and the windows appeared to let in more light. Adam had an almost irresistible urge to take off his shoes before he stepped into the room. His Mum once saved for years to get a new carpet for the living room and, when he trailed mud from his training shoes through the house, she took a rolled up newspaper to the back of his head. Since the renovations, Koloschenko's office looked like a movie set and whilst Adam resisted the temptation to lose the shoes, he waited for Slatkin to give him the nod that it was OK to cross the threshold.

"Adam, thank you so much for joining us. Sit… please sit. Tea… coffee… what can I get you?" Slatkin smiled and gestured towards a plush leather chair at the head of Koloschenko's conference table.

122

"I'm fine thanks… nothing really."

Adam didn't know what to make of it all. The call to meet a man he thought was from Security had left him feeling unnerved. Slatkin's enthusiasm should have put him at ease. It only served to increased his confusion.

"Adam, I'm only here to pour the tea. I wanted to introduce you to Stephen Lester." Slatkin nodded in the direction of the window. Adam hadn't noticed the short, slightly round man who was staring out of the window. Lester turned and offered a chubby hand and a toothy smile. Slatkin continued.

"Stephen has a problem and he's hoping you can help him fix it. I'm going to leave you to it… if that's OK." Slatkin appeared to bow as he backed through the door. It wasn't a mark of respect for Buckley and Lester, just force of habit whenever he left Koloschenko's office.

Lester smiled as he dropped into the chair opposite Adam.

"Adam… is it OK if I call you Adam?"

Buckley nodded and Lester continued.

"Sorry about this but Yuri's a bit nervous. He's an old mate of mine and he's doing me a favour with this introduction. I doubt that his boss would be too pleased if he knew that we'd fixed this up, but I gather he's back in Moscow, so we should be alright."

"Mr Koloschenko wouldn't be happy about this meeting? I don't think I can ummm…" Adam was suddenly nervous, but Lester gave another broad toothy smile.

"His interests and mine are not exactly the same, I make footballers rich and sometimes that puts me on the opposite side of the negotiating table." Lester delivered the line as though he'd declared that his life's mission was to end poverty and disease across the southern hemisphere. Adam wished he'd asked for some water as Lester helped himself to a milky coffee with four spoons of sugar.

"I don't want to do anything that Mr Kolo…" Adam stuttered.

"Adam my friend. You don't have to worry. This meeting is about you, not Dimitri, but your owner is a suspicious chap, it's better that he doesn't know about it."

Adam's eyes darted around the room, as though he expected Koloschenko to appear at any second to deliver a terrible retribution for an offence he was, as yet, unable to identify. "I'm not sure that I…"

"Adam, hear me out. Give me two minutes and if you don't like what I have to say, we part as friends. OK?"

Adam nodded.

Lester plucked a leather-covered folder from his briefcase and flicked through to find his notes. It was clear that the meeting with Adam was one of many important engagements he had that day. Einstein scoffed at people who filled their heads with trivia, such as phone numbers, Lester was clearly of the same view, he had to remind himself of the proposition he was about to put before the young footballer. He scanned a sheet that had Adam's photo clipped to the top corner. Satisfied that he was on top of his subject matter he looked up.

"Adam, I represent a lot of top players. All established names, if I told you how many Champions League winner's medals they have between them…" Lester waved his hand idly in the air. "It leaves me with an unexpected problem, one I think you may be able to help me with."

Adam was starting to relax. He nodded as Lester continued.

"I have been approached by a major enterprise, they are looking for a young, handsome, successful sportsman who is on the way up. They have a range of businesses across Europe and their customers are young girls. They want someone who can relate to that demographic. I could ask Lionel, or Cristiano of course, but they are older, it's not the image my client is seeking. Forgive me for the comparison, but they're thinking 'boy band.'" Lester mimed the inverted commas with two fingers of each hand then continued. "Cristiano sets a few hearts racing but we think his appeal is to women, not young teens. You on the other hand would be perfect."

"I would?"

Adam, your face will sell a million magazines, they'll be fighting in the aisles to get a t-shirt with your picture on it, Buckley baseball caps, posters, playing cards, party masks, there could be a book deal. The potential is endless. Interested?"

"Yeah, of course. What do I have to do?" Adam was wide-eyed with excitement, he leaned forward in his seat and stretched his arms out onto the table in front of him. It was as though he was afraid that Lester might try to escape without delivering on the offer, the footballer was poised to stop him.

"Well nothing much at all. You'd be doing me a huge favour. It's embarrassing to admit that I have no one suitable on my books, so I'd want to do this in tandem with your agent. I'd have approached him directly, but I couldn't find his details. That's why I came through Yuri. And, of course, why Dimitri has nothing to worry about. He's not going to object to his hottest property getting a little more attention."

"My agent?" Adam sat back, his hands retreated to his lap. The bubble had started to deflate.

Lester gave an avuncular smile. "You do have an agent don't you? I'm guessing it's one of the top guys, I'll have my work cut out to get a fair share of the fee on this one." The look turned to embarrassment, he'd admitted that he was getting a cut rather than making the introduction out of the goodness of his heart.

Adam was looking lost. Lester took it as a lack of enthusiasm for what he was suggesting.

"Adam, I'm sure he's out there getting you all sorts of deals right now, watches, razors, cars, clothes. I know you're inundated. But I can assure you this is the sort of thing that will take you to the next level."

"No he's not doing any of that stuff."

"Huh?" Lester looked bewildered.

"It's not like he's a proper agent. It's my uncle, he sells houses… well he used to." Adam had taken on the air of a little boy who'd let go of his mummy's hand at the fairground.

"Adam, I don't know what to say. You're missing out on a fortune."

"But what should I do?"

"Well, under the circumstances, it would be unthinkable to put myself forward but I can let you have some names. There are some terrific people out there."

"But you could do it right?"

"Well I could, of course, but there are ethical considerations…"

Adam Buckley decided it was time to take charge, he'd had others pushing him around for too long.


It was twenty minutes before the door to Koloschenko's office opened and the two men appeared. Slatkin was sitting on a leather sofa in the corridor, reading the local newspaper. Toby Thomas had delivered the editorial exactly as promised.

*Coldharbour Town is just ninety minutes from an historic FA Cup Final with either Chelsea or Arsenal. When the semi-final draw was made, our hearts were in our mouths, we all knew the one we wanted. There are no easy games in the FA Cup, but when they pulled out number four and called Sheffield Wednesday, it was hard not to think that finally the football Gods were smiling upon us.*

*Dimitri Koloschenko has been at the helm for only a few weeks and not everyone supports the changes he's made, but no one can deny that we're already going to Wembley and it's a Division One side that stands between Coldharbour Town and the greatest day in the history of our fine club. Neutrals are already taking about the Russian Cup Final, the decider between the oligarchs. This is an end to the season that we could never have envisaged. Premier League survival is in our own hands, there could be a FA Cup Final round the corner. The Coldharbour Echo doesn't throw it's cap into the ring with everything the club's new owner has done, but now's not the time to focus on what divides us. We need to get behind the club and everyone who has contributed to what could be Coldharbour Town's greatest ever season. Time for a truce and for everyone who loves the club to pull together. Come on the Town!"*

Slatkin had wanted something considerably more upbeat, but Thomas explained that he knew his audience and they'd never buy it. In the end the Russian got something that might help to see them through until the sale was agreed, and Thomas got a two-week, all expenses paid trip to Koloschenko's private villa near Sorrento. Slatkin told him he could bring a woman of his own or they'd have one delivered, two if he preferred. The Russian jumped up as Lester and Buckley appeared at the door.

"All done?"

The warm handshakes being exchanged by the two men were answer enough.

Adam gave him a beaming smile. "Thanks for organising this Mr Slatkin and you know…" he touched the side of his nose and winked in an unnecessarily theatrical fashion. Slatkin nodded his appreciation.

"Adam, one thing before you go." Buckley was halfway down the corridor, but turned back. Slatkin continued. "Have you even got a sister?"

The footballer looked confused then shook his head.

"No I thought not," the Russian said and guided Lester back into the office.

"So how was it?" Slatkin made a point of standing just inside the room, he had no intention of entertaining Lester for any longer than was strictly necessary.

"Piece of cake. Just as you said, he fell for the whole thing. He thinks I'm a big shot agent and I'm going to make him a fortune. I played the ethics card like you said, but he practically begged me to take him on. I mentioned Cristiano and Lionel and he almost came in his pants. Thank Christ I didn't have to say which one plays for Barcelona, might have blown it there and then. But what happens now? He'd have to be a halfwit not to see it's all a scam when nothing comes of it. What on earth are you doing this for?"

"Stephen, my reasons are my business. Your job is to get him to sign a five-year contract with the club, then stick with him for a year. We'll keep enough money coming in your direction to make it worthwhile for him and for you, but you have to make sure that he doesn't ask for a transfer. That's it, that's all. It's worth a lot to Dimitri if Buckley's still onside in a year's time. This struck me as the most elegant way of doing it."

"What was that stuff about his sister?"

Slatkin shook his head, "Let's just say that Dimitri had another idea for securing his loyalty. I decided that a footballer who's had his ego massaged is going to be more use to us than one who's shitting himself every time there was a knock on the door."

Lester knew there was no point in asking the Russian to elaborate. "So what happens now?"

"You call him next week to say you've negotiated a fantastic new deal and he'd be a fool not to sign it. You can string him out on the other stuff… the endorsements. We'll stretch those out over the next year so he stays committed."

"So I don't actually have to be his agent?"

"Don't be ridiculous Stephen, what do you know about being an agent? You're on the payroll because your years at drama school were not entirely wasted and our previous encounters indicate that there is little that you would not do for a reasonable fee."

Lester looked genuinely disappointed. He'd hoped that a new career might be opening up for him. He'd wanted to be an actor, but was regularly told that he had neither the looks nor the talent. A brief spell as a life insurance salesman made him realise just how easy it was to talk gullible, lonely old people into parting with their money. It occasionally tugged at his heart strings when they wrote out the cheque and he delivered a worthless document that he'd knocked together on his desktop the day before. Lester truly believed he had an ability to read people and their motives. He doubted the widows he conned were truly convinced of the need for life insurance. It was more likely that they didn't want to disappoint the nice man who'd come and had tea with them several times before they put pen to paper. They were paying for the fact that he'd taken an interest in them and their lives, so in a way it was a fair trade. Lester's greatest talent was self-delusion. He quickly expanded his offering to include investment products and home renovation. Old and vulnerable people across England would sign up for a couple of new cupboards and find, weeks later, that they had acquired a complete, but badly fitted kitchen at around five times the price they'd have paid on their local high street.

The secret of his success was a willingness to move around the country, thus broadening his target market and reducing the chances of being caught, together with a talent for producing fake documentation and a sharp eye for lonely people with money, but no family or friends to look out for them. There was no end to the number of lonely, gullible wealthy people who'd hand over cash to a stranger as long as he had a convincing story to tell and was happy to sit and share a plate of custard creams while he told it. Lester wasn't sure that being a football agent was necessarily a more honourable profession than being a confidence trickster who'd only twice been convicted for his crimes, but he was damn sure it would be better paid.

***

There were fourteen missed calls on his phone. Had he been bothered to check voicemail, Tony Drake would have heard his line manager's transition from anxious colleague, to inconvenienced superior, then through a descending spiral of concern to,

"Don't bother to show your face in this place again Drake, or I'll rip it off with a fucking angle grinder. Whatever you've got, I hope it's fucking terminal."

Nearly three weeks had passed since Tony had turned up for work. At first he'd called in regularly, assuring his boss that although it was a particularly virulent strain of flu, he was on lots of medication and was confident that he'd be on his feet in no time. As the ketamine took hold, the calls became even more convincing, he sounded listless, confused and weary. It was ten days since he'd called in and the messages from his manager started two days after that. They even sent someone round to his flat, the neighbours said they thought he was staying with a friend. From concern, to urgent pleas because they were understaffed, then a reminder of the terms of his contract of employment, then a deadline which passed unacknowledged. Then the final call saying he should not return. Tony was oblivious to them all. He used the phone only to text Tim the dealer. There was a new landlord at the Harbour Arms, he'd installed cameras in the main bar and one was pointed at the corridor leading to the toilets. Tim had shut up shop and outsourced distribution to his fourteen-year-old brother and a couple of his friends. Orders were received by text and the merchandise was delivered within three hours, cash only, no credit. The price went up a little to pay for this service enhancement, but Tim's customers didn't care. It was the great advantage of selling stuff like ketamine, he didn't see much prospect of his customers flying into an aggressive rage, however he treated them.

Tony never saw the delivery boy. He'd ring three times on the entry phone to be let into the building. The front door had a mini camera, which should have let Tony identify his visitor but the boy's hoodie was complemented with a black scarf that covered the lower part of his face. Sunglasses completed the disguise. Three knocks on the apartment door and, leaving the latch chain secured, Tony would open it just wide enough for a small package to pass in one direction, a cash filled envelope in the other.

His "maid" turned up every other day, to make sure there was food in the fridge and that the flat was reasonably clean. She'd stopped buying fruit and vegetables after a week, he never ate them. By day ten in his new home, Tony was living on yoghurt, biscuits and microwaved pizza. She'd arrive around ten a.m. and be gone within an hour. Tony had already locked himself in the bathroom and all her attempts to make contact were ignored. The dreams were a thing of the past, at least the full-length, HD quality dreams of old had not recurred. They were like an arcade game, where he played a starring role in the action. The ketamine had taken him to a quieter, more detached place. Tony had always been a fan of war documentaries, he'd marvelled at how the black and white footage from World War One made the events look as though they were from another universe. It was terrible for sure, but these indistinct little figures, with their staccato movements in shades of grey were not like real people at all. The new dreams were like that, only in colour and Tony was no longer centre stage. He was in one of the VIP seats at the back of the theatre where you got extra legroom, a free drink and popcorn. The special effects were awesome, it looked like the guy really had stabbed the girl, the look on her face was real fear, then pain and disbelief. The acting was extraordinary. You got to hate the villain, but in an abstract way… this was the movies, not real life. Tony would wake, his heart beating way too fast, but the terror was gone. He knew he was responsible for the deaths but it created only a feeling of resignation and disappointment that a life so filled with promise had sunk so low.

The maid had stopped making any attempt at communication. At first she'd called through the door to ask if he needed anything and if he was happy with what she was doing for him in the flat. After a couple of days she'd resort to listing out the food she'd left him and the chores she'd completed round the flat. On day ten, she left without saying a word. Tony couldn't identify the fear he felt about her presence. It wasn't that he thought that he'd hurt her, but something bad might happen and he didn't want to be there to witness it. Better that he sat with his back to the bathroom wall and closed his eyes until she was gone.

The only person he'd spoken to in weeks was Adam Buckley. His friend visited him every day at first, they watched TV together and chatted about old times and what Tony would do when he got himself sorted again. The visits tailed off, but Adam still popped in from time to time. He even left some money, in case Tony wanted to go out. It came in handy, when the delivery boy came and rang the entry phone three times.

The maid left fifteen minutes before Tony finally dragged himself from the floor of the bathroom. He'd made it to the sanctuary of the sofa before he realised that she'd left the TV switched on. It was a quiz show with over-excited fat people and a bored looking host whose demeanour screamed, 'where did my career go wrong, how did I end up doing shit like this?' Tony stared at his watch, he'd texted Tim hours ago, and his next delivery was overdue. He tapped out another message, there was no acknowledgement of the last one. There was a little stab of fear in his gut, a little burst of unwanted adrenalin at the thought that Tim had forgotten, the delivery boy had got lost, worst of all; the police had caught them all. Where would he get his stuff then? He couldn't remember how he found Tim in the first place, there was no way he'd find a new supplier. The tension was rising in his gut and he began to perspire, it was crazy, the room wasn't warm and he was only wearing a t-shirt and shorts. Tony started to gasp for breath. The images on the TV screen were getting sharper, there was the face of a girl. She was blonde, pretty… very pretty. Then there were four faces, four names and a rolling news banner at the bottom of the screen that said, "Coldharbour Ripper Claims Another Victim." The screen was filled with each face in turn,

132

Annie, Natalie, Zainab and now Angelina. Tony knew for sure he'd killed the first two, and he'd seen reports about the Arab girl, it happened around the time he moved into Adam's apartment. There wasn't much doubt that it was the same killer, especially when her face came back to him over and over again in his dreams. Now there was a fourth victim.

Why was it so hot? Why did he feel like he was burning up? Where was that little bastard with his package from Tim? Tony had to get out of there, he grabbed the duvet that the maid had folded neatly over the side of the sofa and stumbled towards the door.

***

"Peter, we have to find Drake, he's our only lead." Davenport looked vulnerable for the first time since they'd started working together and Sergeant Gray thought for a moment that he might have to reach for a handkerchief. The Inspector looked lost, she'd taken no satisfaction from the knowledge that her instincts about Koloschenko's bodyguard had been correct. The man was still in custody, but he wasn't the killer. Angelina Miynarczik was murdered while he was in his cell and his victim was suddenly backtracking on her evidence. She was a bit drunk too, she told them, he wasn't really that threatening, even if he had groped her a bit. It wasn't the end of the world and she really couldn't face a court appearance, she wanted to put the whole horrible experience behind her. Davenport was certain that she'd been bought off, but it hardly mattered. There was nothing to link him to the murder victims, her change of heart would get him off a charge of sexual assault, all they had left was drink-driving and possession of an offensive weapon. Koloschenko's would shortly secure his release on bail.

Gray recognised Davenport's despair. It wasn't for herself, it was for the victims the killer had already taken and for those still to come, if they couldn't stop him. It was the first time she'd called him Peter instead of by his rank or surname. It was a sign that the chase had become personal.

"Ma'am, Drake's disappeared. No one's seen him for weeks. We're trying to get warrants to search his flat and to track his phone but we're still getting the paperwork sorted. I've got a team of four guys going round there as soon as we get the nod."

"Has anything come out of the background checks?"

Gray looked rueful. "First time round we just looked at him rather than his family. There was nothing… not even a parking ticket, he was a regular boy scout." He picked up a file that was about four inches thick and placed it in front of Davenport.

"His father ma'am, Alan Drake. Jailed for fifteen years for killing a girl… with a knife."

"Jesus… How did we…?"

Gray slumped into the chair opposite his boss. "I'm sorry ma'am. Tony Drake was nowhere in our records, if he had been; there's every chance that we'd have made the connection. He wasn't, so we didn't. It looks like a cock-up but I don't know how we could have picked it up. Alan Drake went inside so long ago, and they didn't even live round here when it happened."

Davenport flicked through the file. The physical resemblance between the two men was remarkable but the crimes were far from identical. Drake senior had been drunk, the motive was almost certainly sexual and he left plenty of incriminating evidence at the scene. DNA profiling was unheard of, but they had fingerprints, a chunk of hair gripped in the victim's right hand and blood on the girl's clothes. A scarf he was seen wearing earlier in the night was found next to the girl's body and a neighbour recognised Drake as he was leaving the scene. When police visited his house the following day, he came quietly and never disputed the evidence that was placed in front of him. It was the antithesis of the crimes they were now trying to solve. That didn't mean Tony Drake was not the killer, but he was certainly not copying his father.

Davenport scanned the first page of the file.

"What about the father? Is he in the frame for this?"

Gray shook his head. "His alibi is as good as that Russian gorilla. He was in Lewes nick when both Annie and Natalie were killed. It's impossible."

"But you think Tony might be cut from the same cloth as his old man."

"He must know about his dad, it's got to mess your head up. And there's a load of stuff on how Drake senior used to knock his wife about. There's every chance he did the same to his son. Most of the nutters we end up dealing with have been abused in some way when they were kids. The more you look at it, the more Tony Drake fits the profile of a killer."

There was a sharp knock at the door, before either could respond Sergeant Lewis appeared at the door. "I sent a team to pick up Drake. They found him half an hour ago." There was a look of triumph on Lewis's face, once again the uniforms had shown the glory boys… and girls, how it's done.

Gray jumped to his feet. "How did you find him?"

Lewis laughed. "Looks like he tried to flee the country, but he didn't make it."

"They picked him up at the airport?" Gray looked at Davenport, she'd instructed him to send a notice to all points of departure a couple of hours earlier. They'd finally got a break.

"Not exactly." Lewis was enjoying his time in the limelight.

"Spit it out Lewis, how did you find him?" Davenport stood up and advanced on the uniformed officer.

"Of course ma'am. He definitely tried to fly, but he was obviously worried that we'd have the airports covered, so he improvised."

"Lewis…"

"He jumped ma'am. Twelfth storey of that posh new apartment block out on Ranmore Hill. Lady who lives opposite says she spotted him, she was talking to her daughter on the phone and admiring the view, when he climbed onto the wall that runs round the rooftop. He waved at her apparently, then he jumped. She said it will haunt her till her dying day. He started to wave his arms around like they were wings and he looked really surprised when they didn't work." Lewis launched into a camp mimicry of Drake's final seconds, flapping his hands ineffectually, followed by a look of terror and finishing with his eyes crossed and his tongue lolling from the side of his mouth.

"He's dead." Davenport made it a statement not a question.

"Well, when I said we're going to pick him up, we're taking a shovel and a bucket."

Lewis paused for only a second or two to enjoy the look on his detective colleagues' faces. Then he turned and made his exit.

"What do you think?" Davenport wasn't sure if the case had just come together or fallen apart.

"Must be him ma'am. Guilty conscience. The woman saw him jump, so there must have been something that drove him to it. There was no one else involved."

"We have to find where he's been staying. There's got to be some more forensic to link him to the victims."

# 13

Yuri Slatkin had produced a detailed analysis of the club's remaining fixtures and those of their fellow strugglers in the Premier League relegation zone. Key factors were identified for each team, such as injuries, suspensions and any plausible stories in the Press that might have a bearing on their form between then and the end of the season. He'd even had a go at predicting how many points each might gain in their remaining matches. The good news was that all of Coldharbour's rivals had at least one game against teams in the top four of the league. Less positive was that two were playing each other, so someone had to get something from the remaining games. Coldharbour had thirty-three points and it looked like thirty-seven would keep them up. There were four games to go.

"Can we buy the points?" Koloschenko always liked to make things as simple and as certain as possible.

Slatkin had anticipated the question. "We've made some confidential enquiries about who might need a lot of cash but we've drawn a blank. It would have to be a centre half with big gambling debts or a goalkeeper with a coke habit, best of all; a referee who's mortgaged the house because he's got a string of mistresses on the side. Even then we'd have to make the approach look like it came from one of the Asian gambling syndicates. If it came out and could be linked back to you, that would blow the deal with the Americans. They're insisting on a punitive clause in the contract to cover any malpractice while we were in charge. We thought about a honey-trap situation, getting a key player into a compromising situation and then threatening him with exposure, but I doubt that would work."

"It's served us well in the past." Koloschenko was clearly disappointed.

"Dimitri, it has worked with politicians and senior businessmen who are concerned that their image will be damaged. Footballers wear sordid revelations as a badge of honour. We could film the entire first team of our next opponents snorting cocaine off the naked bodies of a bunch of schoolgirls and, the next day; their wives and girlfriends will be declaring undying love and unqualified forgiveness. The week after that a tabloid newspaper will pay them to tell the story of how the whole thing has made their marriage stronger." Slatkin put two fingers just inside his mouth as though he was trying to regurgitate something awful he'd consumed. He found the insight nauseating, but it was certainly true.

"Trust me Dimitri, these guys are bomb proof."

"So what is our plan to ensure survival?" Koloschenko checked his phone for messages as he spoke, as though the fate of his football team was of only passing interest.

Slatkin was desperate to find an angle, but had nothing.

"Dimitri, it's down to Boris and the team. They have to get you the points on the field."

Koloschenko slipped the phone into the inside pocket of his jacket, closed his eyes and slowly massaged his temples with the tips of his fingers. Then he jerked his head towards the door. Slatkin knew that he was no longer required. His boss had said nothing, but it wasn't hard to guess what he was thinking.

What had possessed him to get involved in a business that operated in a manner that bore no relation to those he'd encountered before, legal or illegal. It was a matter of days until the contract was due to be signed with the purchasers of Coldharbour Town. If the team dropped into the Championship the deal was off and he'd be stuck with the club.

\*\*\*

Adam Buckley had been advised that the apartment he'd lent to Tony Drake would be hard to shift but he still gave instructions for it to be sold. Within days of it going on the market, dozens of people had booked a viewing before the sale was suspended. The agent informed his client that he was yet to

138

meet a serious purchaser. They all wanted to see where the Coldharbour Ripper had holed up before he killed himself. Adam told his team mates he couldn't bear to go near the place and the idea of taking rent for it just made his stomach crawl. He'd flatly refused to talk to anyone about his old friend preferring, he said, to deal with the loss his own way.

***

Toby Thomas drained the last of the Rioja, ruing the fact that he'd bought only half a case just three days earlier. There was only one plate in the kitchen sink, that was from Monday night's takeaway. For the next two evenings, he'd eaten his char sui pork, egg fried rice and prawn spring rolls straight from the cardboard containers. It always looked pretty cool when they did that on American TV shows. Staring at the remnants of a half eaten meal, he decided that was just the magic of television. Lukewarm meat in a watery sauce had to taste like shit whatever country you were in, even if it was out of one of those stylish little pop-top boxes they have in the States. He'd tried to talk to Tobias again, but his, other, 'rational self' was unmoved.

"I'm telling you mate, unless they find the killer you've got a serious problem. You know why you never see a policeman on the street anymore?"

Toby knew, of course, but waited for Tobias to answer his own question.

"Well it's because most of them can't be arsed and the rest are up to their necks in paperwork. But when they can be bothered to try to solve a crime, they do it with computers. They look for patterns, things that link the victims. And that's where it all goes so badly wrong for you my friend. Those hotels and fancy restaurants, someone's going to remember that the lovely looking dead girl came in with a bloke who was nearly old enough to be her Dad."

Toby was hurt, he'd always been sensitive about the age gap and Tobias wasn't done.

"Toby, sure you never took her out in Coldharbour. It was always London so you might think it was anonymous, but it doesn't work like that. Remember that restaurant you went to with Fairhurst? Really good-looking couple in their early twenties at the next table. That boss of yours couldn't take his eyes off the girl, but I doubt either of you could describe the man now and all you'll remember about the girl is that she had a great body."

"So what's your point?"

"It's different when you see a fabulous looking girl with an old man. Everyone's fascinated by it. They're staring at the bloke, wondering if he's married, what's he got that let's him snare a beauty like that... presumably money. They're searching his face for any sign of guilt. Then they're looking at the girl, trying to decide if she's a hooker, or a scheming employee looking to trade sex for a pay rise or some sweet innocent being seduced by a ruthless pervert. You might as well have a fucking great arrow over your heads. Someone, somewhere is going to remember you. Once they start publishing some decent pics of Natalie that show her when she's dressed up, the penny will drop and they'll be on your tail. Unless they find the real killer."

Toby was indignant. "I paid cash wherever we went, so there's no paper trail. We booked in her name not mine. It'd be my word against there's. And I'm thirty fucking eight for Christ's sake. The age gap was sixteen years."

"Toby, you're missing the point. Yes you could argue that it wasn't you that killed her, and they'd never be able to prove it, but that doesn't matter any more. This is Britain in the twenty first century. You should know this better than anyone, given what you do for a living. If anyone finds a link to Natalie, someone at the paper will remember that Annie Radford came to see you. Then your picture is in the papers and Katie Enright fingers you as the train pervert. Case closed. Later they'll work out it couldn't have been you, but your career will be shot to shit by then."

"So what do I do?"

"Keep your head down, get your takeaways delivered, order your Rioja online and pray they find the killer."

***

As an Academy member, Adam Buckley had read the stories of what footballer's got up to and he could hardly wait for his first away trip with the team. That had been several months before, so he'd had time to adjust to a relatively disappointing reality. He had images of naked models lounging in baths filled with champagne at wild parties where A-list celebrities let their hair down, safe from the prying eyes of the paparazzi. As a Premier League footballer, every door would be open to him. The reality fell someway short, even if it was still beyond the wildest dreams of the average twenty-something. Most of the first team were older than Adam and had already settled down. If they had a bit of fun on the side, it certainly wasn't in public. Under Jack Enright, the players were also less well paid than at most other clubs, some were still on contracts they'd signed when the club was in the lower tiers of English football. That, combined with the fact that the town itself was in decline, had seeped into the mentality of the players. The older ones had all bagged themselves great looking wives or girlfriends, some had kids, but the parlous state of the football club and the general air of decay that seemed to hang over Coldharbour and its surrounding area made it all feel fragile. They were living the dream but they might just wake up at any moment. There were whispers that Per Sunstrom had a mistress he flew in from Stockholm whenever his wife was away, Tom Barker, the defensive midfielder was rumoured to be shagging a Romanian stripper from Coldharbour's one and only lap dancing club and Olivier Gremeaux, the team's French right back was seen, more than once, in the corridor of the team hotel with a woman who was definitely not his wife. They were enjoying the fruits of modest celebrity but out of the glare of the media.

Adam was one of only half a dozen single players in the first team squad and, as the new boy, was yet to be fully accepted by the others. They'd been in the side for a couple of seasons, they'd won promotion two years before, they'd played at Anfield, at Old Trafford and St James's Park. Adam had been in the team a couple of months, only because the guys ahead of him in the pecking order were injured or absent. He'd nicked a few goals, mainly against weak opposition and suddenly he was the golden boy. Feathers were ruffled and egos were bruised. He'd kept his mouth shut about being taken on by Stephen Lester, it would only widen the rift. There were no celebrity parties, the lead singer of the new hot girl band had not pounced him on, nor had he walked the red carpet of a single film premiere with a supermodel on his arm. There had been a string of one-night stands with local girls he picked up in the bars and clubs of Coldharbour. There were afternoon trysts with women who'd asked for an autograph and more when he was wandering around town, and the occasional quickie in the back of his car, in the woods on the eastern edge of town, even in the car park at the football club. There were plenty of suitors but it was a million miles from the glitz and glamour he'd craved as an eager Academy member.

The players occasionally made an appearance at Digital or The Moon, or one of the other clubs in town. Once in a while there'd be trouble, a player had a drink or two too many and started throwing his weight around, or a local guy got jealous of the attention lavished on the footballers and wanted to settle their differences "like men." The players knew how far they could push their luck. The owners always ensured a couple of bouncers were on hand when local celebrities were on the premises. If there was trouble, it wasn't a tough call to decide who'd be deemed to have started it. A footballer running a bar bill that could run to thousands or a factory worker who won't be back until next month's wages got paid. Usually the clubs were convenient places to have a couple of drinks then find a partner for the night. Adam was occasionally allowed to tag along, but he was the outsider. One day they might make him part of the inner circle, but not yet.

There'd been a brawl in Digital only the previous Saturday. Adam couldn't be bothered with even the limited courting ritual required of a professional footballer. He'd spotted a girl called Maddy who'd previously made it clear that she was always available if he was interested. He hadn't even spoken to her that night, he just noticed her looking hopefully from the other corner of the bar. Adam jerked his head towards the door. The message was, "get your coat, you've pulled." Maddy squealed with delight and raced over to his side. Then the trouble started.

Jack Galloway joined Coldharbour when the Scottish Champions released him three years earlier. He was the club's rising star, until Adam Buckley came along. He wasn't going to let go of his exalted status easily. When Galloway and his team mates visited a club, the owner usually cordoned off a small area of the bar for their exclusive use. Some invested in a few brass uprights, a length of gold coloured rope and an intimidating looking heavy to keep the riff-raff out. None of the clubs in Coldharbour had the resources for a separate VIP area, this was the next best thing. Girls would congregate close to the rope hoping to get the nod and be allowed to join their heroes. There were no prizes for subtlety, for those who liked to play hard to get, for those whose allure depended on an air of mystery or for those who drew a man in with wit, humour and intelligence. The recipe for success was to get as much flesh on show as the law allowed and to perfect a look that screams,

"Let me cross the rope and all this is yours."

The newer players could barely believe their luck, pick one out of the line, tap the bouncer on the shoulder, point and he'd collect and deliver. Awesome. Galloway was bored with it all. There was no thrill of the chase, he decided to inject a bit of interest into proceedings. He'd spotted a stunning Asian girl and had her summoned to side. The girl was bouncing with delight and her friends patted her on the back as she made her way to the rope. The response would hardly have been any different had she been heading for the stage to collect an Academy Award. The winner was thrilled, flushed with pride but slightly nervous as to what she was going to say when she got to centre stage. Her audience looked thrilled for her, inside they were burning with envy. The girl was only feet from Galloway when he raised his hand to indicate she should stop. He looked her up and down like an antiques expert appraising a piece of furniture, he stroked his chin and cocked his head to one side, then furrowed his brow. The girl stared nervously, her eyes wide and expectant. Then Galloway raised his hand and made a twirling motion with his index finger pointed towards the floor. He wanted the girl to turn.

"Give us a twirl sweetheart," he said.

She spun round as requested. Galloway looked disappointed and repeated the motion slowly.

"Again darlin', only don't be in such a hurry."

She turned slowly. The footballer looked around at his companions as though they should offer him some guidance, they were grinning, some knew what was coming next. Then Galloway shook his head,

"No thanks love, my eyesight must be going."

Then he waved the girl away with the back of his hand. He was mistaken, she had a certain appeal from a distance but, close up, it was clear that he'd made a terrible mistake. Galloway had standards and this girl simply failed to meet them. He turned back towards the bar, his team mates collapsed in fits of laughter and the girl scurried back to her friends in floods of tears. She was, by any measure, the most beautiful girl in the club, and that was the fun as far as Galloway was concerned. Most men would clamber over hot coals to be close to her, all her friends would kill to be like her, but Galloway could crush her in a second with a dismissive wave of his hand.

That was the power of being a professional footballer. And he didn't even have to take the consequences. Nobody spotted the tall, muscular young man standing yards away from the girl when she walked towards the rope. Nobody saw his look of utter dismay as the footballer humiliated his sister in front of a club full of people. He launched himself towards the rope and was inches from Galloway when the first bouncer grabbed him round the neck. A second man was required to subdue the interloper and drag him towards the exit that led to an alleyway running along the side of the club. The two men intended to give the trouble maker a strong reminder that he'd not be welcome back and the main street was no place for that.

Galloway laughed and ordered another round. Adam grabbed Maddy by the arm and led her from the club.

Adam knew about the post match parties that Galloway and his coterie had in their rooms. Sometimes the girls outnumbered the players, sometimes a single female was somehow convinced that she should provide the entertainment for a group of young men. Adam listened with envy and fear. He wanted to be the ringleader, the guy they looked up to, the one they all wanted to be,

"Hey lads look at Adam, he's going to wear that chick out. Don't know where he gets the stamina."

"Come on fellas, the party's in Adam's suite, can't miss that. They're always a blast."

Then the cold light of reality dawned. It started at school, Adam couldn't use a urinal if someone was standing next to him. Even if he was desperate to go, the arrival of another person in the adjacent slot would slam the door shut on his bladder. With that track record, Adam wasn't going to be playing a starring role in a footballer's sex party any time soon.

Two months into his first team career and Adam had adjusted to the fact that Coldharbour players were masters of what they surveyed. The problem was that it was a dilapidated little seaside resort and a football club that was hanging on to Premier League status by its fingertips. As the season drew to a close, their new owner sought to make the odd gesture to suggest that Coldharbour Town might be a club of substance. They'd only played in London the night before but the team were booked into a hotel after the game.

Adam woke with the feeling that a large metal clamp had been attached to either side of his head. His mouth was dry and his stomach felt bloated. It took a minute or so to orientate himself to his surroundings. The players weren't sure whether to celebrate or not, a dour goalless draw against the team at the foot of the table was not the result they wanted, but it kept them on course for the target of four points from four matches. And the fixture was away from home. All in all, not a bad outcome, their opponents would now almost certainly be relegated. One down, two to go.

The warning from their Russian coach had been unequivocal.

"One glass of wine with dinner, one soft drink in the hotel bar. That's it. No night clubs, no drunken brawling, nothing that puts you in the papers. Mr Koloschenko owns a salt mine in Siberia, if you want a transfer there, then you simply have to ignore what I am telling you."

As Adam looked around his hotel room, the events of the previous night started to seep back into his mind. TV had decreed that the game didn't kick off until after five o'clock, they were hoping for some drama as two relegation threatened teams fought out a titanic battle to stay in the Premier League. What they got was ninety minutes plus of dour, timid, often cynical football. The opposition made the occasional foray into Coldharbour territory but there was little conviction. Had they scored, it's likely the crowd would have been stunned into silence. One newspaper described it as being how they imagined the trenches in World War One. Two sides, both resigned to their fate, neither with any expectation of survival, just desperate for it to all to be over. Occasionally the troops were ordered forward in a futile and inevitably unsuccessful attack, it would be repelled and they'd return to their positions grateful that they'd suffered no lasting damage to themselves. Adam barely touched the ball and when he did, a man mountain of a centre half ensured that the experience was short lived. Sometimes fairly, more often with a subtle nudge, a swift tug of the shirt, once with a raking tackle that felt as though it might have severed his Achilles tendon. The game ended without a goal and the TV highlights lasted less than a minute.

Boris made good with his promise of a glass of wine over a subdued dinner in the hotel restaurant and, by ten o'clock, most of the team had retired to their rooms. When Adam arrived in the bar for his one and only soft drink, a group of younger players were heading in the other direction. They brushed past without even acknowledging their team mate. Jack Galloway didn't look in Adam's direction but raised his voice, just a little, to ensure that his rival knew what he'd be missing.

"I swear, there'll be five of them. It's that little slapper I had after the Swansea game. She said, if I invited her back she'd bring her mates. I slipped her the key so they should be up there now."

There was much raucous laughter and back slapping as they disappeared into the lift.

As Adam entered the bar, there was only one other Coldharbour player present. Alexei Katsov had recently split from his wife, she missed her family back in Russia and had told him Coldharbour was bleak, desolate and miserable. She was returning to Yakutsk, less than three hundred miles from the Arctic Circle where winter temperatures regularly hit minus thirty. He beckoned Adam to join him and the two young women who were sipping vodka tonics on adjacent barstools. Nine hours later, one of them, although he couldn't remember her name, was lying next to him in bed. Boris had banned them from drinking in the bar, he'd said nothing about room service. At least that was the logic his team mate had used to justify what happened next. Adam had a vague recollection of the four of them going back to Alexei's room. The Ukrainian tipped the concierge generously and he'd organised for a selection of spirits and mixers to be delivered which were paid for in cash. There was no way they could go on the room bill. Drinking games followed and Adam lost heavily. Alexei had taken a liking to the red-haired girl and Adam vaguely recalled watching him slowly undress her on the sofa. The blonde had already established that his room was just three doors down and that's when she led him there by the hand.

She stirred in her sleep, her eyes opened slowly and she saw him staring at her.

"Oh my God, I shagged a footballer." The look on her face was of genuine horror, the voice was refined and educated.

"Sorry?" The response was not one that Adam had encountered before, he was more used to a hopeful, starstruck smile and a desperate plea that he call the girl, soon.

She shook her head vigorously and wiped her eyes, when she opened them again her face fell. It was as though she'd hoped the action might eliminate the image in front of her. Adam would be gone, replaced with a man more deserving of her favours.

"I always vowed that I'd never be one of those slappers who dropped her knickers for a footballer."

Adam was suddenly embarrassed and involuntarily pulled the duvet up around his neck. The girl laughed.

"Don't be shy, the damage is done now." She reached below the covers and started gently massaging his groin.

"I'm Lucy... you're Alan right?"

Adam shrugged, this one could call him whatever she liked.

# 14

"So have we interviewed Buckley?" Maggie Davenport appeared calm on the outside but was burning with frustration. Every time she thought the case was under control, it fell apart in her hands. It felt like one of those cup and ball tricks she'd seen on a weekend break in Paris with her boyfriend. They'd watched a thin-faced Arab with a wispy beard place a ball under one of three upturned cups. The punter placed his bet and then watched while the Arab moved the cups quickly across a wooden board. Surely, it was obvious where the ball would be found. The man paused, then pointed. The cup he'd chosen was lifted and there was the ball. They watched again when the bet was repeated for higher stakes. Like the gambler, they both correctly identified the correct cup.

"I've got to have a go at this," her boyfriend had said.

He wouldn't be persuaded, the winning gambler bore a strong, possibly familial relationship to the Arab. There were no other tourists around. It all screamed "scam." Mercifully, the loss was only twenty Euros and she dragged him away as he reached for his wallet a second time.

Davenport stared at the white board, for her it still did not fit together. She'd looked at every strand of the case, it was like that ball, she watched it go under the middle cup. Then the cups moved faster and faster, but she kept track of very turn, then she'd point at the one she'd kept her eye on the whole time, it would rise by an invisible hand and the ball was gone.

Her colleagues had all declared victory. The Coldharbour Ripper had thrown himself from the twelfth storey of an apartment block whilst under the influence of hallucinogenic drugs. Job done. Case closed. Davenport could see that Tony Drake could easily be the killer, but nothing they had was conclusive. It was the ultimate dilemma as far as she was concerned. If they announced that the killer was dead, another murder would shatter any confidence the local people might have in the police. But what was the alternative? An announcement that Drake might be the killer but they weren't that sure, was probably equally damaging. They had another forty-eight hours at most before they had to make some sort of public announcement. The only resolution to the dilemma was a conclusive link between Drake and the killings or, God forbid, another victim.

Gray checked his notes.

"Ma'am, we spoke to Buckley as soon as we identified that it was his flat where Drake was holed up. He said that he was just helping a friend, the guy was sick and obviously didn't have a lot of money. Buckley put him up and paid his bills for a month or so. He said he had no idea he was taking drugs and he seemed to be devastated that his mate had killed himself."

"Did you make a link to the killings?"

"Not explicitly ma'am but we asked if Buckley knew what his friend was up to on the nights the girls died? I reckon he made the connection himself. He kept saying that Tony would never hurt anyone, he was a 'top bloke who'd lost his way.'" Gray read the quote from his notes.

Davenport shook he head wearily. "So all we have is the fleece?"

Gray's face brightened. "Yes ma'am, but it's pretty strong I reckon. Drake's boss told us that each member of staff has a couple of the jackets we found in that flat. Drake only had the one."

"And the fibres definitely match the ones we found on Zainab's clothes."

Gray nodded, "Definitely the same type of fleece, but the fibres are not from the jacket we found at Drake's place. They're from an older garment."

"So it's not conclusive."

"It's all we have." Gray looked anxious, as though there was something he wanted to say, he just couldn't find the words. Davenport had noticed.

"Well?"

"Ma'am, only a couple of days ago, you thought it was probably Drake. We were all hot for it being the Russian bloke, but you thought it was more likely to be Drake. Then another girl gets killed and he chucks himself off a roof. Now you don't seem so certain at all. I don't get it."

Davenport nodded. "Peter, I didn't say it was Drake. I just thought it probably wasn't the Russian. Drake was the only other lead we had. I agree, everything points to it being him, but I'm amazed there is so little forensic evidence linking him to the killings. The jacket is circumstantial but it won't help us get a conviction. The guy's dead, but all we have on him is that he has a jacket *like* the one worn by the killer. How many black fleeces do you think there are in Coldharbour? Let me take a guess, I'd say you've got one, I know I do, and so has my boyfriend. That means, based on the evidence we have, there's as much chance of convicting any one of the three of us as there is of getting a charge to stick to Tony Drake."

Gray knew she was right. He did have a black fleece, worse that that, he'd just realised that in a town where the local team had played for years in black and white, there was probably at least a couple in every house in the area. Davenport continued.

"I don't want to close the case until we have something that would convict him in a court of law."

Gray could see the logic, he was at a loss as to how they'd achieve that objective.

"Peter, you know I want to be certain about this, whatever announcement is made about Drake has to be right. I want us to keep probing for a couple of days, let's see if anything comes up."

"Of course ma'am. But where do we look?"

"What about Buckley. If Drake is the killer, this guy's been sheltering him for a month. Why? Drake could have stayed in his own place, Buckley could still have paid his bills, taken care of him. Why did he have to be hidden away? What if Buckley's involved?"

"Well we know he didn't kill the girls ma'am."

"How so?"

"Angelina. She died sometime before midnight. He was on the team bus coming back from Southampton. They didn't get back to the ground until after one."

"Interview him again. Tell him outright that we think Drake killed the girls. Suggest it might make him an accomplice."

***

The game at Fulham was expected to be a drab affair. Coldharbour's opponents were also in desperate need of points and neither side had shown much appetite for free flowing football in recent weeks. Koloschenko flew into a rage when Boris told him that Adam Buckley would not be playing. They'd not even included him in the squad.

"Boss, his Achilles is giving him trouble. If he plays he could do some serious damage. I have to rest him." It was common sense but not what Koloschenko wanted to hear.

"Boris, we will not be relegated. This team will be in seventeenth place or higher on the last day of the season or there will be consequences. Buckley appears to be the only player who can secure us the points we need and you are telling me he will not play. You can understand why this is not what I want to hear."

Boris hadn't focused on much of what Koloschenko said to him after the word 'consequences.' He was too busy trying to imagine what those might be. Nonetheless he got the gist. The boss was not convinced.

"Dimitri, we have two games left after this, we need only three points and I hope to get at least one today. We have come for a draw, my plan is to stop Fulham from scoring, we will secure the points we need in the two remaining home games. If I am to be without Buckley for any game, this is the one I'd choose. This problem with his Achilles is real. If I play him today, that could be the end of his season. Trust me."

Koloschenko stormed from the dressing room.

The plan that Boris had drummed in to his team all week worked like a dream for exactly eleven and a half minutes. He'd rejected the old fashioned 4-4-2 formation, in Sam Chalmers' day they often went for the more aggressive 4-3-3. It was hard to tell exactly but as Coldharbour shaped up to deal with Fulham's first tentative advance, it looked a lot like 5-5-0.

Had aliens, unfamiliar with the game of football, been observing the match they might have wondered why the pitch was very short but rather wide and what on earth were those net things doing on the side-lines. It's an easy impression to get when both teams flatly refuse to move forward and every pass goes sideways. When the goal came it was as much a surprise to the attacking team as it was a disappointment to their visitors. Fulham played fourteen passes without making any significant inroads into Coldharbour territory. The Sky TV director gleefully switched the shot to a young boy in the crowd who was yawning so widely it looked as though his jaw was locked. The commentators were quick to say they knew how he felt. Suddenly it was as though a couple of the Fulham players had failed to read the script. One ran into the space behind Coldharbour's right full back, another laced a perfect pass though the massed ranks of red shirts. Olivier Gremeaux, the full back was quick to give chase. The Fulham player decided to turn so he could cross with his right foot and Gremeaux got the slightest of touches on the ball. The attacker tried to let it roll out for a throw-in, around four yards short of the line that marked the edge of the penalty area. There'd been an incident in the game at Coldharbour, earlier in the season. The same players had gone for a fifty-fifty ball and Gremeaux came off worse. It was time for payback, nothing serious, just a little tap on the ankles to remind his opponent that the Frenchman hadn't forgotten. A throw-in became a free kick and Coldharbour had brought the pressure on themselves. The back line was still remonstrating with each other when the cross came in. Everyone missed it, the ball flew across the penalty area, its impetus halted only when it struck the inside of the far post and bounced into the net. One – nil.

Less than twelve minutes gone and Boris's master plan was in tatters. He had no Plan B. Buckley should have been a substitute, at least they'd have had the option to use him. All they had on the bench as an attacking alternative, was an eighteen-year-old Academy kid who'd never played a first team game in his life.

It wasn't just that Coldharbour had no attacking options, their defence was suddenly under far more pressure. They couldn't just lump the ball upfield and have Buckley chase it down and hang on to it, while the rest of the team regrouped and took a breather. The goal appeared to ignite Fulham's self-belief. In minutes they were toying with their opposition, it was only a matter of time before the next goal came. And the one after that.

Boris trudged down the tunnel at the end of the game, 3-0 was a humiliating score against fellow strugglers and hardly the preparation they wanted for the upcoming Semi-final. Slatkin was waiting at the dressing room door.

"Dimitri's gone. You're lucky he only lives up the road and I think the lovely Alina is waiting for him. He's not happy."

Boris nodded wearily. He remembered the message he'd given the team before the Southampton game. The threat of a transfer to one of Koloschenko's salt mines. That was his little joke, but he feared that Dimitri might have a much worse fate in store for him if he screwed up again.

\*\*\*

Three months earlier, Eddie Taylor would have relished his upcoming meeting with Toby Thomas. He had a "world exclusive" and a sleazy story that would have the genteel folk of Coldharbour gasping with horror... then hoping for a bit more detail... especially if there were photos. His editor hadn't been the same man recently, he was preoccupied, detached, the editorial meetings were routine, no speeches, no set piece theatrics. For the last couple, Thomas had been waiting in his office when the team began to gather. There were stories that he'd split up from his wife, a rumour that he was screwing around with a girl in Coldharbour. Everyone assumed that his wife had found out and shown him the door. As Taylor approached the office, Victoria grimaced but nodded for him to go in. It was going to a difficult half hour.

Thomas was sitting at his meeting table, idly leafing through the last copy of the Coldharbour Echo. The smile was friendly enough, the kind you might give a shop assistant when she handed you your change. Eddie's arrival hadn't made his day, but it wasn't the worst thing that had happened to him.

"So where are we Eddie?"

"Boss, they've got the Coldharbour Ripper."

Thomas's head jerked up like he was a string puppet, the look on his face turned from surprise to contentment and what Eddie might easily have taken as relief.

"Are they sure?"

"Lewis at the nick gave me the inside track about thirty minutes ago. We'll need to give him a bit extra this month, this definitely falls into the "scoop" category and our deal was always that he got a bonus if he delivered one of those."

"If this is true Eddie, you can pay to have his teeth fixed if you want. Who is it?"

"Who *was* it?" Eddie corrected. "Remember that kid Drake, the junkie who jumped off the roof over on Ranmore Hill? It was him."

"What's the link? How are they so sure?"

"Lewis says he was on the list all the time. They suspected him from the start but couldn't join the dots. Remember that Becky? She was the Simpson girl's best friend. Seems they met up with Drake just before he killed her, she said it was obvious her mate was terrified of him. Lewis put her in the frame for me and I phoned and checked it out. She confirmed it, but that's not all."

"Go on." Thomas had a broad smile on his face for the first time in weeks. Tobias had been right, the police could easily link him to Natalie or Annie Radford and if that Enright girl fingered him for the incident on the train, he'd be in it up to his eyebrows. The only thing that could lift the cloud would be if they found the killer. Today was liberation day.

"Lewis is relaxed about us quoting Becky but the next bit we have to keep under our hats. If we use it they'll know there's a leak at the station. He said he was only telling me so we knew the story was solid."

"What's he got?"

"There were black fibres on the clothing of the Arab girl, they're a direct match to a fleece jacket that Drake wore to work. They've nailed him."

"So the case is closed?" Thomas looked less confident of what he was hearing. "If that's so, why aren't they shouting it from the rooftops. This is the news the town's been waiting for, how come they're not rushing out a statement?"

Eddie was one step ahead. "I asked him the same boss. He said it's all down to the Davenport woman. He says she's a checklist freak, and she's gagging for a promotion. He reckons she's trying to get her ducks in a row so she comes out with all the credit. They'll announce it in the next forty-eight though. If we want the scoop we have to get it out there quick."

"Nice one Eddie, go for it. But I want the forensic stuff in, you don't have to say it's black fibres but we have to have something to hang the story on and the Becky angle isn't enough."

"What about Lewis?"

"Fuck him. He'll be pissed with us for a while then he'll remember all those nice brown envelopes we put his way. He'll be back."

156

Eddie would have preferred to keep the confidence but he could see the argument that the forensic angle made it a much stronger story. Thomas was probably right about the cash too.

"Boss, I've also got a cracker for the weekend edition, local footballer shags TV star, while the wife is at home with the kids."

"Tell me." Thomas sat back and tugged at another chair with the tip of his right shoe. He was suddenly feeling very relaxed and it would make a handy footrest.

"You remember that thing we did about Per Sunstrom talking to a Swedish agent? Well one of the interns spotted him in the car park at that Aldi superstore on the edge of town. He recognised the personalised number plate and thought it was a bit odd that he was waiting when the shop was shut. Then someone picked him up in a hire car and the intern followed. Thought we might get another photo of him."

Thomas looked perturbed by what he was hearing and Eddie was getting nervous. He was sure the punch line would be to the editor's liking and decided to get straight to the point.

"Our guy followed them to the Premier Inn down the road. It was some six-foot Swedish bird. Legs up to her armpits, long blonde hair. She went in to check in, then they both went to a room across the car park. They didn't leave until six a.m. and I don't think they were playing dominoes all that time."

"That's the story?" Thomas sounded disappointed. Eddie was dismayed the lukewarm reaction but thought he had the clincher.

"Our guy recognised her, she's on one of those Scandinavian murder series on TV now. She's a fucking TV star and she's married."

Thomas shook his head. "Eddie, it's not the time. We've got a stack of stuff on the Ripper story, that's going to be our lead for weeks. Also I don't think the people of Coldharbour will thank us for shafting their skipper at such a crucial time in the season. Drop it for now and we'll come back to it in the summer."

Eddie was deflated. The London based tabloids would have a field day with a story like this and Thomas was telling him to drop it. He'd have to come up with something good for the intern who thought he was on his way to a Pulitzer Prize.

"Anything else?" Thomas had drawn the line firmly under the Sunstrom story.

"Not really boss. Just an update on something we were looking at but it's a non-story. Remember you told us to check out Mayor Williams?"

Thomas furrowed his brow, the impression was that he might have done but had no clear recollection.

"We've got some stuff on him but I don't think we can go there."

"I'll be the judge of that, what have you got?"

"Well the first thing was a stroke of luck. Dave in marketing's got a brother who cleans the windows at that massage parlour in Stonehaven. I guess Williams thought nobody would recognise him, but Dave's brother's in Coldharbour all the time. He spotted him."

"Proof?" Thomas was suddenly interested.

"Dave's brother saw the angle straight away, he got these." Eddie dropped half a dozen photos on the table. All were of a middle-aged man trying unsuccessfully to hide his face, beneath the sign advertising "Thai Touch, the authentic experience." It was Williams.

"Anything else?"

"We sent a guy round to the pubs near his house. Met a girl called Sally who used to work in his stables. She gave us some stuff but I don't see that we can use it."

"Eddie…" Thomas was losing patience.

"She worked in the stables and he hit on her a couple of times, but she wasn't interested and he backed off. She reckoned he did it all the time. Some girls were OK with it

158

apparently, most brushed him off but he got a few of them to polish his horse brasses."

"How old were they?" Thomas knew the answer he wanted to hear.

"All nineteen, twenty, sometimes older. I asked her if any younger girls worked there and she got my drift straight away. She said Williams wasn't that kind of bloke, he was just a sad old geezer who wanted a shag."

"But he's married right?" The righteous indignation in Thomas's voice would have done justice to a Methodist minister.

"Yes boss, but that's exactly why I don't think we can use it. His missus has got cancer, they reckon she's got six months to live max. A story like this would be a shocker for her and her family."

"He holds public office Eddie. If he didn't want his wife to know he shouldn't have started down this road."

"Boss, there's rumours that the massage place offers the odd 'happy ending,' but he might be going there to sort a dodgy back. We've got nothing to say that he did anything wrong when he was on the premises."

Thomas picked up a photo from the collection that Eddie had placed on his desk. Phillips looked furtive, he was clearly hoping that nobody would see him leave the premises.

"Body language Eddie, body language. This is like a signed confession. You don't look like that when you've had a spinal adjustment or a shoulder rub. This is a man who's been relieved of a quantity of bodily fluid. Plain as day." Thomas looked triumphant.

"What about the stable girls boss? None of them have ever complained. This Sally says he's quite the gentleman. I'm not sure what the story is here."

Thomas fixed him with his steeliest look. Disappointment oozed from every pore.

"He's supposed to be a pillar of the community, but he uses prostitutes and preys on young women, exploiting their love of horses and their need to work. And his wife is on her deathbed. The voting public need to know the sort of man they've got as Mayor."

He stood, the meeting was over. "I want it on the front page at the weekend. Ripper is the main story, but give this the right hand sidebar and a decent chunk of page three. See how much this Sally wants for a photo and few direct quotes.

Thomas felt as though he floated back to his desk. His first call was to William Fairhurst, proprietor of the Coldharbour Echo. Mayor Williams had been a thorn in his side for years, their businesses were in direct competition and the Mayor's office was less than helpful when it came to planning consents. Thomas brought his employer up to date as though he was imparting grave and distressing news. His employer played along, expressing his regret that a public figure should behave in this appalling manner and reluctantly agreeing that the newspaper was obliged to report what it knew. Fairhurst chuckled at the imminent humiliation of his old adversary, then shook his head in bemusement as he replaced the receiver. How could Williams have been so stupid? Going into a place like Thai Touch where he ran the risk of being spotted. For a modest supplement the girl would come to the customer's house. He checked his diary, he had nothing until six that evening, Mrs Fairhurst was not due to return from the visit to her sister's house until Friday and, he told himself, his back was feeling a little stiff. A massage would do the trick very nicely. He picked up the phone and dialled the number of Thai Touch from memory.

Thomas's second call was to Yuri Slatkin. The Russian was grateful for the tip off about Sunstrom. He'd get the lawyers onto it immediately and whilst it was unlikely they'd get an injunction, he'd get a letter in the post that would give Thomas a sound excuse to kick the story still further into the long grass. The editor of the Echo expressed a preference for Ruinart over Bollinger in response to Slatkin's question and thanked the Russian for his generosity, especially as Slatkin

160

told him there would be a quantity of cash at the bottom of the case.

Toby Thomas looked out over the town of Coldharbour. The sun was shining and he was suddenly feeling blessed. He had a job that he loved and hardly a care in the world.

\*\*\*

Everyone saw the Chelsea versus Arsenal game as the real FA Cup Final. Whoever won that game would surely go on to lift the trophy on May 21. Coldharbour and Sheffield Wednesday were fighting it out to see who'd be cannon fodder on the day. The prize, however, was more than just a loser's medal for the two underdogs. The two London sides had already qualified for the Champions League for the following season. A semi-final victory guaranteed a place in the Europa League regardless of the outcome of the final. Marketing people in Sheffield and Coldharbour were waiting on the outcome before they finalised the sponsorship contracts for the following year. European football and more TV coverage meant sponsors would pay extra to feature their brand on shirts and perimeter advertising. Dimitri Koloschenko would also pocket a further increment to the sales price if Coldharbour got to the final. That increment multiplied if they won the cup. If they were to beat Chelsea in the final, he'd be lauded as the man who took on Abramovich and won. He could hand over the keys to Coldharbour Town to the Americans and leave as a winner, with a very healthy cheque in his pocket. Failing in the FA Cup would be a devastating blow, failing to secure Premier League safety would be a catastrophe. He'd be stuck with his investment.

# 15

Chelsea versus Arsenal was a TV pundit's dream, pitching the cold, calculating and apparently ruthless tactician, Jose Mourinho, against the games' self professed, leading advocate of fast, free-flowing, attacking football, Arsene Wenger. Neither man had a good word to say about the other in public. Wenger lamented his opponent's often dour, disciplined approach to the game. Mourinho gleefully pointed to a trophy cabinet bulging with silverware. There were few neutrals on the subject of the match, most supporters of other teams had a violent antipathy to one side or the other, usually borne out of some real or imagined grievance arising from a previous encounter. Tottenham fans would ideally have liked both teams to lose, if pushed they tended to despise Chelsea a little less.

The game was far from the thriller for which many had hoped. Arsenal a little more reticent than expected, Chelsea only occasionally bursting forward with the fluency many of their fans hankered to see more often. Nobody remembers the losers in the semi-final and that appeared to dominate the thinking of both teams. Arsenal fans held their breath when the ball dropped loose from a corner in the eighty-seventh minute. It fell to a blue shirt and the goal was at the mercy of the Chelsea forward. A red-socked leg stretched out and made the block, but the forward tumbled to the ground. Every blue-shirted soul in the stadium screamed "penalty," apart from the Chelsea players on the pitch. The Arsenal defenders turned to defend the corner that was surely about to be awarded. Then uproar. The referee pointed to the penalty spot. Players jostled, yellow cards were brandished and the clock had ticked well past the ninetieth minute by the time the ball hit the back of the net. Six minutes of added time brought little more in the way of goalmouth action. The whistle blew and Chelsea was the first team into that season's FA Cup Final.

It was twenty-two hours before Per Sunstrom led his team out onto the Wembley pitch. Boris had given them the team talk of his life. Alexei told Adam he was impressed, not just with the fact that the players were on the biggest win bonus they'd ever been offered but Boris spoke about winning the game as though his life depended on it. They were not to know, but Boris actually feared that might be the case.

Neil Davies inspected his boots and picked a couple of imaginary specks of dust from the gleaming leather. In just fifteen minutes he'd be running out at Wembley for the first time and he knew that on the soft pitch they'd be dirty before the game was five minutes old. That was not the point. Prince William was there, and their handshake would be the curtain raiser on a day that would live with him forever. Davies was a true professional, that's what got him and his team to the final. Shaking hands with the next King of England was not something you did with dirty boots.

His mother would be watching, a few friends and many adversaries stretching back to his school days would see him lead his team out at Wembley and those who called him a loser, would choke on their words. He was a runner at school, he was fit, he was quick and he had medals to prove it. The problem had come when sporting equipment was introduced into the equation. He couldn't throw or catch, bats and racquets became deadly weapons in his hands and the only person he was likely to hurt was himself. As a boy Davies threw himself into football, it was his passion. He could name the home football ground for every team in the four divisions, he could name the managers, the club colours both home and away and every time a fuel company or magazine gave away stickers or league ladders, he had to have them. Those collections were still in mint condition in the bedroom of his flat on the outskirts of London. At first they laughed at his aspiration to make the school team, eventually Steve Sims, the sports teacher, included him in the squad. Neil Davies was the one lad who could be relied on to turn up for every game regardless of the

164

weather, regardless of what the rest of the team got up to the night before. Davies was sure he just needed a chance, a few games under his belt. He'd never be a star striker, he'd never be a skilful winger, but he was dependable. If they needed a volunteer for goalkeeper duty his was the first hand to shoot up. Anywhere as long as he was in the team. Sims quickly realised that he'd be better off with ten players than to use Davies anywhere on the pitch. He had no facility for the game whatsoever and his presence served only to sow the seeds of chaos amongst the other players. What a terrible waste, a guy who could run, who was desperate to be part of the squad, whose knowledge of the game and its rules was encyclopaedic, but was as hopeless a footballer as the teacher had ever seen. The squad met for training and they were dividing into two teams for a game of seven-a-side. The nominated captains took turns to pick a player until only Davies was left. Mr Sims watched the forlorn, solitary figure, the last boy in line. The captain of the second team shook his head in dismay, he didn't even bother to confirm his seventh pick. Davies looked crushed. Sims tossed him the whistle.

"Neil, why don't you referee this for us, I fancy a game myself today."

Davies picked the whistle out of the mud and gave it a quick polish on his shorts. He'd tried to catch, as Sims threw it in a gently looping arc, straight to his right hand. It had slipped between his fingers. For a full ten seconds Davies stared at the whistle as though it was an alien object. Then he started to smile and a dream was born.

At the age of just twenty-eight it was a huge honour to be given charge of a FA Cup Semi-Final and Neil Davies was bursting with pride. He'd dreamt of leading a team out at Wembley and the fantasy was about to be realised. It was only a team of three, him and his assistants who ran the line, but it hardly mattered. He was recognised by the football world as a top achiever, he was on first name terms with players and managers that most football fans only ever saw on TV. He was on the inside, where he'd always dreamed of being.

He reviewed all his performances on TV. Thank the Lord, or Sky TV at least, for wall-to-wall coverage of the Premier League. He'd made a few bad decisions over the years but nothing too dramatic. He was known as a solid dependable official who was scrupulously fair. At the end of the game, he might take a glass of wine with the home manager, it was always good to have them shake his hand at the end of the game. It never effected his decisions he was sure of that. One pundit suggested that he had a tendency to give the benefit of the doubt to the big teams, but that wasn't fair. It had nothing to do with post match hospitality, or rubbing shoulders with world famous figures, refereeing was as much an art as a science and ex footballers were never going to understand that.

Neil Davies was ready. He'd have preferred the Chelsea Arsenal game but this was a nice stepping-stone. Maybe next year.


Sheffield Wednesday had come from nowhere to make the semi-finals. They might make the play offs from Division One, the incongruously named third tier of English football after the Premier and Championship, on the other hand they might not. It was as close a contest as anyone could remember for years and anyone down to twelfth place in the table was in with a shot of returning to Wembley in May. Most lower league semi-finalists had at least one major scalp from the campaign. Wednesday had beaten two teams from the middle of the Championship, four from other divisions, but none from the Premier League. Coldharbour Town were going into a huge game in the very unfamiliar position of being favourites.

Members of the Press later lauded the participants for offering up a game that was far more thrilling than the Chelsea – Arsenal tie from the previous day. It was not necessarily a compliment. There's much to be admired when two highly professional, totally disciplined, technically excellent teams play one another. The problem is that on occasions it can be as dull as dishwater. As thrilling for the layman as watching two chess grand masters play an elaborate game of cat and mouse for the world championship. The Sun described the Coldharbour – Wednesday game as being like pub football. Two teams throwing themselves at each other, because they really didn't have any better ideas. Clear cut scoring opportunities were squandered by both sides, defensive howlers littered the game and anyone who didn't know the answer already would have been hard pushed to spot which was the Premier League side.

Wednesday took the lead. The giant killing was on. A careless back pass was intercepted and a tame shot rolled through the legs of the Coldharbour keeper. Sunstrom equalised from a corner. He was quickest and strongest in the aerial battle and Neil Davies and his team failed to spot that Adam Buckley had a firm grip on the goalkeeper's shirt. Buckley himself nicked the second, Jack Galloway knocked the ball into space behind the Wednesday back four. He'd never admit that, since Adam arrived, it had become the default option for a team that had run out of ideas. Had the keeper come for it straight away it would have been no contest but it looked like the central defender had it covered. When he slipped, Buckley was certain to get their first. Everyone knew he liked to dummy his first shot to draw the keeper into diving, this time his opponent was ready for him. He'd stay on his feet and wait for the Coldharbour forward to try to go round him. Buckley took one touch and then lifted the ball over the keeper's advancing frame. Two – one.

Wednesday got their equaliser with ten minutes to go. A shot from thirty yards from a player who'd not scored for three years. Some even claimed it was a cross. Regardless, it took two exhausted teams into extra-time and a penalty-shoot out. Few who have not had to do it themselves can understand why it's so hard to beat a goalkeeper from twelve yards when the target is eight yards across and eight feet high. Most players look like they just hit, and hope the keeper will dive the other way, all too few have mastered the art of hitting the parts of the goal where no keeper could reach. Adam Buckley had practiced for days like this, he was an adherent of the Alexander technique. Graham Alexander played most of his career for clubs in Lancashire and had an astonishing success rate from the penalty spot. He never did a cute little shimmy on his run up, he never dummied the shot, he never waited for the keeper to dive before he rolled it down the middle. It appeared that he also never missed. He'd practice without a goalkeeper, the logic was that if he hit it where he intended, no keeper could ever reach it. He had two types of shot, top right, top left. It rarely failed.

Coldharbour and Wednesday were eighty per cent of the way though a penalty taking master class. Only a couple would pass the Alexander test, but with eight penalties taken, it was four each, Wednesday to take the next one. The ball struck the inside of the post and flew along the goal line into the arms of a grateful goalkeeper. Adam Buckley was up next.

Adam had dreamt of a moment like this, he'd have preferred it to be the final, but when this went in, he might get another chance on May 21... when, not if. He could see the fans behind the goal, what looked like acres of black and white, with the odd dot of red to match Coldharbour's new colours. They were singing but he all he could hear was a dull roar, the words were indistinct. The ball rolled a little as he placed it on the spot, he walked back calmly and repositioned it on the left edge of the spot. As he took his run up, there was no keeper, nothing between him and a bucket that in his mind, was attached to the stanchion at the back of the goal. His run up was six paces, this time the keeper guessed right but the ball was past him just as his hand crossed its flight. Coldharbour Town would play Chelsea in the FA Cup Final.

\*\*\*

Maggie Davenport was grateful that the Chief Constable agreed to do the Press Conference. She had no desire to declare victory in the hunt for the Coldharbour Ripper, a term she'd forbidden her team from using on the grounds that it lent a degree of mystique to a man who liked killing women. Her instincts told her that Drake was a suspect, but she was convinced that the forensic evidence would emerge once they discovered where he'd been hiding. There was nothing. No sign of the jacket from which the fibres found on Zainab Mansour's clothing had come, just confirmation that Drake owned one like it. Alan Drake had a cast iron alibi for the first two murders, he was still in prison, and he'd laughed at the suggestion that his son could be a killer. Davenport took Gray to see Natalie Simpson's parents, who'd continued to express their doubts that Tony Drake could be the killer. Natalie was upset when it ended, they said, but she was forlorn, regretful, not angry about an acrimonious break up. Still Davenport had to agree, there had been no attacks since Drake's plunge from the roof of Adam Buckley's apartment. The only real evidence that Tony Drake was the perpetrator was the fact that he'd killed himself. They re-interviewed the old lady who saw him jump, later they found another neighbour who caught the whole thing on camera. His recorder was frequently trained on the apartment block because of the young woman in 1104 who did her stretching routine in her underwear. He'd delayed coming forward until he could secure a reasonable price for the footage that appeared on the net under the title, "The Birdman of Coldharbour…. Not."

Davenport was furious when the story was leaked to the Echo. They were forced to bring the press conference forward by thirty-six hours and, in their haste, allowed the message to be more conclusive than intended. Tony Drake was the killer and now he was dead. Maybe, but they'd never have been able to prove it.

\*\*\*

Adam Buckley stared at Lucy's photo. It sent goose bumps down his spine. He'd never met anyone like her before. She was smart, beautiful and dangerously sexy. Most compelling of all she appeared to be genuinely interested in him. There were none of the mind games that soured the few relationships he'd had that lasted more than a day. She just said what she meant. None of that,

"Well I know I said you shouldn't get me a present but…"

"I don't care what movie we go to, just not this one."

"When I said I don't mind you going out with your mates, I meant…"

Lucy was straightforward, honest without an ounce of deceit in her. "I'm probably not cut out to be a lawyer," she'd said last time they'd met. They'd laughed about their first night together.

"I was trying to find a footballer for my friend. She's desperate to be a WAG." Lucy blushed at the recollection.

"How did you know where we were staying?"

"That's the embarrassing part. The law firm I work for is doing some stuff for your owner. I spent the afternoon taking notes in a meeting with that Russian bloke, Yuri Slatkin. We promised to hand deliver some documents to your hotel before you left in the morning. I was the delivery girl." She gave a mock salute and a little bow.

"But you were all dressed up for a night out."

"That's what's so mortifying. When I told Sophie, she went crazy, begged me to take her along. I said we could go for a couple of drinks but that was it. Then we met Alexei."

"And me."

"Yes you." Lucy tried to look rueful, only when Adam's smile vanished did she start to laugh. "I really wasn't looking for someone, but you were very sweet. Not what I expected at all. I thought all footballers were brash and flashy. Then there was all that vodka, then Alexei and Sophie got all hot and heavy with each other and it's been a while since I… you know." She blushed slightly.

"No regrets?" Adam asked. That first night with Lucy still confused him. She was a fabulous looking girl but he'd not been in the mood, a poor performance on the pitch and Galloway's obvious snub in the hotel corridor were still preying on his mind when they got to Alexei's room. He'd made no attempt to get her into bed, he was polite and courteous but nothing more. Adam left it to Alexei to talk about the famous names they'd met, the places they'd stayed, the cars they drove and the time he'd drunk champagne out of Madonna's shoe at a London club. It was the fourth time he'd heard Alexei tell the tale and each time it was a different pop star and a different city. Adam had no recollection of anything he'd said to Lucy. He'd asked her what she did for a living at one stage, but couldn't remember what she'd said in reply. He nodded from time to time, but was trying to work out why the centre half got the better of him so easily that day and why Jack Galloway was such an arsehole. Alexei suggested the nightcap in his room, and then they'd started drinking in earnest. It wasn't even Adam who'd suggested that Lucy stay. Getting the slappers into bed was never an issue, but with classy girls like Lucy, even a footballer had to put in a bit of effort. Adam felt like she'd fallen into his lap and he was delighted that she had.

They'd had only four dates since that first night. Adam was happy to take the train to London each time, he was smitten. He'd opened up to her, told her about his insecurities, how everyone thought he had it made but he still stumbled from day to day thinking it might all get snatched away. He even told her about Tony Drake.

"We should have been playing for Coldharbour together, maybe it was my reckless tackle that ended my best mate's dream."

"You can't blame yourself Adam. It was his choice to play again before his knee had healed." She'd stroked his hair as she spoke.

"I guess so but, in some small way, I'm partly to blame for the deaths of those girls. Something must have come apart in Tony's mind to turn him into a killer. He was the one destined for glory, not me. That must have had something to do with it."

Lucy kissed him tenderly. "Tony's problems went back a lot further than that. He was from a broken home, his father was a killer. He saw his mum getting roughed up every day and then read about all the terrible things his dad got up to when it all came to trial. That's what screwed him up, it's nothing to do with you."

She was so calm, so logical. Lucy was the best thing that had ever happened to him. She made him laugh and feel like he should be pretty happy with his lot.

Adam Buckley had dreamt of being a professional footballer, of having his pick of the best looking girls. The reality hadn't quite lived up to his expectations. Of course he couldn't complain about the attention that had suddenly been lavished on him, but it felt empty. It wasn't only the women he'd met, everyone wanted to latch onto him because he was famous. They didn't care about Adam Buckley, they craved a piece of the celebrity lifestyle. He wanted a woman who'd say, "look at my boyfriend, isn't he great," instead of "look at me I've got myself a footballer." Lucy was completely different, he believed her when she said she wanted to avoid the celebrity circus, she'd certainly shown no interest in parading him around like a trophy. And she was single, she said she hadn't had a boyfriend for months. She was obviously pretty picky when it came to men as a girl like that must be inundated with offers. Lucy had chosen him and he couldn't be happier.

*** 

Dimitri Koloschenko had summoned Yuri Slatkin to his apartment overlooking Hyde Park in London. It was a relatively new development, each property had been on the market for seven million pounds. Koloschenko bought two and had them knocked together. Slatkin had the feeling that he was walking into a photo shoot. The furniture was exquisite, the pictures and wall hangings were tasteful but were used sparingly across the brilliant white walls. Light flooded through huge picture windows that commanded a spectacular view of London's most famous park. One wall was dedicated to a series of black and white photographs of an exquisitely beautiful young woman. They were in the style of the publicity shots issued by the Hollywood studios back in the 1950s. The subject would not have been out of place alongside Grace Kelly or Audrey Hepburn. Her face had a feline quality with wide green eyes and a delicate pert nose. It looked as though she wanted to snuggle into your arms and, if you gave her the attention she deserved, she would lavish affection upon you. Neglect her at your peril. If she felt ignored, the sharp teeth and the claws would be in your flesh in an instant. Slatkin thought it was a tribute to the girl's star quality that a single look into a camera lens could convey the essence of her personality. The first time he'd seen the pictures he was sure he was looking at old photos of Kristina, Koloschenko's ex-actress wife. They were of Tatyana, the couple's only daughter. Koloschenko adored the young woman and indulged her every whim, which was why she was studying in Paris instead of being where he would prefer, at her father's side.

There was a South American theme to the statues and ornaments that were set carefully around the huge living space where the two men were seated. On the table was what appeared to be couple of modelling portfolios and a pair of hand-made miniature racing cars.

Koloschenko waved his hand dismissively.

"Our new toys," he said. "Alina wants to launch her own fashion range. I need you to help her with the… the details."

"Of course Dimitri, I'll fix a meeting this week. And the cars?"

"I'm drawn to motor racing Yuri, so much more glamorous than football. I need you to look into it. How would I set about getting involved? I think it is closer to the image I want to portray than running a grubby little football team."

"One that is in the FA Cup Final." Yuri offered, hoping that Koloschenko was coming round to the idea that it was not all doom and gloom.

"The final is a double edged sword. If we win I get more from the Americans and, of course, I will enjoy a drink with the owner of our opposition. Should we lose, I will always be remembered as the man who lost this 'battle of the oligarchs.' I'm not happy with this prospect. And we still have two games to go in the League. We cannot be relegated Yuri. That is an outcome I simply will not tolerate."

Slatkin was at a loss. In business they always found a way to get the result they wanted. Koloschenko was a gifted and decisive businessman, when that didn't deliver what he wanted, he wouldn't hesitate to use coercion, bribery or even violence to achieve his objective. If those tactics could be brought to bear to secure the three points they needed, they'd not have hesitated. It just did not seem to be possible. They'd given Stephen Lester, their favourite confidence trickster, time off from pretending to be Adam Buckley's agent, to approach the goalkeeper of their next opponents. He'd explained that he represented an Asian betting syndicate and would be happy to make it worth the man's while to let a couple slide through his fingers. Lester reported the failure of his mission from the local Accident & Emergency department where he was advised that he'd be taking his meals through a straw for a week or two.

"Dimitri, we were unlucky in the last game. We missed Adam Buckley. I think we might have got a win had he been playing, he's back for the next match. Two games and we only need one win. The last game is at home to a team below us in the League. The bookies are saying we're favourites to stay up now."

"Well that's alright then Yuri, when have the bookies ever got it wrong?

"I'm sorry Dimitri, I don't know what else I can say. We've done everything we can and I think we'll get there. A team that can make the FA Cup Final will get three points. If Buckley stays fit, you'll get the sale and you can go to the Final with every chance of putting one over on Roman."

"So the killer was a friend of Buckley?"

"They went to school together, it was Buckley's apartment block that he jumped off. It looks like he lost it after he killed that Polish girl. His timing was exquisite for us, the police were convinced that Victor was their man, then this boy Drake delivered another victim and himself. Perfect."

"Drake didn't kill the Polish girl."

Slatkin had feared a connection since the day he saw the murder reported in the Press. A couple of days earlier he'd told Koloschenko there was no easy way to get Victor out of jail. His boss had made the logical connection. The one thing that would prove Victor's innocence was another murder while he was in custody.

"You killed Drake too?"

"Yuri, I killed nobody. I explained our dilemma regarding Victor to a good friend of mine. He arranged for a copy of the first killing. The Polish girl was unfortunate, pretty little thing from what I saw in the newspapers. I could not afford to have Victor as the suspect in a murder case and I certainly did not want them to re-examine the killing in Kiev. One day we will have to repay the favour my friend has done for us. As for Drake I never heard of him until he made his little splash."

"Why didn't you tell me at the time?" Slatkin was struggling to keep his voice even. He felt confident he had Koloschenko's trust as long as the man involved him in everything. This was a very unwelcome development. Slatkin's position in the organisation relied on him being the guy who got things done, however grubby they might be. He had to hope it was a one-off, maybe a gentle prod to remind him he wasn't indispensible.

"You were busy and I knew the man I could trust to do it. I'm telling you now. There is nothing else to concern yourself with."

Koloschenko rose and headed for the bathroom, it was a minute or so before Slatkin could hear the shower running. The meeting was over. He gathered his papers and made for the door.

***

Adam returned to first team duty for Coldharbour's penultimate league game. Three points were still required for safety and the match was at home to Newcastle. The Geordies were safe in the middle of the table and had little to play for, Coldharbour was playing for survival and for Dimitri Koloschenko's ticket out of the worst investment he'd ever made. A win would make their final game irrelevant if other results went as expected.

The absence of Jack Galloway was a major concern for Coldharbour. He'd been mugged on the doorstep of his house three days earlier and was out for the rest of the season, including the Cup Final. An Asian man was identified as the prime suspect, based on Galloway's description and their dispute involving the man's sister in a nightclub a few weeks earlier. CCTV evidence placed the accused in the main bar at The Moon at the time of the attack so he was released without charge. It was just as well, he'd promised to drive his twin brother to the airport that evening for his flight back to Hong Kong.

Buckley's first goal was fortunate, the keeper fumbled, the referee should have given a free kick for Sunstrom's clumsy challenge but when the ball dropped it was at Buckley's feet. He scuffed his shot into the ground, but that only served to lift it over the outstretched leg of the final defender. One - nil.

The second was the kind of strike that had the pundits purring and the media adding millions to his transfer value as they picked names from a hat for the next rumour as to who was going to buy Coldharbour's rising star. The comparison with Real Madrid's Gareth Bale would be trotted out all over again. It was a hopeful ball, had it dropped ten feet left or right; one of the central defenders would have dealt with it. As it fell exactly half way between the two players, they both hesitated. That was all Buckley needed. Once he'd got a toe to the ball it was a test of pace and neither of his opponents was going to catch him. The keeper dived as he made to shoot to his right, Buckley delayed the shot and spun to the keeper's left. He could have rolled the ball into the empty net, but he fired the ball hard into the corner, it was satisfying to see it strike the stanchion precisely where he placed the bucket in training. Two - nil and halftime.

Phones were forbidden in the changing room but Adam had sent Lucy some roses, a promise of Cup Final tickets for her and her family and a copy of the itinerary he was planning for their summer holidays. Two weeks on a small Caribbean island. Business class and private planes, five star accommodation all the way. He couldn't wait to hear her reaction. It was a text.

*"Adam, you're a sweetie, the holiday sounds great and I'm sure there's someone who'll love to go with you... not me I'm afraid. You caught me on the rebound, I told you about Stuart, we split because he was going to the USA. It didn't work out and now he's back, said he couldn't live without me. Thanks for a fun couple of weeks. Love Lucy x"*

Buckley sleepwalked through the first ten minutes of the second half. Newcastle had equalised by the time Boris brought on a substitute in his place. At the final whistle it was 5-2 to the visitors. Coldharbour had one game to secure Premier League survival, a golden chance had been squandered.

Buckley had gone when the rest of the team returned to the dressing room. There'd be a fine but he didn't give a shit.

He'd convinced himself that Lucy was different. She was a classy girl who'd taken a genuine interest in him. The fame thing was great, girls were literally falling at his feet. He loved the attention, he loved being able to click his fingers and see women who wouldn't have given him a second look a year before, jump with joy that Coldharbour's new idol had chosen them. Lucy opened him up to a different experience. She was a girlfriend, a mate, they talked, they laughed, he'd told her stuff he hadn't even admitted to himself. Most of the girls he'd met recently wanted to bag a footballer, for an hour, a night or for a life of comfort and celebrity. It was easy street, kudos with their girlfriends and all the money they could possibly have hoped for. They didn't want him, they wanted a tiny taste of what the WAGs they read about in Hello magazine could take for granted. Women, he decided were all vicious, greedy and shallow. Lucy included. She'd used him as a fill-in while her ex made up his mind whether she was more important to him than a job in the States. Well he'd get his comeuppance soon enough, when she tossed him aside for something better.

# 16

The meeting had gone extremely well. Slatkin attended with his legal team from Parris & Hopcraft, a London firm that had initially advised on the purchase of Coldharbour Town from Jack Enright. The Americans came mob-handed. Seated on the opposite side of the table were four executives from the holding company that would make the purchase, and two teams of lawyers, one from the States, one from another London firm. They'd reminded Slatkin that failure to stay in the Premier League would void the contract, but they were ready to sign. Last minute negotiations yielded an increase in the premium to be paid if they won the FA Cup and Slatkin handed over a copy of Adam Buckley's new contract. Koloschenko was entertaining Franklin Thornberry, the incoming owner of the club in his office. Slatkin wondered why so many Americans had two surnames instead of a proper first name. It made them sound like a firm of provincial accountants. All that was left to do was to call the two principals in, get their signatures on the contract and then crack open the Krug Clos d'Ambonnay that was chilling on a side table. At over three thousand dollars a bottle, Koloschenko thought it was an appropriate way of toasting the deal.

Slatkin made the call and knew that it would be at least ten minutes before the two men arrived. It was not the done thing for a billionaire to jump when minions called. There was time to thank his legal team, in particular the very presentable junior who'd assisted on the deal. He'd seen her once before, but couldn't recall where. This was almost certainly her first big negotiation as she looked nervous throughout. He shook her hand warmly, and tried to catch a glimpse through the gap between two of the buttons on her shirt. The clamminess of her palm was a bit of a turn off but suddenly the idea of getting his legal team out for a celebration dinner wasn't such a bad idea. He suspected the girl might be very diverting company if she had a few drinks inside her.

Koloschenko and Thornberry returned for the signing ceremony. There'd be no announcement of the sale until after the club's future in the Premier League was secure, but the Russian's personal photographer was there to record the event. The champagne was poured and Slatkin looked around for the cute blonde, she was chatting to one of the American lawyers. The bubbles from her first sip seemed to have gone up her nose, she giggled then placed her hand on the man's arm. He moved a little closer and appeared to stand a little more upright, then flashed a broad smile, revealing impossibly straight, white, even teeth. Slatkin wondered how much they'd cost him. He had competition but that was fine, he wasn't used to losing.

\*\*\*

Maggie Davenport was already seated at the conference table when Sergeant Gray arrived. The idea that they might be working on a new case together had put a spring in his step. He'd seen what a good detective she was, but the Drake case was like wading through treacle. They were never on the front foot, the case kept leading them up blind alleys and just when they thought they had something, like Victor, it turned out to be a dead end. There was some satisfaction in knowing that Drake was dead, but it was a hollow victory. Gray's father was a gillie on a Scottish estate, like his grandfather. Duncan Gray told the story of his pursuit of a magnificent stag one cold November morning. A couple of English bankers had paid a small fortune for the hunt. Peter vaguely remembered the men, they were pompous, patronising and indecently excited about the prospect of killing a beautiful animal. He remembered wishing the stag could have shot back, failing that he prayed for it to escape. They pursued the stag for hours across the heather, through the stunning, rolling landscape of the Highlands until one of the dogs picked up the trail. Then they found their prey, lying prone at the edge of a small stream. Duncan said it must have been a heart attack. One of the clients wanted to shoot it

180

anyway, and get the photo he'd craved from the start of the trip. At the very least, they wanted the antlers. Duncan drove them to the railway station, without the trophies they sought and quietly suggested that it would be better if they did not return.

Like his father's stag, Tony Drake had just fallen into their hands. There was no victory, he'd never stand trial for his crimes and the girls' families could only have closure for their loss if they unequivocally believed that he was the killer. If there was the slightest doubt, even a tiny worm of uncertainty, they'd spend the rest of their days feeling that their daughters had not got the justice they deserved.

The people of Coldharbour were in no doubt at all, partly because of the coverage given to the case by the local paper. The Echo was triumphant in proclaiming that the terror was at an end. Tony Drake was a psychopathic drug addict who had terrorised the town for a few weeks, but he'd got his just desserts. They wondered how no one spotted it sooner. Plenty of locals were willing to give their two pennyworth.

An unnamed ex-girlfriend explained how he ruthlessly seduced her when she was only seventeen and then cast her aside when he'd got what he wanted.

Anonymous classmates told how everything changed after his football injury. He was supposed to make it big, but then it was his best mate, Adam Buckley, who signed for Coldharbour Town. Drake wasn't the same after that, he was consumed with envy and bitterness that his pal could be such a success when he was selling screwdrivers and chisels at the local DIY store. Maybe they should have spotted it, maybe they should have seen that there was a potential killer in their midst.

Toby Thomas launched an appeal in aid of the families, "For the Victims of Tony Drake, the Coldharbour Ripper." A portion of the money raised, would go to a local charity for women who'd suffered domestic and sexual abuse. Thomas would shortly attend a lunch in aid of the charity to present the first instalment of the money raised. William Fairhurst, proprietor of the Echo, had given the cause a flying start with a donation of ten thousand pounds.

Tony Drake was a guilty man, few would argue. The jigsaw fitted together if you didn't look too closely, he had to be the killer. That was some sort of closure, some sort of victory.

Davenport greeted Gray with a casual wave of the hand and pointed to the table in the corner, there was coffee and a couple of stale danish pastries. Gray was anxious to get started, then dismayed to see the pictures laid out on the table. Annie, Natalie, Zainab and Angelina.

"Peter, I want to go through this one more time. It's driving me nuts."

"Yes ma'am," Gray took one sip of cold coffee and tossed the pastry back on the table before taking a seat.

"Tony Drake was, as you said, like a boy scout before all of this. When we did the initial pass and his name came up as an ex-boyfriend of Natalie Simpson, nobody had a bad word to say about him… even the parents of the girl herself. All we know is that they had some sort of mystery falling out and neither of them was happy about it. He gets to twenty-two years of age, there's not a blemish on his record and suddenly he's a junkie nutter and everyone's wondering why they didn't spot it before."

"He did kill himself ma'am."

"But we're looking at a perp. who's supposed to be descending into an hallucinogenic spiral. A man whose grip on reality is getting more and more fragile as the days go by, but look at the pattern. Three killings with what we think is probably the same type of knife. Then Angelina. This is just before Drake tries to fly from the top of an apartment block, we've seen the video, we've seen what was left of the body. He's out of shape, he looks half starved, the guy looked a hundred years old. But the Polish girl's killing was the most clinical of the lot. When Zainab died, it looked like he was getting careless… the fibres on her clothing. There wasn't a trace of forensic on Angelina's body and the wound was almost certainly from a different weapon."

"Are you saying there are two killers?"

Davenport looked exasperated and exhausted. "Peter, the truth is that I don't know what to think. If Drake hated Natalie, why did he kill Annie first? If he was imploding, why is the final murder so much more expertly carried out than the one that immediately preceded it? Why is there no forensic at all to link Drake to the killings? Where is the black jacket?"

Gray looked helpless. Everything his boss was saying was true, but just as they had nothing to point to Drake, they had nothing that pointed anywhere else either. He was grateful for the urgent knock on the door, it was Sergeant Lewis, looking less than his usual smug self.

"Ma'am, they've found another body."

*** 

Yuri Slatkin received the call from Coldharbour Town's head of Security at ten minutes past seven that evening.

"Mr Slatkin, it's the police. They've asked us to send over all our CCTV footage between midday and five p.m. They haven't said why."

"I'll be right over, don't give them anything."

Slatkin switched off his TV and grabbed his car keys. They'd found the body of a young woman close to a walking trail in the woods close to the edge of Ranmore Hill. The news programme he'd been watching had no further details.

It was less than a twenty-minute drive to the football ground, Hanif Shah, the club's security chief was at the entrance to let him in.

"Hanif, do you have any idea what they are looking for?"

"No idea Mr Slatkin. It actually wasn't even an official call. I used to be in the local force and their Sergeant Lewis called to give me the heads up. He said they'd be round early tomorrow and he wanted to make sure I had time to get it all ready before he got here."

"Hanif, you know why I'm concerned about this, don't you?"

Shah shook his head, he didn't know and he wasn't sure he wanted to. They didn't pay him to worry about anything other than making sure the club's premises didn't get robbed or burned to the ground.

"Mr Koloschenko was here yesterday and he signed a very important contract. The recording might show him leaving with the man he dealt with. There's nothing shady about it, we just can't afford for news of the deal to get out before we're ready. Understood?"

"Completely." Shah moved to the far corner of the room and began sorting though a pile of files that might have been there for years.

The girl left the signing ceremony at twenty past midday. Most of her colleagues were still there, enabling the police to pinpoint the earliest time she could have gone missing. Slatkin remembered checking his watch seconds before she'd grabbed his arm to say goodbye. Something about having to get back to the office because she was going on holiday that night. The conversation in the room ebbed a little as she left, most of the men turned to watch her make her exit. It was a straightforward matter to locate the relevant clip.

Slatkin watched the footage. The clock in the corner of the screen showed twelve twenty four as she strode across the car park. She'd done the girlie, "oh gosh, champagne goes straight to my head" thing in the meeting room, but she was stone cold sober. Just before she got to the door of her car, she paused and looked round. Somebody had called out to her. There was a look of concern, maybe disappointment, not fear. It was obvious they knew each other. The man came into view and they spoke for little more than a minute. She was clearly anxious to leave and turned towards the car, but he grabbed her arm. She pulled it away and then he raised his hands as though he was apologising, she nodded slowly at first, then more rapidly and got into her car unimpeded. Then the man walked round to the other side of the vehicle and got into the passenger seat. The girl took a second or two to secure her seat belt then drove out of the car park.

Slatkin pocketed the disk, it covered the whole of the previous three days. He'd removed the evidence but now there was a gap, it would stand out a mile when the police came to call.

"Mr Slatkin, you know those cameras are quite unreliable." Shah was still on the opposite side of the room. "I was looking for a section of tape the other day and all I got was seventy two hours of fuzzy interference. You couldn't see what was going on. I kept the tape, so I could show you when I put in my bid to upgrade the system. It should all be on hard disk really."

"Where is this fuzzy tape?"

Shah walked back to the desk where Slatkin was sitting and opened a drawer. It took him a second or two to find what he was looking for. Having located the disk, he slipped it into the space left by the one nestling in Slatkin's pocket.

"So what are my chances of getting a new system Mr Slatkin?"

Slatkin's fingers closed round the precious disk. "I'd say they're zero Hanif. But you're a dead cert for a bonus at the end of the month."

Shah smiled. "Happy to be of service Mr Slatkin."

***

Toby Thomas was in his element at the charity lunch. In his pocket was a cheque for ten grand, written out by his employer. He could play the grand benefactor, but it wouldn't cost him a penny. Most of his audience were female and many appeared to be overwhelmed to have a local celebrity at the top table. Thomas was not just the impressively youthful editor of a local newspaper, he made regular appearances on Coldharbour Radio and, on one occasion, he was interviewed on BBC's South Today. Desserts were left untouched, it wouldn't do to be stuffing one's face with black forest gateau with a TV star in their midst. Middle-aged women, throughout the room, were sucking in their stomachs, pushing out their breasts and doing their utmost to look coquettish when Thomas sought to make eye contact with his audience and his gaze fell upon them. He was lapping up the attention, as he reminded everyone of the coverage the Echo had given to the terrible slayings that had terrorised the town. It was as though his lurid pieces were responsible, at least in part, for shaming the murderer into hurling himself from the top of that apartment block. The Echo, he told them, had a long tradition of championing the rights of women, without elaborating on any specific initiatives. He was delighted to be able to offer their outstanding charity some truly practical help, with that he plucked the cheque from his pocket. A keen history student might have noticed that the gesture looked remarkably like Chamberlain on his return from Munich in 1939, brandishing a document that promised peace in our time. Thomas milked the applause as he handed ten thousand pounds of someone else's money to a charity that he didn't even know existed a week before. The Echo photographer stepped forward, then moved to the left. Thomas had already explained that was his best side. He'd be on the front page of the Echo at the weekend and he was determined to look dashing. What he hadn't bargained for was that he'd be on the front page of a lot of other newspapers too.

Katie Enright slipped her IPhone into her handbag, a marathon texting session complete, she turned to her grandmother.

"Sorry Nana, Ben's being a real pain in the butt. He thinks I've gone off him because I chose to spend the weekend with you and Granddad instead of being with him."

"And have you?" Carol Enright chuckled as her granddaughter rolled her eyes in mock despair.

"I hadn't until he started pestering me, now I'll have to give it some thought. So what have I missed?"

"Mr Thomas from the local paper. He just gave the charity ten thousand pounds."

"Brilliant, which one is he? Katie peered around the room, she was late arriving and rushed straight to the table. She'd only seen about four men and then only from the rear or the side. Throughout Thomas's performance, her eyes had never lifted from her phone. The chairperson of the local Women's Institute chose that moment to approach their benefactor and introduce herself. There were other good causes in town that could do with a cash injection. Thomas stood to shake hands.

"Oh my God it's him." At first Katie looked shocked, then she giggled. "It's the pervert from the train. I can't believe it."

It was early evening by the time the Enright's finished their family conference. Jack and Carol were adamant that the police had to be informed. Katie had identified Toby Thomas as the man who tried to assault her on the train a few weeks earlier. There could be no doubt that he should be held to account. Katie was equally determined that the matter should be forgotten.

"Nana, I've pushed it from my mind. All I remember is that he was a bit too friendly so I pretended to be asleep then he nudged me a bit, then I felt his hand on my leg. He's going to say it was an accident."

"But Katie what he did was obscene. He probably does it all the time, you owe it to other women to put a stop to it." It was her grandfather.

Katie shot him a look that made him flinch.

"Granddad, have you got any idea how this works? Young female turns up at the police station and tells them she got felt up by a celebrity three weeks earlier. I can see them rolling their eyes right now. 'Why didn't you report this earlier miss?' Even if they took him to court, he'd have a lawyer who'd try to make me look like the criminal. 'What were you wearing?' 'Had you been drinking?' 'How many men have you slept with?' They defend their client by attacking me. That's how lawyers work."

Enright flinched again. The thought that his precious granddaughter had slept with any men at all turned his guts to ice. He'd taken some time to come to terms with Katie's conception and the implications that had for the chastity of his daughter.

"Katie, I'm sure it's not..."

"Well I'm sure it is. One of my best friends was assaulted on the tube in London and she reported it. Their lawyers portrayed her as a drunken whore. There's not a way in the world I'm going through that."

Katie switched on the TV, it was her way of conveying that the debate was over. Her grandmother made one last try.

"What about those poor girls who were killed? Maybe..."

"Grandma, please leave it. They got the killer, he jumped from the top of a tower block. This Thomas bloke is just a sad little wanker who's not getting any action at home. I'm not reporting it."

She increased the volume on the TV remote, the presenter was summarising at the end of an item that was illustrated with the picture of an exceptionally attractive blonde girl only a few years older than Katie.

"Lucy Barker's body was discovered on Ranmore Hill near Coldharbour around four o'clock this afternoon. Local police have yet to confirm whether there are similarities with the four murders that rocked the seaside town over the last few weeks. The case of the so-called Coldharbour Ripper was closed with the suicide of Tony Drake, a local drug addict. Today's events appear to raise the spectre that the Ripper may still be out there."

Katie stared at the screen long after they'd moved on to the next item. Her grandparents both realised they had to wait for her to speak first.

"Can you drive me to the police station?"

***

Yuri Slatkin was not surprised to see a woman in Dimitri Koloschenko's office. He'd not expected it to be the man's wife. Kristina was forty-four and at a respectable distance, she could comfortably pass for a woman in her mid twenties. Closer and the hot money would be on thirty-five tops, but a discerning eye might spot that her lips were a little too full, her eyes and mouth were drawn back so that she looked in a constant state of surprise and her skin had a polished look as though each imperfection had been scraped from its surface. When youth and a healthy diet ceased to deliver the appearance she required, she hired a professional make up artist. When the canvas on which they worked started to sag, Kristina had no hesitation in turning to a surgeon to help maintain her image. She was a promising stage actress when she met Koloschenko at a party. He was a decorated war hero at the time and there was something about the young soldier that convinced Kristina that he was the best prospect out of the many suitors seeking her hand. Twenty years on, she was very satisfied with her decision. She knew of his mistresses, but had come to terms with it. As long as they were married she could indulge the merest whim, if they divorced she'd become a billionaire in her own right. Heads she won, tails was much the same. Kristina knew that her husband had a ruthless streak, she knew that he wouldn't hesitate to kill if it delivered the outcome he desired. Nonetheless, she felt invulnerable and had good reason to do so.

The couple had lived in Kiev for three years before Koloschenko decided to come to London. There was a young model with whom her husband had become hopelessly infatuated. The girl was local but long straight flaxen hair

suggested one Scandinavian parent, clear light caramel skin
suggested the other might hail from the Mediterranean. Kiev is,
after all, a couple of hours by plane from both Stockholm and
Rome. It was easy to see what drew her husband in. Those
huge vivid green eyes were wide and innocent. Combined with
a cute retroussé nose and a small but perfect rosebud mouth,
she did vulnerability to a tee. Her face was enough to secure a
lucrative career in modelling but she was particularly blessed.
Five-feet eleven inches in her silk-stockinged feet, long
willowy limbs and full, pert breasts ensured that her first
contract was for a range of lingerie. Koloschenko was invited
to the designer's opening show and was captivated before she'd
reached the end of the catwalk. She was flattered and
completely overwhelmed by the power he could wield
throughout the city. No door was closed and he lavished her
with expensive gifts. It was the least she could do to sleep with
him a few times. Kristina doubted that her husband had fallen
in love with a girl less than half his age, it was far more likely
that she spiked his pride. He was a married man, it never
occurred to his new mistress that he'd be faithful to her during
what turned out to be a brief fling. The problem was that she
thought that was a two way street. On the days she wasn't
seeing Koloschenko, she was conducting a passionate affair
with a male model who often shared the same catwalk.
Koloschenko confronted her and demanded to know why she
was seeing another man. Lyudmila Semolova laughed and
pointed to a magazine she'd left open on the sofa. It was
obvious that was what she was looking at when he arrived. The
picture was of her lover, wearing only the tightest briefs his
highly toned, sun-tanned frame was glistening with oil. The
picture was intended to be answer enough. The Russian was
being asked to draw his own comparison between the Adonis in
the picture and himself. Lyudmila's look was scornful.
Koloschenko carried a small knife tucked into a leather pouch
that was strapped to his leg. As she turned away, he palmed it
and severed her spinal cord with a single fluid movement.

Victor was summoned to dispose of the body and that's when Kristina got her insurance policy. Unaware that Koloschenko was with a woman, he'd brought along Kristina's brother, another ex-soldier who'd recently joined the family firm. Koloschenko became wary of his brother-in-law, who was the type of man who took precautions, He'd have told someone of the incident, it was doubtful that he had proof, but he certainly knew enough to make life awkward for Koloschenko. If anything happened to him or to Kristina, that information could easily leak out. The man was an enemy, but Koloschenko believed in the old adage, "keep your friend's close and your enemies closer."

There was a more positive reason why Kristina knew that her husband wanted to see her live to a healthy old age regardless of the state of their marriage. Tatyana was nineteen and studying at the Sorbonne in Paris. Their daughter was the one human being on the planet who could wrap Dimitri Koloschenko round their little finger. The Russian worshipped his only child and would never do anything that might cause her distress. Kristina and Tatyana had an unbreakable bond that Koloschenko envied. If anything happened to his wife, Tatyana would be heartbroken. That was a price that Koloschenko would never be willing to pay.

"Yuri, English rain must suit you. You are more handsome than ever." Kristina loved to flirt with her husband's associates, she could usually see the fear in their eyes as they tried to see how Koloschenko would react.

"You are too kind Kristina, you grow more beautiful every time I see you." Slatkin was a little tougher to crack than some of the others. "Are you here to watch Dimitri's team in action?"

"My God no. I have no idea what possessed him to do this in the first place. It's Dimitri's fiftieth birthday on Thursday, we are having a small party for him and I have some very special surprises. I do hope you can join us."

Slatkin smiled and bowed slightly. "I have already replied to your kind invitation. Of course I'll be delighted to come."

As Kristina turned to find a chair, Slatkin flashed a beseeching look in Koloschenko's direction. He took the hint.

"Kristina, give me a few minutes with Yuri."

She shot an angry look at her husband before she picked up her handbag, then gave Slatkin a smile that was utterly devoid of warmth or humour. To her the man was keeper of her husband's secrets and that meant he had something over on her. Knowledge was power. There was silence until Kristina departed.

"He's really very good isn't he?" Koloschenko had turned to stare out of the window. His view was of the training pitch attached to the back of Coldharbour's ground. There was only one of the first team still practicing together with a couple of Academy players who were acting as little more than ballboys for their hero.

"Dimitri?"

"Buckley, he's quite a player. I understand why the Americans are so keen to keep him, although I suspect they have something up their sleeve to ensure he pays back a chunk of their investment."

"Dimitri, I have to talk to you. It's about the girl they found in the woods."

Koloschenko turned and walked slowly towards to his desk.

"Ah yes, another twist in the case of the Coldharbour Ripper. A copycat perhaps."

"Dimitri, I can only speculate on who killed the other girls but I know who killed Lucy Barker."

Koloschenko was expressionless. Slatkin had downloaded the CCTV footage to his computer and then synched it to an IPad. He continued.

"The police knew she was here, but everyone she met has an alibi. She was the first to leave and everyone else was still in the meeting room after our CCTV picked her up leaving the car park."

"So?"

"This footage shows that she didn't leave the car park alone."

Slatkin pressed play. Lucy reached her car before she heard her name being called, the disappointment was clear on her face, but she obviously knew the person walking towards her across the parking lot. There was a brief discussion but they clearly agreed that Lucy would drive him somewhere. She got into the driver's seat and seconds later Adam Buckley got into the passenger seat.

"No one else has seen this?"

"No Dimitri. The police told us that they were coming for the recordings. I removed this one and Hanif was happy to tell them the camera malfunctioned. Another camera picked up her car leaving the car park and, from the angle, it looks like she's alone. The police think she met her killer after she left the ground."

"Maybe she did." It was clear that, for Koloschenko, it didn't matter much either way.

"Dimitri, I had someone gain access to Buckley's flat."

Slatkin had pressed stop when the clip showed Lucy Barker's car pull away. He pressed play.

"This is what he found."

There was a brief clip taken from a handheld camera. The initial shot panned round a large open plan living room, then zoomed in on a desk with an Apple IMac and a laser printer. Scattered across the working surface was a series of photos, some were of Lucy alone, some were of her and Buckley together, 'selfies' taken by one or other of them. The last was a shot of Lucy sleeping, she was naked apart from a tiny white G-string.

"Great tits," Koloschenko said with an approving nod of the head.

"Dimitri, for fuck's sake, she's dead."

"So?"

"Buckley killed her. They were a couple. Alexei mentioned only a couple of days ago that Buckley was out of sorts. He said he was seeing a girl and they'd split up. Buckley was devastated apparently."

A cloud descended on Koloschenko for a second.

"Did Alexei ever meet the girl?"

"Yes, and I asked him if she was hot and he just shrugged. He admitted they were drunk but he was so eager to get into her friend's pants that he wouldn't recognise Buckley's girl if she was sitting opposite him."

"Do you believe that?"

"They're in the player's lounge right now. The girl's face is all over the news, he didn't recognise her."

"Maybe it's a different girl."

There was one final image that had been captured inside Buckley's flat. The intruder had opened a drawer, inside was a collection of flick knives.

"Dimitri, it's the one piece of information that they never released to the public. The police think this is the type of knife used for the first three killings. Our man inside the police station has confirmed that."

For the first time, Koloschenko looked flustered, even angry.

"This was information I would have liked to receive before we killed the waitress. Small but important details."

Slatkin could barely believe what he was hearing. Koloschenko was unconcerned that his star player was a psychopath, he was angry because the information Sergeant Lewis had given them would have enabled him to ensure the Polish girl's killing was a more credible copy of the others.

"Dimitri, I didn't know that you were planning on replicating the crime. How would I? I really don't see that as the problem here."

"So what is the problem?" Koloschenko looked genuinely puzzled.

"Buckley is a killer, the other guy was just there to take the blame. We should have seen it before, he was in Buckley's flat for fuck's sake. Dimitri, what are we going to do?"

"Nothing." Koloschenko stood and picked up his briefcase.

"Nothing?"

"Yuri. In eleven days, we will complete the sale of this piece of shit. All we need to do is to win our next game. I can apply none of the usual levers that are available to me to secure the outcome I desire. All I have is a mediocre team of footballers, one of whom may just be gifted enough to secure the points we need. He may also allow me to go out with a little glory in this FA Cup thing. If we lose, it is to be expected, if we win, I will have one over Mr Abramovich for the rest of his days. Adam Buckley will play for this team in the two remaining matches. After that I do not care what happens to him. The Americans have recourse only if he demands a transfer, they were smart, but not smart enough to draft a clause that covered the discovery that he is a serial killer. When the money clears our accounts you can serve Mr Buckley to the authorities on a silver salver. Until then this conversation goes no further. Do you understand?"

Slatkin nodded.

***

Adam Buckley was a slow starter. As a teenager, girls showed an interest but as soon as he got close, his chest tightened, he couldn't think of anything to say and they lost interest. There were the odd fumbles at parties but, while his best pal Tony Drake, was getting off with anyone he chose, Adam was left with the spotty one that no one else fancied... until the party just after his sixteenth birthday. She was too drunk to care about small talk and clearly eager to find a corner where they could get to know each other a lot better. The act was over in seconds, the humiliation never passed. It would have been bad enough had it remained between the two of them, but she'd sobered up and returned to party. He'd watched as she told her friends about the brief and unsatisfactory encounter, he saw her extend her little finger, then allow it to slowly descend until it pointed meekly to the floor. Then she pointed to the stain near the hem of her skirt and then to him. He didn't need to be a lip reader to hear she was saying "five seconds, that was it, five seconds," with theatrical incredulity. Her friends covered their mouths with their hands in mock horror and giggled. Six years had passed and his cheeks still burned when he thought of that night and the scorn he'd suffered at the hands of Annie Radford.

Then there was Emma Simpson. He knew he should have steered clear, the girl was barely fourteen but she was besotted with him. There was a randomness about schoolgirl crushes, most girls liked the same boys, but Emma had a bit more spirit than the others. She might have even chosen Adam Buckley because no one else did. Her older sister found out and went absolutely berserk. She didn't want Emma messing around with a loser who was nearly three years older, the more she made the case, the more Emma declared her undying love for the target of her affections, Adam Buckley. Natalie Simpson begged him to stay away from her little sister and he agreed, on one condition. She had to stay away from Tony Drake. He'd had enough of the golden boy gliding through life, he decided to put a little bump on the road for him. And in case Natalie decided to run to her boyfriend there was an extra incentive.

"Your baby sister would do anything for me, and I mean anything. If you breathe a word of this to anyone, especially Tony, I'll pop round to see her and prove my point. When I've finished I might have a bit of fun with you too. Understand?"

Natalie nodded, there was no price too high to keep Adam Buckley away from his sister. She never spoke to Tony Drake again.

196

Adam started carrying a knife when he was about fifteen, he couldn't imagine how he might use it, but Coldharbour could be a rough town and it was better to be safe than sorry. It became a habit. His first flick-knife was a gift from an aunt who imagined he'd spend his days whittling lumps of wood into ornaments and handy household items. Within a couple of years he had about a dozen of the same brand of knife in a range of colours. He liked the tiger emblem engraved on the handle. The night he'd met Annie Radford again, he was carrying his latest acquisition. It had an elegant light green handle, weighed nothing in his hand and was a snip at twenty-three pounds. Adam had taken to jogging late at night and spotted the young woman standing by a bus stop. She looked angry and a little drunk. When she spotted him, she smiled, an automatic reaction whenever Annie saw a young, fit man close to her own age. Adam never missed an opportunity for an encounter with a drunk and vulnerable woman.

"You OK?" he asked.

"Not really, some dickhead abandoned me here. Expects me to get the bus home."

"Well if I can help…" Adam approached but still had no idea that he was talking to Annie Radford, the girl from the party six years earlier. He'd taken in the short skirt, the low top and the battle the girl was fighting to stay upright on her stilettos. Standard procedure was to call a cab… his place or hers and then part company after an hour or in the morning depending on how much fun she turned out to be.

"Oh my God it's you."

Adam smiled, it was a typical reaction from a female fan. "Yes, it's me." He made a half-hearted attempt at a modest smile.

"Hamster cock." The girl covered her mouth and laughed just as she'd done all those years before at the party.

"What the fuck?" Adam was starting to make the connections in his head. He knew the girl and was about to place her.

"Oh God, I should have told Toby Thomas, I had an exclusive. Imagine the headline, 'He shot he scored… all over my new skirt.'"

"What the fuck, you're Annie…."

"And you're a famous footballer, who'd have thought it. God you were such a loser, I don't know what possessed me to even let you touch me." She appeared to shiver as though the recollection caused her physical discomfort.

"Look you little bitch…" Buckley stepped forward as Annie turned away. He reached to grab her shoulder but she pulled hard to free herself. It gave Buckley just enough time to locate the knife, free the blade and plunge it into her neck. Annie staggered for a couple of seconds and retreated towards the bus shelter. The life ebbed from her body as her back hit the thin plastic sheeting. She slid into a sitting position her legs splayed out in front of her. Buckley stared at her with contempt.

"You were always a slut. Jesus you can't even keep your legs together when you're dead."

He kicked the back of her right leg so that it straightened in front of her. One stiletto shoe snapped at the heel under the impact. He then picked up her other foot and delicately crossed her legs at the ankles.

"Bitch," he said. The killing was an impulse, he glanced around to see if anyone might have witnessed what happened but the street was empty. Few ventured out after ten in Coldharbour during the week. They saved their money for the weekend

He'd woken with conflicting emotions. Shock that he'd killed someone, but comforted by the feeling that an account had been settled. Six years on, memories of his first encounter with Annie Radford made his stomach tighten and his cheeks burn. Now they were even. There'd been an hour or two of panic, what evidence had he left at the scene? He'd touched her leg with his shoe and picked up her foot with a gloved right hand. The rain would have helped but he shouldn't be blasé. There was a bottle of white spirit in the kitchen. Handy for

198

removing paint stains, equally effective as an accelerant when you choose to burn a pair of thin cotton gloves in the sink. He washed the knife carefully and returned it to the drawer with the rest of his collection. There were splashes of blood on his t-shirt and shorts, they went straight into the washing machine.

Natalie hadn't been planned either. Buckley switched his jogging route to the promenade after he killed Annie. A hoodie prevented anyone from recognising him, Coldharbour weather ensured there were few people around the pier at that time of night anyway. He recognised Becky, the girl from the pub, first. The temptation was to say hello, she'd made it clear that she was up for it and exercise made him horny. Then he'd spotted Natalie. They were barely seventeen when he'd spent three months trying to pluck up the courage to ask her out, then bloody Tony Drake beat him to it. What's worse, it was love. He was besotted with her. Then little Emma gave him the opportunity to get even with both of them. Buckley put it to the back of his mind until that afternoon in the pub and the look that Natalie gave him as she walked out. He'd have taken hatred, but that was contempt. Who the fuck did she think she was?

At first he thought he was too far away to confront her, but suddenly she gripped her stomach and made for the low railing that ran around the promenade in front of the pier. It looked as though she was about to be sick, but then recovered herself and started to search through her handbag for something. It gave Buckley time to cover the thirty yards that separated them, when she turned he was standing in front of her.

'Hi Natalie, see you've still got your nose in the air."

Natalie tried to step past him but he moved across to block her.

"What do you want?" She tried to sound assertive but fear coursed through her. The threats Buckley had made years before were still fresh and raw.

"Just saying hello. How's that little sister of yours? Must be nearly twenty now. She'd have done anything for me back then, she'd be pissed off if she knew it was you that stopped her seeing a famous footballer."

Natalie looked at him with disgust. "She was a child and you're a revolting pig."

"Local hero actually, how about you and I...?" Buckley nodded towards the steps that led to the beach. "Come on sweetheart, how about a quickie, your sister would have been up for it back then if you hadn't stuck your nose in. I'm guessing you're just as much of a slut as she was."

Natalie spat in his face and turned. Buckley was amazed that a single wound to the neck could have despatched Annie Radford. He'd checked it out since on the internet and it seemed that he'd just got lucky. This time he knew where to strike. Natalie fell against the railings and tumbled into the sea below.

Again Buckley felt no remorse, it was another account settled, another slight avenged. The Arab girl was a momentary flash of rage. He'd watched the news that day and seen how a suicide bomber killed four allied servicemen in Baghdad. They showed photos of the soldiers, two weren't out of their teens, one had a wife with a baby on the way and the fourth was two days away from the end of his tour of duty. Then some fucking raghead killed them for no reason. When he saw a women walking towards him wearing a veil, something snapped. She'd crossed the road, she'd tried to get away from him, she obviously had something to hide. It was hardly pay back for the death of four soldiers but it was a start.

He'd not gone out that night with the intention of killing anyone, but he'd worked out that it might not be helpful if he was recognised jogging through the streets when a killer was on the loose. Someone, somewhere might start to ask questions. He'd taken Tony Drake's old fleece out of impulse. It wasn't a deliberate attempt to implicate his old friend, just one of those lucky breaks. It occurred to him that he'd probably made contact with the Arab girl, she'd moved too fast and he had to pull her back. Killers were often caught based on the tiniest of residues left at a scene. Buckley was confident that if he'd left any traces, it would be from the fleece. A short trip to the woods at the back of Ranmore Hill, with a shovel and the white spirit had sorted that out,

When they said there was a fourth victim, he was unable to conceal his astonishment. Buckley had been on the team bus returning from Southampton. He was shocked, there was obviously a nutter out there.

***

The ladies and gentlemen of the press were out in force, unaware that Toby Thomas had departed the marital home weeks earlier. TV crews laid siege to the house and were dismayed when the man who came to collect the newspaper from the doorstep in his pyjamas was clearly not the editor of the Coldharbour Echo. Mrs Thomas hadn't heard of her husband's arrest and began to remonstrate with the crowd that had gathered. There had to be some mistake, they'd obviously got the wrong address. The news programmes were obliged to pixelate the faces of the Thomas children as they were driven to school, the same courtesy was applied to the car number plate of Richard Hawkins, the school teacher who had occupied the other half of the Thomas marital bed for some weeks. It was a token gesture, anyone who watched a few minutes of the report would be able to identify the house to which they'd laid siege. In hours the road was crammed with people trying to catch a glimpse of the lair of Britain's latest serial killer.

Maggie Davenport had interviewed Katie Enright herself. She promised that unless they could find sufficient evidence to link Thomas to the other killings, the file would be closed there and then. Katie would only be asked to give evidence if there was a murder case to answer. It was the e-mail account that initially appeared to nail him.

They already had all the e-mails from Natalie's side. They'd got those within days of her death. It tracked the illicit relationship from start to finish, right down to the last one from "Tom," the name used by her lover.

"It's not over, it can't be. It's not over."

It was a Hotmail account, all mails had been sent from a pay-as-you-go phone. Armed only with the information from Natalie's side it was a dead end. Davenport knew her luck had changed when they found the phone in Thomas's bedside drawer when they raided his flat. It had some photos of Natalie that Thomas hadn't wanted to delete but was too frightened to download elsewhere. He'd looked at them repeatedly in the days since her death and couldn't bring himself to toss the phone in the sea.

Thomas himself admitted the link to Annie Radford. He knew that someone at the paper would tell the police he'd met her. Thomas decided on a strategy that went against everything he'd ever been taught, against every instinct he'd developed in all his years in journalism. He decided to tell the truth, with no spin, no angle, no hidden agenda.

"Yes Inspector, I did meet Annie Radford the night she died. She offered to come to my flat, I was tempted and we walked as far as the bus stop. Then I realised I was making a mistake and I gave her the money for a taxi home. I swear I have no idea what happened after that."

"You chose not to come forward with this information."

"I couldn't have told you anything you didn't already know. She was at the bus stop and then this lunatic found her. She was alive when I left her."

He took the same tack regarding Natalie.

"I was in love with her, I offered to leave my wife for her, but she laughed at me… said it was just a bit of fun as far as she was concerned. Sure I was gutted, but I'd never have hurt her, I swear."

Once again Maggie Davenport was far from convinced that they had their killer. He was plausible and appeared to be sincere. Only the recollection of all the fiction masquerading as fact, published twice weekly in the Coldharbour Echo kept her on her guard.

\*\*\*

Eddie Taylor was trying out the leather recliner in his new office when William Fairhurst, proprietor of the Coldharbour Echo arrived to wish him good luck.

"Well done Eddie, it's a well deserved promotion."

"Thanks boss, but it's temporary right? Until Toby sorts out this…"

Fairhurst shook his head. "Thomas didn't kill those girls, but he's finished here."

"I knew he didn't have it in him Mr Fairhurst, but you're sure he didn't do it?" Taylor was a little embarrassed by his lack of confidence that Thomas was innocent.

"He was having dinner with me the night the Arab girl was killed and he was a guest of the football club in Southampton when the Polish girl died."

"That's what I mean, once he's out…"

"Toby Thomas is finished Eddie. What is not in dispute is that he terrorised a young woman on a train and he was screwing another girl behind his wife's back. We wouldn't be able to take a moral stance on a single issue with him at the helm. The job's yours unless you've got any skeletons in the cupboard."

Eddie looked almost disappointed that there were none. He got his carnal pleasures vicariously, writing about the sexual indiscretions of strangers.

"I get that Mr Fairhurst, but it's hardly the rap sheet of the Boston Strangler and Toby's name is going to be associated with this paper for a long time to come."

Fairhurst fought to hide his irritation. "Not if you do your job right Eddie. You have to break that association in the minds of our readers. There's more dirt on Thomas out there and you have to find it. Then I want the Echo to be right out in front when it comes to revealing what the little shit got up to. I don't want to see anything that involved the paper, but your job is to convince the public Thomas was a schizo. Highly professional newspaperman by day, sad little pervert by night. Get it?"

Eddie nodded but he wasn't sure he got it at all. It was a high-risk strategy that involved skewering the man who'd given him his chance to run a news desk and who'd given Fairhurst a profitable newspaper.

"You wouldn't prefer to go with, 'Thomas is innocent, he dined with me the night of the third killing, says Echo proprietor.'"

Fairhurst closed his eyes and took a deep breath.

"Then the Sun comes back with 'Local paper defends its sex fiend Editor,' and what if he did kill one of the first two girls. It's possible the other two were copycats."

Eddie shook his head wearily. "I guess."

The weight of his job as new editor of the Coldharbour Echo was taking its toll and he'd been in the position for less than forty minutes.

"Eddie, you have to go after Thomas or there will be no paper for you to edit."

"Got it boss."

The men parted company, each to make a phone call that they hoped might rescue them from the dire predicament they now faced. Eddie called Sergeant Barry Lewis at Coldharbour police station. He needed anything he could get on what the police had discovered. Fairhurst called his lawyer. They'd received an offer for the Echo Media Group from a Yorkshire based publisher wanting to expand their operations to the south.

"Sell it," he told the lawyer. "And quick."

\*\*\*

"It's not him is it?" Sergeant Gray broke the silence. He and Davenport had finished the latest interview with Toby

204

Thomas ten minutes earlier. They were watching him pace the room via a camera located over the entrance.

"We know he didn't kill Zainab or Angelina, Fairhurst at the Echo has vouched for him on the first one and the entire Coldharbour first team say they saw him in Southampton at ten thirty that night. Until we can be sure that all the girls were killed by the same person he's not off the hook for Annie or Natalie."

"And Lucy?"

"He was at a charity lunch from one thirty and we know she was alive at twelve fifteen. It's possible, but highly unlikely. We're getting CCTV from a service station over by Stonehaven. He claims to have filled up there at 12.45. If that checks out, he's in the clear.

# 17

Only Yuri Slatkin and Dimitri Koloschenko knew the true identity of the Coldharbour Ripper. Courtesy of Katie Enright's statement and his connection to the first two victims, Toby Thomas was found guilty of the murders of all five girls without ever making it into a court of law. The media took on the role of self-appointed prosecutor and judge. Cast iron alibis for two of the killings were not enough to deter those who believed the old saying, "there's no smoke without fire." There was a public outcry that he should have been stopped after the first killing. An Echo intern discovered that a young woman had been robbed and sexually assaulted at the same bus stop three years earlier. If only the local councillors had heeded the warning and installed CCTV in what was obviously a crime black spot. Colleagues at the London newspaper where he'd worked, prior to the Echo, came forward with a series of sordid revelations. Toby Thomas had seduced a series of teenage girls. He was cautioned for mooning a police car the night he passed his A level exams, and a series of photos emerged of Thomas at a party trying to make out with a girl who appeared to have consumed her own body weight in vodka. The Echo led the revelations that Thomas was a dangerous, predatory fiend. They omitted to report that it all happened around the time of his eighteenth birthday. For most people, Thomas's late teens would have been a party-filled rite of passage, the envy of his friends. His own employer turned it into conclusive proof that he was capable of the cold-blooded killing of five young women.

Details of his meeting with Annie Radford hit the headlines days after his arrest, and the gaping holes in the story were quickly filled in with conjecture and groundless speculation. Thomas must have hit on the poor girl during the interview, but been rejected. Seeing her in the street a few weeks later, he could not control his rage at the snub. The Echo failed to cover that, on the grounds that it put the paper in a bad light. They majored on the Natalie Simpson angle. Sergeant Lewis knew that sharing the content of the e-mails could cost him his job and pension. He just gave them enough to run with the headline, 'Sex cheat Thomas told poor Natalie she could NEVER leave him.'

Toby Thomas had become the most reviled man in Britain. There could be no doubt that he was guilty. His trial was not in court, no judge or jury were present. Thomas faced trial by media, where there is no test of admissibility for the evidence that is presented. If it draws a gasp, a disapproving shake of the head or, better still, a sly salacious grin then it's fair game. Thomas had mud thrown at him from every angle. Whatever happened, some would never wash away. As their investigation progressed, Davenport became increasingly convinced that he was not the right man. It was possible that there were two killers. Angelina's killing was subtly different to the others, the forensic team believed that the angle of attack was shallower; suggesting a shorter assailant and the knife was almost certainly wider and longer. No forensic traces had been left, it was a more professional job than the killing that preceded it. But Thomas had a cast iron alibi for that and the killing of Zainab Mansour. When the CCTV footage arrived, he was in the clear for the murder of Lucy Barker too. He'd filled his car with fuel at exactly 12.45 that day, forty minutes drive from where Lucy was found and the same distance from where he'd attended a charity lunch. He'd have to have been in two places at once.

Maggie Davenport knew that they'd have to drop the harassment case relating to the incident on the train. She'd promised that to Katie Enright. All they had was a possible charge for impeding a police investigation. Thomas should have come forward as a material witness to the Annie Radford murder. Within twenty-four hours they'd release him. She'd decided that he was an unscrupulous, self-centred, egotist who'd put his own interests before finding the killer of a woman he'd spoken to on the night she was killed and of a woman he professed to love. Toby Thomas was not, however, a killer and she doubted that he deserved the savage treatment he'd received in the press, much of it by his own paper. Their next meeting was not for an hour, she had to wait for his lawyer to arrive. Davenport picked up her coffee and turned to the front page of the Echo, bracing herself for that day's scrapings from the bottom of the journalistic barrel and praying that whatever they had was not a leak from Coldharbour police station. To her astonishment the Echo had dropped the Thomas case. There were two more deaths in town that week, but they were in no doubt as to who was responsible. The killer had left a note.

Veronica Williams had been diagnosed with lung cancer some years before. Doctors had long since given up any sort of treatment, she was receiving only palliative care and her husband had spent a fortune ensuring that she could receive that at home. He'd been a successful businessman and, on retirement, became mayor of Coldharbour. There was the usual thing about fat cats feathering their own nests and favours for his cronies, but most locals thought he was a pretty decent guy. Until the Coldharbour Echo ran its expose.

He was, they said, a vile predator who lured young women to his sprawling country estate with the promise that they could work with horses. Not satisfied with slaking his lust on the teenagers of Coldharbour, Williams was a regular visitor to a "massage" establishment in Stonehaven. Eddie Taylor had taken Thomas at his word, there was no need to speculate on what went on behind closed doors. They had three things to satisfy the prurience of their audience. First the establishment was Thai. Everyone knew that apart from fried rice and noodles, the only thing Thais sold was sex. Second, it was a "massage" parlour and placing inverted commas around the word massage did the trick there. Finally… the photos. Mayor Williams looked like he might die of shame as he stumbled through the front door and hurried to the car he'd parked three streets away.

The readers of the Echo were invited to draw their own conclusions.

Williams never recovered once the story appeared. His children were aghast, his neighbours avoided contact and his work at the town hall became impossible. Conversations stopped as he approached, old friends found any reason they could to avoid meeting for coffee. He never recovered from the shame he'd brought on his family. When he decided to take his own life, he realised that he could trust no one to take care of his wife in the few short months she had left. He couldn't bear to think of the stress his own suicide might cause her, so he took a pillow and smothered her first.

The Coldharbour Echo decided to lead with, 'Sex pest Mayor in double killing."

***

Yuri Slatkin had mastered the art of appearing to be calm even when he was boiling with rage and frustration. They were seventy- two hours from their final league match, at home to Norwich City. A win for Coldharbour would consign the East Anglian club to relegation. Seven days after that they'd play at Wembley in their first ever FA Cup Final. The opposition was Roman Abramovich's Chelsea. They had one crucial asset in the games that remained, Adam Buckley, killer of four young women. The deal with Thornberry was due to complete the following Monday, provided Coldharbour secured the points they needed to preserve their Premier League status. The purchase price would be adjusted upwards by fifteen per cent should they beat Chelsea in the Final. Slatkin had to keep Buckley out of trouble and make sure he played in both games. He'd detailed two of Koloschenko's best men to tail Buckley whenever he left the company of his team mates. No chances would be taken with so little time to go. Then that stupid bitch Kristina insisted on a party for Koloschenko to mark his fiftieth birthday. She'd chosen a fabulous location to be fair. Forty miles from central London, it had been used for a G20 conference and a meeting of the infamous Bilderberg Group, who some believe to be a shadowy organisation bent on world domination. Slatkin decided that would echo nicely with Koloschenko, who hoped that one day he'd get an invitation, maybe this was a sign. It was a vast country estate set in fourteen thousand acres of woodland, rolling lawns and intricately manicured gardens. A small army of security men had been detailed to ensure that no one could enter or leave without presenting a digitally encoded invitation card. Guests were advised to ensure they were in possession of the card at all times. Plain-clothes security staff mingled with the party-goers, armed with a small device that would identify anyone who did not have valid accreditation about their person.

Slatkin was not directly involved in the arrangements but it was another thing to think about in the most crucial week of his tenure as Koloschenko's advisor. He knew that his position depended on the deal going through and therefore on Coldharbour's survival as a Premier League club. It wouldn't be his fault if that failed to happen but that mattered little to Dimitri Koloschenko. If something went wrong then clearly someone had failed him. Heads would have to roll. Slatkin could only hope that, should he be one of the scapegoats, the head rolling would be of the metaphorical variety.

"How are things Yuri?"

Slatkin jumped at the sound of Koloschenko's voice.

"Wonderful Dimitri, it's a great party. Kristina is an amazing woman."

"Kristina is a tiresome shrew Yuri, but she is the mother of my beautiful daughter, therefore I tolerate her. My car must be here at eight, Alina is waiting for me and I don't want to disappoint her."

"Of course Dimitri. It's done."

"And I was not enquiring about the party. The deal, I'm four days from getting rid of this weight round my neck. Tell me nothing can stand in the way."

Slatkin answered, feeling only a fraction of the confidence he tried to inject into the reply.

"We have done all we can, Buckley has been wrapped in cotton wool since we found out about him. Two men trail him as soon as he leaves the ground each day. He's been the model professional. Most nights he goes home alone, twice he has picked up a woman and taken her back to his flat. Both times the girl survived the encounter."

"And had that not been the case?"

"As you instructed Dimitri, our men would have disposed of the evidence."

"So our young superstar is ready for the challenge ahead."

"Most definitely, Boris is thrilled with his form and his attitude in training. There's just one thing…"

"Yes Yuri." Koloschenko hated problems, he expected his men to report solutions not issues.

"Buckley is a killer, he won't stop. He might be distracted by the big games coming up but, at sometime in the future, that switch in his head will flick again. At some stage he'll be caught and they'll start looking at us all over again. What did we know? Why didn't we stop him? The Americans will sue. It's not the image we want Dimitri."

"Yuri, I'm disappointed that I have had to take the initiative on this. I expect more from you, but this issue will be resolved."

"It will?"

"The Americans have recourse only if Buckley signs a contract with another club or if we are found guilty of some form of malpractice. That does not cover a situation in which Buckley dies in a tragic accident days after we celebrate our Cup Final win. A car crash, a house fire, murdered by a thwarted groupie. I'll leave it to others to decide the detail, but today Buckley is crucial to our ambitions, once the deal is complete and we have this FA Cup, he becomes a loose end. I abhor loose ends."

Slatkin nodded. Koloschenko was right. As long as Buckley's death looked like a tragic accident, they were in the clear.

Kristina was hopping with excitement as she approached, she pressed herself against her husband as though she couldn't wait to be alone with him, then planted two kisses into mid air, several inches from either side of his face.

"Dimitri, I'm so excited. I have a very special surprise for you."

Slatkin was reminded of the old joke, what do you give to the man who has everything? Answer... Penicillin.

"My darling I will open it with the other presents, be patient." Koloschenko turned back towards Slatkin to ensure his instruction was understood, Kristina tugged at his arm again.

"Dimitri, it's not really a present," then she turned towards the door as though anticipating the arrival of an honoured guest. Koloschenko recognised Vasily, an ex pro-boxer who was assigned to Kristina as bodyguard. Koloschenko suspected that he offered her a more intimate service as required but was unconcerned. His wife's personal life was of no consequence to him as long as there was no public embarrassment. Vasily whispered in Kristina's ear and her look of concern turned to relief then amusement.

"It seems you'll have to wait. She won't be long."

A tiny worm formed in Koloschenko's mind and started to burrow.

"She?" Koloschenko grabbed his wife by the arm and started to shake her.

"Be patient Dimitri and let go, that hurts."

"Tell me you don't mean Tatyana." Koloschenko scanned the room, most of the Coldharbour players were present but he couldn't find the face he was looking for."

"Of course I mean Tatyana. I wasn't going to let her miss her father's birthday. She'll be here shortly, calm down for God's sake."

Koloschenko looked like a man possessed.

"Where the fuck is she, you thought she was here but she isn't. Where the fuck is she?" Kristina was still in the vice like grip of her husband's right hand and was struggling to stay upright on four-inch stilettos as he continued to try to shake the information out of her.

"She'll be back in a moment I'm sure. I bought her a Porsche Boxster and she's taking that young footballer for a tour of the grounds."

"Who? Who the fuck is she with?"

All conversation had stopped and all eyes were on the extraordinary scene playing out in the corner of the room. Slatkin reached for his phone and speed-dialled the man in charge of keeping an eye on their star striker.

Kristina had half an eye on her guests as she answered. "Adam Buckley, your little superstar. She has a crush on him, and you know our daughter, if she wants something she goes for it."

Koloschenko appeared to freeze for a couple of seconds, as though he couldn't process what he'd heard. There are many things that a father would not wish to hear about his daughter, but what Kristina had told her husband was beyond his worst nightmares. There were no words to express his anguish, only an ear-piercing wail that came straight from the soul. He brushed his wife aside and as Vasily stepped in to protect her, Koloschenko felled him with a single punch to the side of the head. Guests stepped aside to clear his path to the exit and Slatkin trailed in his wake, clutching a mobile phone to his ear.

"What do you mean you're waiting at the gate? I told you to follow him."

There was a pause then, "I know he's supposed to be with the rest of the team, but he isn't. Find the little fucker now. He may be in a Porsche Boxster."

Adam Buckley laughed as Tatyana spun the wheel and the rear of the car slid round the last corner before the lake. The wheels clipped the grass and mud flew up from the rear tyres, but she gunned the accelerator and in seconds they were half way down the final straight.

"Where did you learn to drive like that?"

Tatyana gave a nonchalant smile. "I'm Daddy's little girl, but I think he wanted a boy. He taught me to drive when I was twelve, I've flown his plane and I'm pretty good on the family yacht too. My mother hates it, but she's old." She spat the final word as though the whole concept of ageing was incomprehensible. Tatyana could not imagine ever getting old.

"So he's a pretty cool dad then?"

"He's awesome. I just have to give him this look…" Her huge green eyes widened still further, there was the tiniest downturn at each corner of her mouth, then melancholy turned to mirth as she delivered the sweetest smile. They both laughed as Tatyana spun the car to a stop under a vast oak tree twenty yards from the edge of the water.

Buckley had done a double take as Tatyana approached him in the entrance to the house. The thick blonde hair, long slender legs and perfect firm breasts made her a dead ringer for Lucy. The comparison popped into his head and the term made him feel a little queasy. Dead ringer. Lucy still preyed on his mind. All four of them had got what they deserved, but Lucy was the only one he had feelings for. When Tatyana arrived, the other players bowed and scraped as though she was royalty. In a way she was. They all thought she was hot, but clearly off limits. Nobody would risk getting in a tangle with the boss's daughter.

Those who'd met her said she was a very bright girl, studying at a fancy French University and evidently dating the son of a famous Italian industrialist. Buckley recalled the day the players passed round one of those celebrity magazines. There was a twelve-page photo shoot of Tatyana and Stefano. She looked amazing in a white bikini, mesmerising in a simple yellow sundress and fabulous in long black eveningwear. In most of the photos an adoring Stefano eyed his girlfriend with a smug grin. He was clearly thrilled to be in a relationship with such a desirable young woman and, having millions of people across Europe curse him for his good fortune made it even better. Tatyana Koloschenko was quite a catch.

"So how long are you in England?" Buckley's small talk skills had improved marginally since his early days in the limelight.

"Mama had me flown over for the party. I'll be back in France by Sunday. I love my Dad, but..."

"You didn't want to come?"

"God no. Dad's parties are business events with vodka thrown in. They're full of dirty old men who try to grab my ass when they give me a kiss I don't want... and their dried out old wives who can't stand the sight of a young woman because their jealous. That's why I thought we could have a bit of fun."

Tatyana turned to face him and quickly selected the appropriate look from her repertoire. Head bowed slightly suggested shyness, even modesty, eyes wide and hopeful, she tugged gently on her bottom lip with perfect even teeth. The top button of her dress was undone... no bra. The lower buttons were also open revealing the smooth honey coloured flesh of her right thigh.

"I thought we could... you know." The modesty had gone, replaced with the assertiveness of a young woman used to getting her own way.

"And your boyfriend?" Buckley could summon the picture in her mind's eye. A ridiculously handsome and preposterously rich Italian who had everything he ever wanted handed to him on a plate. Including a dazzling girlfriend. The man was already indecently hairy, a few years from now when the pizza and the pasta kicked in he'd be indistinguishable from a medium sized orang utan. Tatyana gave a raucous chuckle. Buckley knew the words he wanted to hear, something along the lines of,

"It's over. It was never very serious. When I saw your photo I knew I had to meet you. Stefano's history for sure."

Tatyana ran a hand along the inside of his thigh and delivered an altogether different reply..

"Oh God, Stefano must never find out, that's why I chose you. It's the curse of being in those awful magazines all the time. You can only fuck famous people. If you do an ordinary person they just sell their story. Besides, I've never had a footballer before and you're cute."

Buckley closed his eyes while he tried to take in what he'd heard. She wasn't interested in him, she was no better than those silly little sluts in the bars of Coldharbour. Lucy had gone back to her ex and Tatyana would go back to her Italian, Buckley was merely a diversion.

Tatyana was certain that she'd made a compelling case for a brief and uncomplicated union. The last thing she expected was Buckley's hand to flash across her face. Blood started to drip onto the pink fabric of her dress as her assailant's hand closed around her throat.

"You bitch, you think you can just click your fingers and I'll do whatever you want. Who the fuck do you think you are?"

Buckley could hear the car engine in the distance. If it was coming in their direction he guessed he had about thirty seconds before it got to them. He reached into his pocket and pulled out an eight-inch flick-knife, the outline of a leaping tiger was embossed on the handle. The colour of the grip was almost identical to the growing spots of blood on Tatyana's dress. It occurred to him how fortunate it was that she'd approached him in the hallway of the house. They were about to pass through the security scanner and the knife would certainly have been found.

The car was closing, Buckley could see that. It had come straight over the grass, ignoring the asphalt trail the Boxster had taken. He could see that Koloschenko was driving and an ashen-faced Slatkin was hanging on in the passenger seat as the car slewed from side to side. He had less than ten seconds before they'd be upon him. That was fine, he looked down at

Tatyana's terror stricken features as he flicked open the blade of the knife.

Ten seconds was plenty of time.

**THE END**

**Please read on for an extract of the first chapter of Vortex, a novel by Matt Carrell**

# Vortex

## by Matt Carrell

## An extract from Chapter One

## When the rain stops…

Piruwat Angsorn ran a hand through his thick mop of greying hair and stared in awe at the seething chaos of Bangkok's traffic. Once again his eyes were drawn to the illuminated display perched high above the junction, ticking down the seconds until the lights changed. The clock turned from red to green three times, but the car was barely a hundred feet closer to the junction of Asoke and Sukhumvit Road. Only the green-jacketed motorbike taxi riders made any progress, along with the occasional *tuk-tuk* dodging from lane to lane, to speed an unwary tourist towards another gold shop or designer outlet. The passenger would be offered a once in a lifetime bargain and the driver, a healthy commission for delivering another eager punter. For most of the other travellers that night, patience was running short, but Piruwat couldn't have been happier. It gave him a little longer to luxuriate in the plush leather seat of the huge Toyota Land Cruiser, watching the city unfold in front of him. He'd never seen so many people before; his village was little more than a network of dirt tracks with fewer than thirty houses. This was his first visit to Thailand's distant capital.

Stroking the smooth wooden finish of the car's interior with rough calloused fingers, he eased himself still lower in the soft hide of his seat. Piruwat examined his cracked, dirty fingernails and the deep brown face reflected in the car window. The locals would pick him out in a second, as a farmer from the poor northeast of the country. A westerner might guess his fiftieth birthday was behind him but outdoor life had taken a heavy toll in Piruwat's thirty-seven years. The plaid shirt was new and the jeans were a passable copy of genuine Levis, but there could be no mistaking a man who made his living planting rice and tending tobacco plants.

*"Mai pen rai."* Never mind… he chuckled to himself. Instinctively he stroked the amulet, the *Phra Kreuang* he picked up at his village market three weeks before. The vendor

promised him good luck and as Piruwat stared down at the face of the Buddha, he promised himself that the seller would share in his good fortune. Things were destined to change, the poem told him so and it had been right up to now.

Piruwat owned a Toyota too, but it was a thirty-year-old pickup truck and much of the vehicle had been replaced, more than once, with parts salvaged from the scrap yard. It got him to the market once a week, as long as he didn't push it too hard. That was the first thing on his wish list, a new truck, or at least a second hand one that still had its own documentation and hadn't been scavenged piece by piece. He'd have to spend a little on the house too, maybe an extra room for his two daughters, they were getting too old to share with their brother. There were so many things he could do with his newfound fortune, so many choices. He never had choices before.

Piruwat smiled again as he picked up the heavy crystal glass from the sleek wooden holder at the side of his seat. He raised the tumbler to his lips and took another sip of the iced Jack Daniels Black Label the driver poured for him as he got into the car. It couldn't have been more different to the harsh bite of his usual Songsam Thai whisky. He knew he'd never have a car like this one, but he might be able to treat himself to a decent bottle of *farang* liquor from time to time.

As the traffic ground to a halt once more, a face appeared at the window, a tiny girl who couldn't have been any older than his six year old daughter, Pim. The girl brushed her long black hair from her face with a thin, dirty hand and looked up at Piruwat with huge brown eyes. She offered one of the garlands many drivers hang over their rear view mirror for luck. Piruwat reached into his pocket to find some change but as he started to lower the window, the car eased forward and picked up pace. The young girl was left standing by the road, her expression unchanged. She often tapped on a hundred windows before anyone bought a garland. But she was already an old hand at the trade. As the Toyota pulled away, she stepped back onto the sidewalk and waited for the traffic lights to bring her the next batch of potential customers.

Piruwat settled back in his seat and stared out at the frantic, bustling streets of the city. Shoppers poured out of the vast Terminal 21 shopping centre, most heading for the Skytrain, knowing a taxi would just have to take its place in the largely stationary traffic of Sukhumvit Road. The farmer took another long hit of the whisky. He was in no hurry, things never moved that fast in his village and he was determined to enjoy every second of his trip. The pedestrians looked gloomily at the sky and their pace quickened as they fled the humid streets like a single being, heading for the stairs and the air-conditioned sanctuary of the Skytrain line that runs the length of Sukhumvit Road. A few raindrops hit the window at Piruwat's cheek and he too stared at the darkening sky. He was new to the city, but no stranger to a Thai rainstorm. He could almost count down the seconds until the heavens opened and a wall of rain hit the street. The lights changed once more before the Toyota passed through, but by the time the car crossed the junction, water flowed inches deep in the gutter and passers-by fought to raise their umbrellas against the deluge. Piruwat was a good Buddhist, and would never take pleasure in the misfortune of others, but he knew he was a very lucky man. Sipping from the crystal glass, his hand closed over the precious slip of paper in his trouser pocket.

Three weeks had passed since the game. He went to the temple that day with offerings for the monks. Piruwat prayed and knelt in silent contemplation for nearly fifteen minutes. He picked up the small wooden container of *kau cim* sticks and thought about the question he wanted to ask. That night he'd be playing *Hi-Lo* with *Kuhn* Karapong and his friends and the farmer wanted to know if luck would be on his side. He shook the box gently until a stick fell to the ground. Painted crudely on its side, was a number that had never come up for him before and he was anxious to check its meaning. A smiling saffron-robed monk beckoned him towards the row of boxes where he would find the poem matching the number on the stick. The verse was short and simple.

*"The spring is here, yet it still rains. When the rain stops, joy comes. The sun and moon gradually rise. The old gives way to the new. To see through this is like going through the Dragon gate. The God and Buddha aid you. "*

Piruwat had driven his battered Toyota to the game that night, through a rainstorm just like the one now drenching the streets of Bangkok. As he reached Karapong's house he saw that stone dragons guarded the stairway to the front door. The original part of the house was a traditional bamboo, stilt construction, raised to guard against flooding and to keep vermin from the living areas. Karapong had recently built a huge extension in modern style, including a vast terrace commanding a panoramic view of the valley below. Underneath was an air-conditioned garage for his brand new Mercedes.

Piruwat thought about how he could get to the door without being soaked to the skin. He decided to make a run for it... then the rain stopped. The dragons... the rain... there could be no doubt about the meaning of the stick, the poem could not have been clearer. When the rain stops, joy will follow.

*Kuhn* Karapong greeted each of his guests as though they were long-standing friends and a young girl was on hand to wash the feet of each of his visitors before they were ushered to the *sala* where the game would take place. There was plenty of beer, several bottles of Songsam and a selection of regional delicacies betraying the host's birthplace of Chiang Mai and his enormous appetite. The table was laden with *tord man plaa, sai kok* and *por pea gung*, easy snacks to eat without distracting the players from the game. Karapong eyed the food and the assembled gamblers as though he could not decide which to devour first.

Piruwat had few expectations of winning before his visit to the temple. He brought five hundred baht and his main concern was to ensure he got his fair share of food and whisky before his pockets were empty. As usual he started cautiously, with low stakes and simple bets, more often than not guessing correctly whether the combined total of the dice would be higher or lower than 7. With each roll of the dice he stroked his amulet and prayed for good luck. As his pile of cash grew, his confidence rose and he began to place more money on outcomes with higher odds. In less than two hours he started to believe the message of the sticks, he'd won four thousand baht and his luck was in. Had he left the table, it would have been disrespectful to the spirits who were smiling on him. More than that, he felt at one with the dice. As Karapong rattled them inside the wooden cup, Piruwat could see the dice turning and ricocheting off one another. As his host slapped the tumbler on the table, Piruwat felt his hands drawn to the bets he should make. Occasionally he must have misinterpreted the spirits who guided him because Karapong would gratefully sweep his stake from the board. More often, and normally when he bet high, his host strained to look nonchalant as he paid out on a winning bet. Piruwat was embarrassed by his success, the pile of baht in front of him grew higher with each throw of the dice and his fellow players stared in awe. He placed higher stakes and chose more improbable bets, he was anxious his host should not lose face in his own home. To lose a little of his winnings would ensure both men could leave the table with honour intact. Yet the dice continued to fall for Piruwat.

As the clock struck midnight, the farmer sat with a little over twenty thousand baht at his elbow. The farm might generate such a sum in a month; he'd won it in just a few hours. The new day gave his host the opportunity to call a halt to the game and the players started to say their goodbyes. Piruwat had no idea how to deal with his good fortune. It would be disrespectful to offer a tip to his host but he was anxious to make some sort of gesture. Only as the local garage owner bade farewell did the idea strike him. The man handed Karapong some baht notes and received a slip of paper in return. Piruwat had forgotten that in addition to the *Hi-Lo* games, his host offered odds on the lottery. Not the official government version but the parallel underground lottery. Choose three digits that match the last three of the number drawn on TV twice a month and Karapong paid five hundred-to-one; choose two matching digits and the pay-out was still a healthy fifty-to-one. The farmer could make a gesture without embarrassing his host.

"May I play too?" he asked as the garage owner departed.

"With your luck *Kuhn* Angsorn, I think it would be better for me if you did not," Karapong replied.

"As you wish," Piruwat said, embarrassed by his clumsiness.

The older man smiled and gripped the farmer's shoulder.

"My little joke, I would be delighted to have the chance to win a little of my money back."

Piruwat relaxed and returned the man's smile.

"How many numbers, *Kuhn* Angsorn?"

"Three," the farmer replied.

"And your bet?"

Piruwat paused, "Two thousand," he answered, reaching eagerly for the wad of notes in his trouser pocket.

The farmer took the paper Karapong offered and wrote the number 795 on one side. As his host returned the signed slip, he handed over two thousand baht. Honour was partly restored in Piruwat's mind.

Piruwat barely thought about the ticket in the days that followed. He bought half a baht of gold, a little over a quarter of an ounce, with most of his winnings; it's the Thai way of saving for a rainy day. Piruwat owed his brother two thousand baht since the previous harvest and the men shared a full bottle of Songsam to celebrate its repayment. His wife and children were able to replenish their threadbare wardrobes and the rest went into a small tin behind the hearth in their house with the lottery slip he received from Karapong.

Two weeks later, Piruwat saw Aiee; his neighbour's daughter, running through the village. Twice a month she sold roughly copied sheets listing the winning lottery numbers. He paid the five baht, more as a kindness than because he wanted to check the numbers. Nonetheless he couldn't resist taking a look. He ran to the house and frantically dug out the tin. His fingers trembled as he looked at the numbers again. The farmer's mind raced and for a moment he thought maybe it was the first three numbers he needed to match not the last. The winning number was 876795. It was the last three on which he'd bet and Karapong owed him one million baht.

Piruwat drove to see Karapong without even telling his wife where he was going. He couldn't bear to raise her hopes without confirmation of his luck. Karapong was waiting for him; he too had seen the numbers and knew the bet was won.

"*Kuhn* Angsorn, I am honoured to be visited by a man who is so clearly blessed by the spirits."

Piruwat relaxed, since he'd expected the man to be hostile.

"*Kuhn* Karapong, it is I who am honoured."

"My friend, I am pleased for your win and I am anxious to get you the money as quickly as possible. I have been in contact with my partner who is in a position to pay you immediately. Will you be taking your family with you?"

"*Kuhn* Karapong, my family does not know about the ticket. My wife would have been angry if I told her about the wager. She will know nothing until I return with the money." He paused for a moment, confused by the question. "Taking them where?"

Karapong smiled and slapped the farmer on the back.

"You will be on the bus to Bangkok this afternoon but you must hurry. I will tell your wife you had to travel on urgent business. She will be thrilled when you return."

"Bangkok?"

"My partner is in Bangkok, we have never lost such a bet before. I am sure you understand we do not keep such a large amount in the village."

Piruwat smiled again and shook his host's hand. Of course, he should have thought about it. Who would keep a million baht in their house?

As promised the man was waiting at Mo Chit bus station in Bangkok, wearing a black suit and a red tie, exactly as Karapong described.

"*Kuhn* Angsorn?" he asked, without offering the traditional *wai* greeting one would expect from a chauffeur.

"I am Angsorn," Piruwat replied.

"*Kuhn* Karapong's partner has been detained in a meeting but looks forward to meeting you shortly. I have been instructed to take you to the Amari hotel in the city centre. There is excellent seafood and my employers were sure you would wish to celebrate."

Piruwat just wanted to get his cash and head back to his family, but the driver opened the door and gestured for him to get inside. Having poured his passenger a generous measure of whisky, the driver got back in the car and they began their slow progress though the streets of Bangkok. The poem came back to Piruwat… the old gave way to the new, just as it predicted. By the standards of the wealthy of Bangkok he was still a peasant, but soon he would be heading back to Isaan with one million baht in his pocket. He would not be boastful of his good fortune but gradually the other villagers would understand he was a man of means, a man to be respected. There are many things in Thailand that can win the respect of one's peers, the most effective of course was money and soon the farmer would have a great deal of that.

The Toyota picked up pace, left the main road and headed east on a small *soi*. Piruwat turned to check he wasn't imagining things. As they passed a sign for the district of Klong Toey he noticed that once again they passed under an arch framed with dragons. The poem again... the old would give way to the new. Piruwat was in no doubt things would never be the same for his family, he'd never had such luck with *Hi-Lo* or the lottery, nor had he visited the capital of his country and it was certainly the first time he'd ever ridden in such a magnificent vehicle. He'd tasted JD Black Label before but, as he swirled the last of the amber liquid in the crystal glass, it occurred to him that it was usually a little clearer than this one. There'd been no strange white residue in the bottom of the glass. He wanted to ask the driver about that, and why they were now heading further from the main roads when the man had explained he was going to a city-centre hotel. He wanted to tap on the screen that separated him from his chauffeur but as he yawned, he couldn't summon the energy. His arms felt heavy, he could barely keep his eyes open and as the car drew to a halt on the dockside he drifted into a deep sleep.

Piruwat was right that life for his family would never be the same again, he was right that his luck had changed completely. The chauffeur opened the rear door and pulled the slumped body of the farmer from his seat. It was no real struggle to drag the man to the edge of the dock. It took a few seconds to go through his pockets, to find the once precious lottery ticket and the small fold of baht bills Piruwat had brought to Bangkok. The driver removed the farmer's watch and searched briefly, and in vain, for any other valuables. Satisfied that, should the body be recovered; it would look like a street robbery, there was only one thing to do before he dropped the limp body into the river. The driver pulled out his knife and drew it firmly across Piruwat's throat. It was a practiced move, the man knew exactly how the blood would spurt from the wound, and he was anxious not to soil his

228

clothes. Seconds later, there was a splash and the driver returned to his seat in the Toyota.


**We hope you enjoyed the extract. If you want to know what happens next, check out Vortex by Matt Carrell on Amazon.**

**Vortex is available as an e-book on Amazon worldwide and as a paperback in the USA, United Kingdom and Europe.**

## About the author

Matt Carrell was born in Brighton, England more years ago than he cares to remember. The son of Irish immigrants, he graduated from London University and then trained as an accountant. For more than two decades he enjoyed a successful career in the Financial Services industry. Matt's work involved a great deal of international travel and he developed a particular affection for Hong Kong and Thailand.

Matt's first published work was a series of short stories entitled Thai Lottery... and Other Stories from Pattaya, Thailand. The idea for the book emerged while watching tickets being sold by a Bangkok street vendor, and hearing from a friend about the perils of getting involved in the parallel underworld lottery. Inspired by enthusiastic feedback from readers he started work on Thai Kiss, his first full length novel, this was published in May 2013. His second novel, Vortex, is also largely set in Thailand and draws on Matt's extensive experience of the investment industry. A Matter of Life and Death is set in England and reflects his passion for football and his belief that the game is being destroyed by avarice.

Matt and his wife divide their time between England and the French Alps, with frequent trips to Asia. They are both passionate about sport, with skiing, football and golf heading the list. Honestly, she really does like football!

### Published works by Matt Carrell
A Matter of Life and Death
Vortex
Thai Kiss
Thai Lottery, and Other Stories from Pattaya, Thailand
Something Must Be Done
Slips, Trips & Whiplash

## Novels and short stories by Matt Carrell

### Thai Lottery… and Other Stories from Pattaya, Thailand

Thai Lottery is the story of the lengths a girl will go to when a debt becomes a matter of life and death, and of the westerners who have bought their own tickets to a more personal lottery. They come to Thailand looking for something that's missing from their lives. Some may be lucky but for a few the result will be utter despair.

### Thai Kiss

Matt Carrell's first novel tells the story of Paul Murphy, on the run from a British drug dealer he flees to Pattaya, Thailand. As he starts to rebuild his life, there are many who want to share in his new-found success, but who can he trust?

### Something Must Be Done

"When bad guys have guns, the answer is to arm the good guys." If you've made up your mind about gun control, this short story, set in the UK and in a US High School, will make you think again.

### Slips, Trips & Whiplash

Steve and Micky each believe they've found the perfect woman, yet every week they meet in a local bar to trade the contact numbers that will deliver the lives they covet. Both harbour a nagging doubt that their girl might be out of their league, but it's Steve that's hiding a dark secret about where he met the lady whose picture he carries inside the cover of his notebook.

## Vortex

On land or at sea the vortex is mesmerising but lethal. Andy Duncan joins an investment firm in Hong Kong and quickly discovers that the same forces apply in business. The lure of power, money and status blurs moral boundaries and for those who covet the immense rewards on offer, one illicit act can lead to another, drawing them into a spiral of deception. Duncan frames a junior clerk to save the career of a high-flying investment manager and is rewarded with rapid promotion. Transferred to the firm's new Bangkok office, he is quickly embroiled in a corporate scandal and the disappearance of a beautiful teenage girl. The only way he can hang on to his career and his new lover is to trash every moral principle he ever held dear.

Prem Boonamee's career is also on the up. Promotion in the Thai mafia is swift for those willing to follow orders to the letter. Since his first kill he has had little compunction about doing his masters' bidding. All that troubles him is a recurring dream, of the girl he abandoned to her fate and what would be their final bloody meeting.

The future of the two men is inextricably linked, when the Thai underworld targets a major financial institution. Duncan appears to be able to trust only his lover and her uncle, the man likely to become the next Prime Minister of Thailand.

Vortex offers an authentic insight into Thai culture and the intricacies of an industry that has a profound influence on the world economy. As "The Wolf of Wall Street" tops the movie charts and Thailand is on the verge of political meltdown, Vortex is a fast paced, often humorous, but generally dark take on what happens when morals and avarice collide.

**All available from Amazon.**
**Please visit my website - www.mattcarrellbooks.com**

Printed in Great Britain
by Amazon.co.uk, Ltd.,
Marston Gate.